Praise fo

Rebel Angels 1:

"The characters of the protagonists are wonderfully portrayed and you can feel the heat waves coming off this book while turning page after page. Highly recommended!"

— Karin, *Cupid's Library Reviews*

Dream Warriors 1: Gareth

"Fast paced, with a well-matched hero and heroine and a variety of interesting secondary characters both human and inhuman, *Gareth* will appeal to fans of paranormal and fantasy romance alike."

— Sondrea Cash, *Romance Reviews Today*

Ontarian Chronicles 1: Taken by the Storm

"*Taken by the Storm* is science fiction romance at its very best. Ms. Friberg writes with humor, passion and rich detail, making *Taken by the Storm* a treat to read. The complex plot and varied characters provide immense entertainment and heartfelt emotion. For a story that will delight, entertain, and keep you on the edge of your seat, I highly recommend *Taken by the Storm* and award it RRT's Perfect 10."

— Terrie Figueroa, *Romance Reviews Today*

Dream Warriors 1: Gareth and *Ontarian Chronicles 1: Taken by the Storm* are currently available in e-book format at www.loose-id.com.

Loose Id

ISBN 10: 1-59632-131-8
ISBN 13: 978-1-59632-131-1
REBEL ANGELS 1: BORN OF THE SHADOWS
Copyright © 2004 by Cyndi Friberg

Cover Art by April Martinez
Edited by Maryam Salim

This book is an original publication of Loose Id® The story herein was previously published in e-book format by Loose Id in July 2004 and is a work of fiction. Any similarity to actual persons, events or existing locations is entirely coincidental.

Printed in the U.S.A. by
Lightning Source, Inc.
1246 Heil Quaker Blvd
La Vergne TN 37086
www.lightningsource.com

REBEL ANGELS 1: BORN OF THE SHADOWS

Cyndi Friberg

Dedication

I'd like to dedicate this book to a group of incredibly supportive people. Without you Gideon would have loitered forever on my hard drive. To Scott, the love of my life, my rock. To the Agents: Michele, Jan and Kally. You are truly the best of the best. And to Cher for always pushing me in the right direction.

Thank you can't begin to express how much you mean to me.

—Cyndi

Chapter One

Krak des Chevaliers
County of Tripoli, Palestine
March 1148

Fidgeting upon the wooden stool, Naomi pushed a lock of long hair behind her ear and concentrated on the manuscript page spread before her. Dust motes danced playfully in the rapidly fading sunlight, but she couldn't allow herself to be distracted. The familiar scent of ink and sandalwood soothed her, helping her focus. She shifted the precious vellum folio to a slightly different angle, catching what was left of the light.

To achieve true illumination, a scribe must release light from within the text, not just decorate the margins. Her design was intricate and interesting, but there was no spark or inspiration. No illumination.

Naomi focused on the entwined figures centered on the page and set her quill aside. Eve's long hair concealed everything but her slender limbs. Adam, on the other hand, had only a strategically placed fig leaf to protect his modesty.

"Perhaps without the leaf I could find illumination," Naomi muttered with a mischievous smile.

"I'd be willing to serve as your model."

Naomi twirled about so suddenly she nearly toppled from the stool. Stifling a startled gasp, she stumbled to her feet, pretending the movement had been graceful.

Raising her gaze to the stranger's face, Naomi forgot her clever rejoinder. She forgot to breathe. She forgot everything except the man standing near the doorway.

His features were harsh and angular, and yet so incredibly beautiful he didn't seem real. Bright with amusement and speculation, his strange golden eyes captured her gaze completely.

"Shall I disrobe?"

The smoky quality of his voice made Naomi tingle. Sleek black hair had been pulled straight back from his face and secured at the nape of his neck. Naomi wanted to trace the slash of his black eyebrows and smooth the faint creases that framed his extraordinary eyes. She wanted to test the resilience of his mouth with her fingertips and...

What was wrong with her?

Shaking away the strange stupor, Naomi forced herself to speak. "I'm not the scribe, my lord, so I require no model."

He walked toward her, his stride long and lazy. "If you aren't the scribe, then what were you doing when I arrived?"

Naomi quickly hid her ink-stained hand behind her back. Her sandals scraped against the floorboards as she moved away from the high, angled table. "I was admiring Brother Gabriel's work. He is the finest illuminator in the entire order."

After so many years, the deception should not rankle, but it did. She hated the prejudice, which required she deny her accomplishments.

He glanced at the manuscript page, then back at her. Who was this man? His garments told her only that he was wealthy. The plush, black velvet surcoat had been elaborately embroidered in gold and the gray tunic beneath was no less costly. He wore no sword, but Naomi sensed the menace that hovered around men of war.

"What business have you here?" she asked. "Were you looking for Brother Gabriel?"

Before she realized his intention, he reached behind her and grabbed her wrist. His touch sent shivers up her arm and Naomi sucked in a ragged breath. Drawing her arm back in front of her, he turned her hand this way and that, inspecting the calluses and stains.

"You're not a scribe?" he challenged softly.

"The order has been charged with illuminating the Holy Scripts, sir." She avoided his gaze as she continued her explanation. "Some learned men believe that women do not possess souls. Almighty God would never bestow talent and inspiration on so lowly a creature. Only a man can be trusted to script the Word of God."

The stranger laughed and Naomi felt her insides clench. He had been beautiful when he scowled; his appeal now made her restless and...hot.

His thumb brushed over her wrist and his gaze settled on her mouth. "Gabriel must have his hands full with you about. Where is he?"

Naomi tried to draw her hand from his grasp, but he wouldn't allow it. The soft stroke of his thumb made her pulse jump and her skin flush. "What do you want with Brother Gabriel?"

"What I want at the moment has nothing to do with Gabriel."

Her hand brushed against coarse stone. She'd backed herself into the wall! Her heart fluttered and she found it hard to swallow. "If you have business with—"

"What's your name?" he interrupted.

His shimmering gaze moved slowly over her features. Naomi felt it like a physical touch. Coolness from the stones at her back seeped through her clothing in sharp contrast to the heat radiating from his body. She shivered, shifting her weight from one foot to the other.

"I do not share my favors, sir. There are women in the village who are willing to...accommodate your needs."

"What would you know of my needs?"

He sounded odd, as if she had struck some dark, painful chord within him. Naomi's chest tightened and her heart pounded. "Nothing, my lord. I meant only to make clear that I am not a harlot."

He released her hand and moved in closer. Pressing his palms against the wall, he caged her with his body. "I would have your name, damsel."

Fear welled within Naomi, but she tried not to panic. The scriptorium was high in a stone tower, secluded and isolated. "Please, my lord. I did not mean to anger you." She spoke in a calm, even tone.

"I am not angry."

But he looked angry. His golden eyes glittered with determination and the set of his jaw seemed dangerous. He was tall and broad, strong and menacing.

"Who are you?" His voice was barely more than a whisper, his eyes searching.

"No one of consequence." She pushed against his chest, shocked by the inflexibility of his flesh. "Let me go."

He smiled, slowly, provocatively. "I think not, on both accounts."

Gideon stared down into the woman's bright blue eyes and felt his fangs begin to lengthen. He quickly closed his mouth, unwilling to reveal his true nature. He was hungry, but it had been many long weeks since he'd touched a woman. He could not decide if he wanted to penetrate her throat with his fangs or feel her body close tightly around his shaft.

Perhaps he'd do both.

He wrapped his arms around her suddenly, molding her body to his. She instinctively arched and shoved against his chest, but this only pressed her lower body more intimately against him. Her eyes widened and the scent of fear exploded in his nose.

"Be still," he commanded her with his dark voice and the flash of his eyes.

She went limp in his arms, her eyes drifting shut, and Gideon chuckled. He hadn't meant the compulsion to be quite so powerful. Her head lolled back into the bend of his elbow, exposing her neck and ending his mental debate. He would feed first and then draw her back to awareness as he slowly seduced her senses.

Burying his face in her throat, he inhaled her scent deeply. She smelled fresh and feminine, with faint traces of fear and— arousal. Gideon parted his lips and stroked his tongue along her jugular, feeling the rhythmic pounding, the power and life. Intoxicated by her scent, it took him a moment to recognize the subtle sweetness of her taste.

Innocence.

With careful restraint, he pricked her skin with his fangs and then quickly withdrew. He intentionally savored the rich complexity of her blood. His heart began to hammer as her nature was revealed. She was pure of heart. Selfless, devoted and true.

Dark hunger slashed through Gideon and he groaned. The age-old battle within his spirit raged out of control, driving the breath from his body and the strength from his legs. He sank to his knees, his hold on the woman constant.

The shriveled remnants of his goodness surged to life, reaching for her, crying out to her, but the evil in him was just as strong. He wanted her as he had never wanted anything or anyone. He threw back his head and roared. Anguish and fury saturated the sound. He longed to drown in her innocence, to gorge on her goodness until...until she was corrupted or dead?

Unsteady and shaken, he sat down on the wood planked floor and pulled her into his lap, cradling her in his arms like a child. His hand trembled as he brushed the hair out of her face. She looked no different than other humans. But something about her held him back. His dark nature demanded that he use her to sate this raw, burning hunger, but he couldn't seem to move.

She shifted within his arms and slowly opened her eyes.

Fear erupted again. He could smell its acrid stench, hear its relentless pounding, taste its bitterness—but it had never been repulsive before.

"What happened?" she asked.

"I frightened you. You fainted."

"I have never fainted." Her voice sounded truculent as she sat up in his lap. She squirmed a bit and then went very still, her hand splayed in the center of his chest.

Her long chestnut hair was tousled, a stray wisp curled against her cheek. She stared up at him with the biggest, bluest eyes he had ever seen, and Gideon knew he would not ravage her. Seduction, on the other hand, was still a very real possibility.

"Then did you pretend to faint so I would take you in my arms?"

Her eyes lit with indignation and Gideon smiled, his dark hunger controlled again, at least for the present.

"Why would I need such a ploy?"

"Because you're not yet ready to admit that you want me, even to yourself."

She laughed and the hand resting against his chest began to push. "Are you always so arrogant?"

He couldn't bring himself to let her go. Her rounded bottom was doing cruel things to him, but he ached with the need to touch her. Taste her. "Kiss me, and I will release you." *If you still want to be released once my mouth is moving upon yours.*

Naomi felt like Eve in the Garden of Eden. "I shall scream and you will be forced to let me go."

"Forced by whom? This chamber is far from the domestic range. We are quite alone."

She didn't move, could scarcely breathe.

Brushing his warm fingers against her cheek, he tucked a curl behind her ear. "Let me taste your mouth. I only want a taste."

She rubbed her palm against his chest, fascinated by the unyielding shape beneath the soft material. Why was she still sitting here? He wasn't really restraining her.

This man was the personification of her darkest fantasies, the illusive, mysterious something that other people whispered about. He was potent, powerful and yet incomprehensible.

His mouth covered hers, driving all rational thought from her mind. She felt the heated slide of his lips, and she trembled. She felt the sensual glide of his tongue, and she groaned. His mouth moved over and against hers, his tongue touched and tasted.

She found his sleek hair and sank her fingers into the cool strands. His fingers were in her hair, too. She felt his hand close into a fist, carefully controlling her. He tilted her head, and his mouth fit more tightly over hers, guiding her lips farther apart.

She accepted the bold thrust of his tongue with a little gasp. Overwhelmed and intoxicated, she felt completely out of control. He was taking too much, moving too fast. She couldn't breathe, couldn't think, could only yield to his passion.

Fear found its way through the haze as he deepened the kiss. He was aggressive now, demanding, his mouth plundering the depths of hers. Naomi shoved against his chest and tore her mouth away.

"More, Naomi, give me more," he growled.

His arms tightened, dragging her flush against his chest. Naomi turned her face away as his words registered. "You called me Naomi."

"Is there some other name you would prefer?"

His mouth moved to the underside of her jaw. She felt the moist heat of his lips slide along her throat. Shoving hard against his chest, she tried to think, to understand what he was doing to her. He had demanded her name, but she hadn't told him.

Scrambling off his lap, she scurried to the other side of the chamber. "How do you know my name?"

For a moment, he sat there staring at her over his shoulder, but in one fluid motion, he gained his feet, and stalked toward her. "You told me your name."

She felt compelled to look at him, to stare into his eyes, but she quickly averted her gaze. "Nay, sir, I did not."

He stood directly across the table from her. It was no real protection. He could easily shove it aside. She sneaked a glance at his face. He was looking at the manuscript page, his expression inscrutable.

"Where will I find Gabriel?"

His voice softly demanded the information and Naomi felt the urge to blurt out his location. "What do you want with Brother Gabriel?"

"Where will I find him?"

He looked up and their eyes locked before she dragged her gaze away. Naomi felt hot, and then cold. "I've no idea. You need to inquire with the castellan. His name is Brother Aaron."

Suddenly, he was beside her, his palms framing her face, and Naomi had no choice but to look into his strange golden eyes. "What is Brother Gabriel to you?"

She struggled against the need to tell him every detail of her relationship with Brother Gabriel. Keeping her mouth firmly closed, Naomi fought the bizarre compulsion. Never would she do anything that would endanger Brother Gabriel, but the need to speak became overwhelming. "He is a member of the Holy Order of St. John. Surely you knew that before you came here."

"What is he to *you?*"

Stubbornly closing her eyes, she allowed Brother Gabriel's kind, serene face to form within her mind, driving back the dark compulsion. "Why have you detained me?"

"Because you're lying." His hand slid down along her jaw, his thumb stroking back and forth across her bottom lip.

A hot golden haze burned through her mind, consuming the image of Brother Gabriel. Naomi's eyes flew open. It was as if he were controlling images inside her head!

"You lied about being a scribe. You lied about Gabriel. You not only know where he is, but he is important to you. What is the connection?"

Someone had to end the stalemate. Although he could easily find out about her, his identity and purpose would be far harder to learn. "Brother Gabriel is the nearest thing to a father that I have ever known. He is a friend and mentor. What is he to you?"

"Gabriel is my brother." With an enigmatic smile, he turned and left the room.

She stared after him for a long moment, her mind filled with questions. Why had Gabriel never mentioned having a brother? Was the stranger a mercenary or had he come simply to visit his brother? What did he want with Brother Gabriel? The stranger's interest had seemed somehow—menacing.

How had he known her name?

Why had she felt almost eager to accommodate his smallest suggestion?

An odd combination of fear and excitement pulsed through her entire body. She had never met a man who made her tingle with just the intensity of his gaze.

She must tell Brother Gabriel that a man claiming to be his brother had arrived at the Krak des Chevaliers, but he was in the chapel attending Vespers. As she should have been, she realized with a small, rebellious smile.

It was all so very strange.

She turned her attention back to the manuscript page, determined to banish thoughts of the stranger from her mind. His striking features refused to stay suppressed. With a helpless sigh, she reached for a scrap of vellum and began to sketch.

Chapter Two

Naomi angled her sketch of the stranger toward the lamplight and felt heat spread across her cheeks. Just his image caused her senses to respond. It was really quite ridiculous.

"I missed you at Vespers," Brother Gabriel said from somewhere behind her. "What kept you so occupied that you neglected your evening prayers?"

Carefully keeping the scrap of vellum turned away, Naomi pivoted on the stool and offered her warmest smile. "Adam and Eve. Well, mostly Adam."

Brother Gabriel chuckled and Naomi tried to relax, but tension gripped her abdomen and refused to let go. She studied her closest friend with new interest as he crossed the scriptorium. There was nothing she didn't know about this man, or so she'd believed until a short while ago.

He wore a long-sleeved black robe emblazoned with the distinctive white cross identifying him as a member of the elite Order of St. John of Jerusalem. Naomi felt proud to be part of such an important order. The Knights of St. John had been serving Western pilgrims as they traveled through the Holy Land for well over a century. One of their grandest accomplishments had been building a hospital in the heart of Jerusalem, and now members of the order were often called Knights Hospitaller.

Naomi focused her attention on the man within the robe. Gabriel's neatly trimmed hair was a bright blending of silver and gold, nearly opposite from the raven-black locks of the man claiming to be his brother. His eyes were a warm brown, but there were shards of gold Naomi had never noticed before.

"Is something troubling you, Naomi? You stare at me as if I have sprouted horns."

"Who is this man?" She handed him the scrap of vellum.

His eyes widened for just a moment before he concealed his surprise. She watched his throat work as he swallowed awkwardly. "Where did you see him?"

"He just left. You may have passed in the bailey."

He set the sketch aside and grasped both of her hands. Fear shone in his eyes as he searched her face and person. "Are you well? Did he harm you? Threaten you?"

Naomi nervously licked her lips. "I am fine. But why would that be your first assumption? Is he your brother, as he claimed?"

Releasing her hands, Brother Gabriel averted his face for a moment before he spoke. "Tell me exactly what happened."

"Nay, not until you tell me why he frightens you. I have never known you to be afraid of anyone or anything, yet I see fear in your eyes."

"Gideon can be dangerous, Naomi. I cannot pretend otherwise. He—"

"Gideon," she whispered. "He did not tell me his name."

"What *did* he tell you?"

"Only that he is your brother. He asked where he could find you and when I wouldn't volunteer the information he became annoyed." She had to fight back a smile as she remembered the heated embrace they had shared. "He can be quite intense."

"Did he touch you?" He took a step toward her. "You said he didn't harm you."

"He didn't harm me," she said reassuringly. "What does he want with you?"

"I'm not certain."

"Why did you never tell me you have a brother?" The faintest edge cut through her tone despite Naomi's effort to conceal her disappointment.

"It never occurred to me that you would meet." He turned toward the door. "I must find him. His coming can only mean trouble, for both of us."

* * *

Gideon leaned against the stone wall of the mercenary barracks and stretched out his legs along the narrow cot assigned for his use. Crispin had chosen the cot on his left; the one on his right was unoccupied. The barracks were spacious and surprisingly clean. Gideon had arrived with eight mercenaries, but the Castellan of Krak des Chevaliers had extended them hospitality without hesitation. The compound was massive; nine additional inhabitants would hardly be noticed, Gideon reasoned.

Men of every shape and variety milled about the open room, conversing with each other, some sharpening weapons. Gideon watched them with dispassionate interest in the smoky lamplight, his mind distracted by his encounter with Naomi.

She had been lovely and spirited, but her emotional connection to Gabriel was what interested him most. Who was she? How had she come to be in Gabriel's care? Did she know her "father's" true nature?

"Does he know you're here?" Crispin asked.

"I've yet to speak with him, but the girl will tell him, I've no doubt."

Gideon had quickly learned that having a human under his control was more than just convenient, it was necessary. Crispin safeguarded Gideon whenever he was vulnerable. Gideon didn't allow him to remember many of the things they did together, but Crispin was loyal. A preternatural compulsion assured his loyalty.

"This girl, is she comely?" Crispin asked with a characteristic grin.

"She is wondrously fair." Gideon felt his hunger stir as he remembered her sweet taste, so pure, so innocent. "Her dark hair has just a hint of fire, and her eyes hold the blue of an endless summer sky."

"How poetic," Crispin teased him.

The raucous sound of numerous conversations diminished suddenly, drawing Gideon's attention toward the main entrance to the barracks. A Knight Hospitaller stood in the doorway, his dark monastic robes decorated only by the large white cross on his chest.

Gideon suppressed his unconscious reaction to the symbol. Revulsion, fury and fear rolled through him, but he managed to keep his expression composed. Instead of revealing his discomfort, he focused on the individual clothed within the robes.

Nearly a century had passed since he last saw his brother face to face, and the confrontation was long overdue. The drab robes didn't distract from the purity of Gabriel's features or the bright splendor of his gilt-colored hair. Gideon watched as he crossed the barracks. Gabriel managed to maintain a serene expression, but his gaze revealed his uncertainty.

"Gideon," he greeted calmly as he reached the cot.

"Gabriel," Gideon replied, his tone mocking.

"What brings you to the Krak?"

Before Gideon could answer, Gabriel noticed Crispin's avid interest. "May we speak outside?"

Gideon smiled. "Why? Do you have words for me that would make my friend uncomfortable?"

"Making people uncomfortable seems to be your goal, not mine."

He narrowed his eyes. How much had Naomi confessed? Surely, she hadn't shared all the details of their meeting with Gabriel. Swinging his legs to the floor, Gideon rose and followed his brother out into the night.

Moonlight caught on the large cross atop the chapel's bell tower, casting a dense shadow across Gideon's path. His steps faltered and his stomach clenched, but he marched through the shape and into the darkness beside the barracks. He didn't stop until they were well away from curious ears.

"How did you find me?" Gabriel asked.

"It's a simple thing to find someone who is following you. Did Michael dispatch you, or do you willingly participate in my punishment?"

"There is only one participant in your punishment, Gideon, and that is *you.*" Gabriel's voice was firm, his expression guarded. "I am here. You cannot change that fact. When did you become aware of my presence?"

"I saw you in Jerusalem. I thought you had some manner of assignment, but the more I thought about it, the more suspicious I became. How long have I *been* your assignment?"

Gabriel smiled and glanced away. "You have been more like a command center from which I am dispatched to other assignments."

"So, you spy on me unless He has something of more importance for you to do?"

"For the most part," Gabriel agreed.

"And you are only to observe? Not give me guidance?"

"Would you accept my guidance should I give it?"

Gideon chuckled, resting one shoulder against the barracks outer wall. "You're nearly as good at avoiding questions as am I. You can speak only truth, so tell me now. What role has Michael set for you?"

Gabriel fidgeted. "I have been told to monitor your situation."

"And report back to Michael, no doubt. How is the study coming? Have I learned my lessons well? How much longer am I to be banished from the light, expected to live off of these mortals?"

"That is, and has always been up to you, Gideon. All Michael did was release your constraints. You claimed that we are slaves, so Michael set you free."

"There is no freedom in what I have become." Gideon sneered.

"You are a creature of your own making. If you are not content, then change."

They glared at each other for a long moment.

"Have all these years taught you nothing?" Gabriel asked.

Anger boiled up within Gideon, tasting foul in the back of his throat. He folded his arms across his chest and began to pace. "Oh, my time with mankind has taught me all manner of things. I have learned to be ruthless and to deceive. I have learned to manipulate others to my own will. I have learned to lust and to covet. I have learned—"

"Nothing you needed to know," Gabriel interrupted impatiently. "Have you not seen the sacrifices they make for each other? Their tenderness and their loyalty, their courage and their honor?"

"Honor?" Gideon scoffed. "Honor is as much a myth as love."

"You have known love, Gideon. I love you unconditionally. You must learn how to *give* love, not how to *be* loved."

Gideon looked away from the hope and the expectation in his brother's eyes. He gazed out into the night, drawing strength from the darkness.

"Are you in love with her, Gabriel?" he asked in a quietly provoking tone. "Do you feel the full range of human emotions, as I do, or did Michael spare you that torment?"

"We speak of Naomi now?" Gabriel asked.

"She is quite remarkable. The most disturbing combination of childish innocence and lush feminine promise."

Gabriel took a step forward, anger hardening his features and brightening his gaze. "Leave Naomi alone. She has nothing to do with any of this."

Gideon grinned, amazed at how well he had guessed what his brother was feeling. "No wonder you masquerade as a monk. Your very nature makes the role effortless. Piety, selflessness and chastity are routine for an angel. You do not burn with lust, do you? You feel protective and responsible, but you feel nothing more for this girl, do you?"

"I have cared for Naomi since she was a babe." Gabriel sounded defensive. His bright eyes narrowed in his perfect face. "Her mother died in my arms, and I have taken responsibility for the child ever since."

A deep chuckle rumbled in Gideon's chest. "She is no longer a child, *Brother* Gabriel, and I will continue her education from here."

"Why are you doing this?" Gabriel demanded, frustration clear in his melodious voice.

"Because I can," Gideon snapped in return.

"I do not understand."

"Aye, you do. That is the reason you stink of fear. You understand exactly what I intend for your precious `daughter'." Gideon started back toward the barracks.

"Will it ease your pain to hurt Naomi?"

"That is what I intend to find out." He tossed the words over his shoulder without turning around.

"She has done nothing to deserve this, Gideon. I will do everything in my power to protect her from you."

"Good." He paused at the corner of the building. Penetrating the shadows with the golden intensity of his glare, he knocked Gabriel back a step. "I welcome the conflict, *Brother.* I have grown quite accustomed to war."

Chapter Three

The following day dawned bright and clear. Arid winds swept over the endless, sun-baked plains and warmed the thick stone walls of the mighty Krak. Naomi spent the day alone in the scriptorium. She didn't mind the solitude, for her work was engrossing.

When she ventured from the scriptorium in search of food and wine, she learned that the castellan, Brother Aaron, had sent Brother Gabriel on an errand. She had hoped to hear the outcome of his confrontation with Gideon, but apparently her curiosity would have to wait.

Naomi heard the bells announcing Vespers and sighed. She'd attended Morrow Mass. Surely God would forgive her for neglecting her evening prayers—even if it was for the second day in a row.

Amused by her thoughts, she rose from her stool and stepped back from the table to see the illumination from a different angle. She was satisfied with the design framing the figures. Eve was suitably evocative, but Adam still seemed flat and unremarkable.

"Still trying to see beneath his fig leaf?"

Naomi refused to be embarrassed. Ignoring the little shocks of sensation that erupted at the sound of Gideon's voice, she tilted her head and continued to study the folio.

"Something is missing," she said.

He laughed and stepped up beside her. His warm, exotic scent touched her nose and Naomi inhaled deeply, filling her lungs with Gideon.

"If you cannot see beneath the leaf, how can you be certain?" he teased.

Thinking herself fortified against the allure of his angular features, Naomi turned and looked at him. Her breath caught in her throat and heat pooled low in her belly. His golden gaze caressed her face, beckoning her.

"Gideon," she murmured.

"You have spoken with Gabriel, I see. He was not at all pleased to learn that I had been alone with you. Is he always so protective?"

"He has never before had call to be protective." Was he drawing attention to the fact that they were alone again? "I have always been treated kindly."

"By monks and servants?"

She smiled, amused by his haughtiness. "I am myself a servant and I've always been surrounded by monks."

"You're no servant." He nodded toward the illumination. "Is that the work of a servant?"

She dragged her gaze away from his face and looked at the manuscript page. "Nay, that is the work of Brother Gabriel," she grumbled.

The warm brush of his thumb along her jaw made Naomi jump. She looked up at him and he smiled. His moods swung from charm to menace and back again with dizzying speed.

"Is Gabriel the only one who knows the truth?" His forehead furrowed and then he asked, "How did you manage the deception? Gabriel has an aversion to lying."

Naomi laughed at the understatement. "Brother Gabriel refuses to lie. I think he fears that his tongue will catch fire if he utters one untrue word."

Gideon chuckled, and tingles coursed down her spine. Why did her senses respond to everything he did?

"Did he teach you the technique or have you studied with other scribes?"

"Brother Gabriel instructed me in the art of illumination, but I don't think he realized where it would lead when the lessons began."

"It is rather complicated to become proficient at something basically forbidden to your gender."

She nodded, trying not to let her anger show. "When my work matured to a certain level, Brother Gabriel took the page to Brother Aaron, the castellan of the Krak des Chevaliers. Brother Aaron told Brother Gabriel what a wonderful job he had done. Brother Gabriel tried to correct the misconception, but Brother Aaron sees what he wants to see."

Naomi bristled each time she thought about the narrow-mindedness surrounding her. She was expected to be meek and mild, obedient and submissive simply because she was female.

Well, Brother Gabriel had nurtured her mind and encouraged her imagination. He had supported her secret passion for illumination, not realizing that the end result would be discontent.

Tossing her hair over her shoulders, Naomi finished, "So, Brother Gabriel has presented each of my pages to Brother Aaron, not bothering with an explanation, and Brother Aaron believes what he will."

"I see."

He turned back toward the table and Naomi took a moment to study him. He was dressed again in black, both his tunic and surcoat. Today his long hair was unbound, falling past his shoulders in soft waves. Never had she seen a man more pleasing to the eyes.

His head shifted toward her and she heard him draw a slow, deep breath.

"What are you thinking about?" He punctuated the question with a salacious smile.

Naomi tried to swallow past the lump lodged in her throat. There was no possible way he could know the nature of her thoughts. And yet he seemed to sense her arousal—or smell it? Was that possible? Worrying her bottom lip, she took several steps away from him.

She crossed to the open window and leaned out, allowing the wind to brush her heated cheeks. After a moment, she turned to face him, resting back against the sill.

"What do you want..." She paused. "Is it *Sir* Gideon?"

"It is simply Gideon." He remained by the table, his gaze intent upon her face.

"Of?" she pressed him.

"I call no place home. I live by my sword and swear fealty to no man."

"Then, what do you want with me, Gideon?"

"I want to know everything there is to know about you. I want to teach you everything there is to know about me."

Naomi disregarded the strange tightening in the pit of her stomach. This was a game to him. He couldn't really care about her; they had only just met. "I've no deep dark secrets, and if you do, I have no interest in them."

"Have you always lived with the Brothers of St. John?" he asked, as if she hadn't spoken.

"I'm an orphan. Many children are taken in by the order."

"I'm only interested in one. Tell me about yourself." His deep smoky voice was almost hypnotic.

Naomi pushed her hands into the pockets stitched to the front of her tunic. "It is not a fascinating tale."

"Let me judge what I find fascinating." He sat down upon her stool and smiled encouragingly.

"As you wish." She relented reluctantly. "I don't even know the name of the woman who gave me life. Brother Gabriel was praying in the Calvary Chapel at the Church of the Holy Sepulcher in Jerusalem when a young woman came up beside him. She pressed an infant into his arms, and then collapsed at his feet. The Hospital of St. John is just around the corner and Brother Gabriel took her there."

"The woman did not survive?"

"Aye. She was burning with fever. The physicians were amazed that she had been able to walk into the church."

"Are you certain this woman was your mother? She could have been a servant or she could have stolen you from your family."

Naomi smiled, but his question made her sad. "I have often entertained such thoughts. I've pictured my real mother appearing one day to take me home to my loving family. I've dreamed that the king of some distant land will suddenly realize I'm his daughter. But they are the wistful dreams of every orphan." She glanced down, tracing the shape of her pocket with her fingertip. "The physicians confirmed that the woman had recently given birth. They believed the infection that claimed her life was directly related to my delivery. There is no one waiting beyond the horizon to rescue me."

"No one inquired about this woman? No one knew her?"

Taking a deep breath to clear her mind of wishes, Naomi continued her tale. "She was delirious for two days before death claimed her. She spoke fluently in several languages and her speech was refined, so the brothers suspected that she was a pilgrim, or the daughter of a Crusader."

"When were you born?"

"In the year of our Lord 1130."

"Thirty years after Jerusalem was reclaimed," he calculated. "The Christian kingdoms and principalities had already formed and the coastal states settled. Why was a noblewoman still in Jerusalem?"

"Many Crusaders found prosperity here and stayed, but I never said that my mother was of noble birth. I have no knowledge of that. The brothers sent word throughout Jerusalem and as far away as Constantinople. No one knew anything about the woman. If she had been someone of consequence, she would have been missed. I suspect that she was the consort of some Crusader. She was likely left behind when he returned to the West."

"Left alone to bear the fruits of their love?"

Embarrassed by the indiscreet topic, she merely nodded. "Brother Gabriel was told to relinquish my care to the sisters of the order, but he refused. My mother died in his arms and her last words were a plea that he take care of me."

"And he has," Gideon concluded, rising from the stool. "He has kept you by his side and seen to your education, but you have been cloistered and secluded from all life has to offer."

She laughed softly, but the nearer he drew the more uncomfortable she became. What did he want from her? Why was he doing this? "What has life to offer that I have been denied? Hunger? Poverty? Uselessness? I have the security of the order's protection. I have been taught languages, theology and history. I have had access to vast stores of information, as well as fascinating fiction. And I have my work. What do I lack?"

His surcoat brushed against her tunic and she shivered.

"Excitement, adventure, the thrill of the unknown," Gideon suggested. "What about love? Do you not want a family? A husband and children?"

"I've not met any man with whom I would care to spend the rest of my life. I feel no Divine calling, so I have not entered the order, but I don't know if I will ever marry."

"You will marry. Your nature would never tolerate celibacy." His eyes captured her gaze and a sly smile bowed his lips.

"You have a very pronounced opinion of me considering our short acquaintance." She managed to speak only after dragging her gaze away from his. Was he able to cast a spell with his strange golden eyes or was she just a lonely fool, vulnerable to the attentions of an attractive man?

He touched her chin, drawing her gaze back to his. "Am I wrong? Could you live without the touch of a lover, forever?"

His thumb brushed teasingly over her mouth and Naomi felt her lips tremble. "If it is required of me."

"Required by whom?"

If he would just stop touching her, she would be able to think. "Brother Aaron has been hinting lately that I should take vows or move on. I'm not a child anymore."

"I noticed," he whispered. Leaning in, he brushed his lips against her temple, inhaling deeply. "You would be utterly wasted in an abbey."

His scent surrounded her. The smooth heat of his cheek rubbed against her, filling her mind with images. She saw his golden skin rubbing and sliding against her ivory skin. Her body ripened and ached. Naomi cleared her throat and braced her hands against the cold stone sill. She could not let him overwhelm her again.

With quick agility, she hopped up onto the wide sill. Only her knees brushed against him now. The stones were cold beneath her bottom and her palms. She welcomed the shock. "That is the story of my life. Are you fascinated and amazed?"

"That is the story of your birth, Naomi," he corrected. He pressed his hands against the stones on either side of the window, imprisoning her within the sill. "Now, tell me the story of your life. Were you happy as a child? Have you ever done something of which Brother Gabriel disapproved? How do you spend your time? What do you dream about?"

Suspicion crept up along her spine, making her fidget. "Why do you want to know these things? What am I to you?"

A definite purpose drove his curiosity. Fear surged through her. They were alone and she didn't understand the way her body responded to this man. He had the eyes of a hawk, sharp and calculating.

And she was his—*prey.*

Naomi ducked beneath his arm and rushed for the door.

Gideon watched her escape, amused and intrigued.

"Fare thee well," he called.

She didn't even pause.

Strolling to the high, narrow window, he waited for her to emerge into the courtyard below. A smile played about his lips. He couldn't remember the last time he'd found anything this stimulating.

A stubborn ray of the dying sun caught in her hair, directing his attention to her slender body. She moved quickly, purposefully across the bailey.

Was she afraid he would pursue her? Or was she off to tell her "father" about their latest conversation?

The scent of her fear still lingered in the room. But a darker, richer scent tantalized him even more.

Danger attracted her, called to a part of her she had yet to recognize. Seducing her would be a pleasure. A pleasure he intended to enjoy to the fullest.

She was the enemy. He must never lose sight of that fact. Humans had cost him too much already. He would surrender nothing more.

Centuries had passed and still the images remained vivid and painful. Gideon stood obediently by, a reluctant soldier in Michael's army, as he watched his best friend Fall.

Lucifer, the morning star, the brightest and most powerful of all the angels shrieked in agony as he plummeted to earth. The Angel of Light hideously transformed into the Father of Darkness.

With a muttered curse, Gideon moved to the other window and stared out into the gathering night.

Everything changed after the Fall. God revealed His new creation and poured out His unconditional love on the ungrateful race of humans. Angels became servants, messengers expected to protect and counsel the very creatures who had displaced them.

Lucifer had been damned for the sort of rebellion God allowed mankind to express freely.

And Gideon would never forget.

Raking his hair with both hands, Gideon lifted his face to the sky.

Naomi.

He whispered her name in his mind and pictured every detail of her lovely face. He would awaken her to passion, make her crave it, make her burn.

He would awaken her to darkness. And her seduction would be all the sweeter because he knew how her "father" would mourn.

Chapter Four

Naomi tried all night to convince herself she didn't care what dark purpose drove Gideon. The conflict raging between the brothers had nothing to do with her.

But this morning she'd awakened restless and confused. Brother Gabriel never kept secrets from her. Why would he neglect to mention something so fundamental? She hadn't seen him since she told him of Gideon's arrival. Was he intentionally avoiding her? The entire situation made her uncomfortable.

One day in seven Naomi was free to do as she pleased. When she couldn't locate Brother Gabriel, she decided to visit Zarrah in the Maronite village to the west of the Krak des Chevaliers. Zarrah was a young widow who lived with her father and small son. Her brother, Jonah, had often hinted that he would like to take Naomi to wife, but she had never given his offer much consideration.

Naomi found the brisk walk to Zarrah's home calming, but a day spent fending off Jonah's advances and watching Zarrah with Benjamin left Naomi achingly aware of all she would sacrifice were she to enter the Order of St. John. All too soon, Naomi was saying her farewells and striding swiftly toward the Krak, anxious to return before the sudden desert nightfall.

You will marry. Your nature would never tolerate celibacy.

Gideon's words echoed back to her and Naomi smiled.

Could you live without the touch of a lover, forever?

The prospect hadn't seemed nearly so desolate before Gideon took her in his arms.

You would be utterly wasted in an abbey.

A warm tingle ricocheted through her and Naomi hurried her pace. Perhaps she should think more seriously about Jonah's offer. If Jonah took her in his arms, would her heart beat so hard she could barely breathe?

The soft thump of hoof beats drew Naomi from her musings. She watched the horseman coming toward her in the distance. Riders seldom used this path, but Naomi simply stepped off, intending to let him pass.

He drew his horse to a halt directly in front of her and Naomi tried not to panic. He might only wish a word with her. His long leg swung over the saddle and he slid to the ground.

Fear crept over her, weakening her limbs and lodging in her throat. She looked around for a weapon, a stone, a stout stick— anything to ward him off.

The man approached, his stride lazy, leading his large bay stallion. The animal wasn't adorned with the trappings of war, but Naomi recognized it as a destrier by the defined musculature and the sheer size of the beast.

She had a similar impression of the man. Though he was dressed simply in a plain tunic and chausses, Naomi could easily picture him in heavy chain mail and brightly colored surcoat.

His hair was a sun streaked brown and his dark eyes met hers boldly. She searched for kindness in his eyes, desperately hoping for some indication that he didn't mean her harm. All she saw was confidence and calculation.

"Good day, damsel," he greeted.

Naomi nodded, praying he'd simply pass her by. Averting her eyes and stooping her shoulders, she tried to move around him. His hand shot out and Naomi gasped. Her heart pounded and moisture evaporated from her mouth.

"Good eventide, sir." She struggled just to form the words with her dry tongue. His fingers encircled her arm with firm, unyielding pressure.

"I've just come from Krak des Chevaliers; was it there I saw you?" A smile parted the dark beard obscuring the lower portion of his face.

"It's possible, good sir. Please, may I pass?" She kept her voice even, struggling to conceal the fear ravaging her composure.

"Are you in a hurry to return to your duties? Can you not abide a few moments with a lonely stranger?"

His grip on her arm became a caress. Even through the thin material of her long-sleeved chemise, she could feel the taunting brush of his fingers.

"If it's companionship you seek, there are women in the villages who are available to you."

He pulled her closer, his smile seductive. Naomi's arms shot up between them, her hands pressed firmly against his chest. Surely, he didn't mean to take from her what others were willing to give! She was breathing too quickly. Her head spun sickeningly.

"Why would I continue on to a village, when you are just to my liking?"

She yanked against his restraining hold. Blood pounded in her temples, drowning out everything but her fear. She couldn't mistake the strength in his simple hold. If she couldn't break the grasp of his fingers, what hope did she have of fighting him off? "Please sir, I do not sell my favors."

"Good." He laughed. "For I don't mean to pay."

Sweeping her up in his arms, he deposited her, face down across the saddle. Naomi screamed and kicked and thrashed, but he quickly mounted, dragging her across his lap.

His large hand smacked her behind, hard. "Be still. You'll do me no good with a broken neck."

He kicked his steed into a gallop and Naomi had to struggle for each breath. His hard thighs jabbed her middle and each rhythmic lunge of the horse caused blood to pound painfully in her head. She prayed for rescue—or death.

When he stopped the horse a few minutes later, Naomi threw her weight backward before he could dismount. She hit the ground hard and her ankle twisted. Strangling on a hysterical cry, she turned and tried to run.

"You foolish girl." He sneered as he swung down from the horse. He easily caught her and shoved her to the ground. "Are you trying to kill yourself?"

Tears trailed freely down her cheeks. "I do not share my favors," she sobbed. He reached a hand toward her face and she shrank away. "Please, just leave me here. I do not want this!"

He grabbed her suddenly and forced her onto her back. Crouching over her, he ground his mouth against hers in a harsh abomination of a kiss. Revulsion rolled through Naomi's belly. His knees forced her legs apart and she went wild. She jerked her head to the side and screamed, desperate to escape his brutal hold. He slapped his hand down over her mouth and began to shove her skirts up.

Naomi put all her panic-empowered strength into the fight, thrashing and kicking, arching and bucking. But the man easily restrained her. His palm remained over her mouth, preventing her from crying out. If he thought she'd given up, would he remove his hand? Was there any chance someone would hear her?

"That's better," he muttered, as she forced herself to stop resisting.

The pressure of his hand across her face eased and Naomi bit his palm as hard as she could. He rocked back onto his haunches with an angry curse. Naomi screamed and renewed her struggles. He batted her hands away and grasped the neckline of her simple tunic. With one vicious yank, he ripped it to the waist. Her chemise still covered her breasts, but his hot gaze settled on the shadowed promise of her nipples.

Naomi was paralyzed by the carnal hunger in his dark stare. He had only to move his clothing aside to complete the act. Dread cramped her abdomen and bile rose into her throat. A ragged sob tore from her as he shifted her wrists into one strong fist and covered her breast with his hand.

"Please, don't do this," she whimpered.

He didn't seem to hear her, or he simply didn't care. He untied the cord at the top of her chemise and pulled the entire length free of the fabric. Without the lacing, the material gaped, revealing her breasts.

Naomi sobbed and pleaded, but he was unmoved by her desperation. His hand returned to her breast, his callused palm hot against her bare skin.

His head suddenly jerked backward and his dark eyes widened. Naomi didn't understand his expression, until the long blade of a sword came to rest against her attacker's throat.

"Up, slowly," Gideon's deep voice commanded.

He dragged the man off her and issued another sharp command. The stranger vaulted onto his horse and galloped away.

For a moment, she was too stunned to move. Then the protective stupor broke and emotions crashed upon her. She rolled to her side and crossed her arms over her breasts, sobbing uncontrollably. She could still see his lustful eyes and feel his hurtful hands.

Gideon knelt beside her and touched her shoulder. She cried out sharply and flinched away from him.

"Naomi."

She clutched her tattered clothing to her breasts, and curled into herself, each breath loud and ragged. He stroked her cheek with the back of his fingers and said her name again. Slowly, she turned her head and focused her gaze on his face. Relief pushed back her terror, but she still trembled with disorientation.

"Gideon," she whispered, struggling to sit.

He helped her, his hands light upon her upper arms. They sat facing each other, hip to hip, their legs angled in the opposite direction. "Are you all right?"

She drew her legs up in front of her and wrapped her arms around her knees, hiding her breasts. She couldn't stop shaking.

"Did he hurt you, Naomi?"

Naomi longed to throw herself into his arms, to bury her fingers in his hair and melt into his warmth. Would she feel protected in his embrace? Would she feel safe? "He...didn't...I twisted my ankle, but that's all."

As if he sensed her silent longing, Gideon pulled her into the cradle of his arms. Without thought or hesitation, she wrapped her arms around his back and buried her face against his chest. She clung to him, soaking in the comfort of simple human contact. She was safe. He would keep her safe.

After a long moment, Naomi eased away from him and looked up into his face. His arms still held her tenderly, the way she imagined a lover might. "How is it you are here?"

His features were all harsh angles, but his strange golden eyes glowed with warmth, and something else. Possessiveness?

"I was looking for you," Gideon whispered. "You missed Compline and Gabriel was worried." He gently touched her hair and pressed a kiss to her brow.

Tears burned her throat, but she stubbornly fought them back. She wanted to stay in his arms, to cuddle against his chest until the last of her fear was driven away. But she didn't know him, couldn't trust him, couldn't trust herself when she was with him.

"How did you know where to find me?"

His hand moved to cup her cheek, his thumb teasing the fullness of her lower lip. "Gabriel told me where to look."

"I didn't see Gabriel before I departed. He didn't know where I had gone." She sat up, still mostly in his lap. He was like a wavering mirage, an illusion created by what she wanted him to be.

His hand settled at the nape of her neck and his thumb stroked up and down along the side of her throat, tracing her pulse. "Someone must have seen you depart. I know not how he knew, but he knew. I am here. You are safe. That is all that matters."

She had to do something, say something to break the tension building between them, or she would shatter. "If this is what you meant by excitement and adventure, I'm more certain than ever I can do without."

He smiled and slowly shook his head. "I was talking about this."

She didn't resist when he pressed his lips over hers. Her hungry fingers found his long hair, and it was as gloriously soft as she remembered. She inhaled deeply his exotic, spicy scent.

He kissed her gently, patiently. Even the brief touch of his tongue comforted her. She was able to banish the other man's cruel face by concentrating on Gideon. A familiar tingle tripped along her spine and she sighed. But all too soon he eased her away.

Almost desperately, she reached for him. "Please," she whispered, "I need...to forget."

A strangled groan escaped him as he pulled her more fully onto his lap. He supported her with one arm, while his mouth settled over hers. "Do you trust me?" His lips moved against hers as he spoke the words.

"Nay." She punctuated the admission with a nervous laugh.

"Let me touch you, Naomi. Let me show you how it should be, how it was meant to be."

A shiver passed through her. "I cannot escape being ravaged only to surrender myself to you."

"That is not what I propose. I want only to give you what you requested, a way to forget."

Temptation. Oh, wicked temptation. And he was right: she had asked him for it. "You will do no more than touch me?"

"Aye."

"With your fingers?"

He laughed. "Unless you beg me to do otherwise."

"Nay! Even if I beg you to do otherwise. You must promise it will go no farther."

"Do you really have so little faith in your ability to resist me?"

She threaded her fingers through his hair, her gaze fixed on his mouth. "I would have your word or this ends here."

"I will touch you with my fingers and kiss your mouth, but nothing more."

"Then, touch me."

She felt the throbbing proof of his desire jerk against her bottom, as if to protest the restriction. The tip of his tongue circled her lips and his hand slipped under the edge of her ruined chemise, cupping her breast.

Her breath hitched and she murmured wordlessly. Heat emanated from his hand, seeping into her flesh, making her ache. Her nipple gathered against his palm, tight, sensitive. Separating the sides of her gown, he offered her breasts to the moonlight, and his hungry gaze.

"So lovely." He stroked the soft underside of her breasts and rolled her nipples between his thumb and forefinger, working them into pebble-hard points.

His dark head dipped, his intention clear, but Naomi dragged his mouth to hers. Kisses were safe, familiar. She didn't understand these other feelings, so she clung to what she knew. His hand continued to caress her breasts, while he kissed her deeply, tenderly.

Abandoning herself to their kisses, she shifted restlessly on his lap. He left her breasts exposed to the night wind and found the hem of her garment. His palm ascended along her bare calf. He deepened the kiss, his tongue dueling with hers.

Tension kept her thighs pressed together. "Relax, Naomi. Open for me." She trembled, but her legs parted and his fingers brushed the damp curls at the apex of her thighs.

For a moment he just cupped her mound, applying gentle pressure. She tried not to panic. No one had ever touched her there. Surely it was sinful. She knew she was wet and she felt…swollen. That seemed to happen whenever he touched her, but why?

His finger sank between her slick folds and she tore her mouth from his, panting harshly into the night. Her inner muscles rippled and pulsed, closing tightly around his finger.

"You are so wet, so ready to take me, Naomi," he whispered into her ear.

With his finger still buried inside her, he brushed his thumb across a spot so exquisitely sensitive it made her whole body quiver. He pushed deeper with his finger and circled her sensitive nub with his thumb. She moaned, clutching his shoulders. The tension inside her spiraled out of control. Heat and tingling pleasure pulsed out from her feminine core. She arched and shook and finally collapsed against him.

Gideon eased her away, his features tight, his expression pained. His hot breath fanned her face in ragged puffs. "Oh, Naomi, how I burn for you."

She could hear desire harsh within his voice, but he set her from him and struggled to his feet. Remaining on the ground, she clutched her ruined dress with one hand, her gaze following him. He dragged deep gulps of air into his lungs and then raised his face to the sky. Naomi felt her skin prickle as she watched him. It was as if he drew strength from the darkness surrounding them.

"Will you please take me back to the Krak?" she asked awkwardly.

He didn't respond. Motioning toward his horse with the graceful sweep of his arm, he waited for her to rise.

"I don't think I can walk," she said, in a soft embarrassed tone.

Without a word, he returned and lifted her into his arms. He carried her to his horse, holding her snugly against his chest. He hesitated for a moment. His gaze moved slowly over her face. Did he enjoy having her helpless in his embrace?

He set her on the saddle and mounted behind her. With quick, efficient movements, he arranged his cloak to encompass them both and set the horse into motion.

"Did you know that man?" Naomi asked, ready for any topic other than her brazen behavior. "He said he'd just come from the Krak. I think he was a mercenary. Was he familiar to you?"

She felt his arm stiffen subtly. He took a moment to answer. "I'm not certain."

"You're not certain?"

"I was mad with rage, Naomi. I saw only your distress and the back of his head."

That wasn't true. After Gideon lifted the man off her, they had faced each other. There had been plenty of time for Gideon to determine if he knew the man. "What should I do if I see him again? What if he returns to the Krak?"

He splayed his long fingers against her ribs and his cheek nuzzled her hair. "You worry for nothing, Naomi. The villain is long gone."

He was trying to distract her with his touch. His attempt made her all the more suspicious. "How can you be certain? There are hundreds of people housed within the Krak's curtain walls. How can you possibly know that I'll not encounter him again?"

Slowing the horse to a lumbering walk, Gideon grabbed Naomi and lifted her into his arms. He swung her legs to one side so that she sat upon his lap. "The danger is gone, Naomi. Trust me in this."

His fierce expression only compounded her misgivings. "Who was that man? How do you know there is no danger?"

"You guessed correctly. I know him and I will see that he never touches you again."

"How?"

His hand tangled in her hair and he brought her face up to his. "I will kill him if you like. Is that what you want to hear? I will spill his blood and laugh as the life fades from his eyes."

"Why? What am I to you? Why would you offer such a thing? Why were you following me?" She was nearly shouting by the time she finished her list of questions.

"Tell me what you want. Name your price. What must I do to possess you?" His voice was thick with desire, harsh and urgent.

Confused and a little afraid, Naomi guided his hand out of her hair. "I have no wish to be *possessed* by anyone, and I want *nothing* from you."

"It did not seem so a few minutes ago."

She started to protest, then simply turned her face away. Untangling her skirts, she maneuvered her leg back over the horse's neck and did her best to ignore her tormentor.

Chapter Five

In the darkness behind the barracks, Gideon stomped the length of the building and back. His hands curled into tight fists, his nails cutting painfully into his palms. One powerful sweep of his mind revealed that Crispin wasn't inside the building. Dragging a long, deep breath into his burning lungs, he spun to face the wall. He had to control his fury before he summoned Crispin or his friend wouldn't survive the confrontation.

He'd saved Crispin's life on the battlefield thirteen years before. Forcing a small amount of his own blood into the mouth of the mortally wounded youth had not only triggered Crispin's miraculous recovery, it had created a strong mental and emotional bond between the two. Crispin was faultlessly loyal, but he was not a mindless puppet. Gideon had allowed him to retain his personality.

Gideon scraped his nails along the wall, and he pressed his forehead against the cold stones. He shook with the need to kill. He was angry, he was hungry, and he was aroused. Focusing on the hunger, Gideon battled back the need for violence and sexual release.

He growled low in his throat and turned to press his back against the wall. He sent out a mental summons, drawing Crispin to him. Splaying his hands against the stones, Gideon concentrated on the rough, cold texture beneath his palms. He allowed the coolness to seep into his body, calming him, soothing him.

A soft, feminine giggle broke his concentration. He sprang away from the wall and crouched, ready for battle. Females seldom traveled alone, even within the castle compound. A young woman stopped short as she rounded the corner and saw him. Held back by a solid red scarf, her long dark hair framed an unlined face. Her dark eyes were wide, luminous with fear.

"Do not be afraid," Crispin said as he stepped up behind her. "He will not hurt you."

Gideon's eyebrow arched at the lie. Had Crispin misunderstood the reason for his command or was this a clever ploy to defuse Gideon's anger? The sexual desire ignited by touching Naomi surged again. He needed release and he needed blood.

Gideon could hear the frantic pounding of the woman's heart. He could smell her fear. The rhythmic surge of her blood echoed through his entire body, and her helplessness excited him all the more.

Wordlessly he raised his hand, casting his thrall and commanding the woman to him. Her eyes stared back at him unblinking and unfocused. She stood before him utterly defenseless.

Gideon glanced past the woman, his eyes clashing with Crispin's. "Do not depart. I would speak with you."

"I will stand guard," Crispin muttered and then discreetly turned his back.

Gideon returned his attention to the woman. She began to tremble with the first brush of his fingers. Despite his mental hold over her, she could apparently sense his power, and her peril. Her features were ordinary, but her skin was soft and supple, as yet undamaged by the unforgiving climate of her home. He ran his fingers across her cheek and along her jaw. Turning her face aside, he stroked her slender neck with his fingers and then his lips.

His body hardened in a painful echo of the desire Naomi had aroused. He pressed himself against the woman, allowing Naomi's image to form within his mind. His hands wandered over the woman's soft form. He cupped her breasts and then her buttocks as he rocked his shaft against her sex, but she was a poor substitute for what he really wanted. If he took her now, would he still burn for Naomi?

Gideon groaned in frustration and banished his sexual need. This creature might be unable to fulfill his desire, but she could certainly appease his appetite. His mouth returned to her throat. Her pulse thundered beneath his lips. He closed his eyes, enjoying the intoxicating thrill of holding a life within his grasp. His fangs distended, growing in direct proportion to the urgency of his need. He traced the pulsing line of her throat with his tongue, tasting her skin, inhaling the scent of her life.

She whimpered, while he molded her trembling body against his chest, supporting her head in the crook of his arm. Gideon scraped his teeth across her skin and waited. The final penetration was so much sweeter when he prolonged the tension and built the urgency.

The erotic give of her flesh beneath his fangs sent ripples of pleasure through Gideon's whole body. Again he paused, savoring the physical connection before he began to feed. He absorbed the energy of her life and renewed his strength with her human essence.

Power surged through him. Hunger gradually abated, leaving in its place a tingling heat. Gideon pulled back, panting softly, before he swept his tongue across her skin to seal the wound.

He closed his eyes. His hunger was fulfilled, but he was not replete. The memory of Naomi's blood, sweet and pure, taunted him. Why was this happening? He must not become ensnared in his own trap.

Pressing his lips to the woman's temple, he took the memory of his face from her and muddled even her memory of Crispin.

"Take her," he told Crispin, pushing the girl away. "Then, return to me. We are not finished."

Crispin returned alone a few moments later. Again, Gideon smelled fear, but none of it showed on his friend's face.

"Did your plan work?" Crispin asked audaciously.

He was clever, this mortal man. The question inferred that any dissatisfaction Gideon was now experiencing resulted from some flaw in *his* plan.

"I told you to frighten Naomi." Gideon spoke in an even, misleadingly soft tone. He stalked toward Crispin, intentionally revealing his predatory nature.

"And was she not frightened?"

A feral growl escaped Gideon as he sprang. In an instant, he grabbed Crispin by the throat and slammed him against the wall of the barracks. He could see the golden glow of his own gaze on the stunned face of his victim. "She was a bit more than frightened, Crispin," he whispered.

"I did what you directed." Gideon's hold stretched Crispin onto his toes, but his features remained in a mutinous scowl. He reached up and clasped Gideon's wrist. "You told me to make her believe that the danger was real. Had I been any less aggressive, she'd not have been convinced."

"How long were you prepared to be `aggressive?' You touched her breast. You tasted her mouth! I should rip out your throat—"

"I acted on your command," he interrupted hoarsely.

Gideon released him suddenly and stepped back. What Crispin said was true. Gideon had arranged the situation. But he had never imagined his own reaction to seeing Naomi writhing helplessly beneath Crispin's big body.

"She should not have this power over me," he muttered, more to himself than to Crispin.

Crispin rubbed his bruised throat and wisely kept silent.

Gideon paced back and forth in front of Crispin, his thoughts chaotic, his emotions seething. "Where is Gabriel?"

"He has retired for the night, as you expected."

"Did he speak with Naomi?"

Crispin shook his head. "No one approached while I was observing him. Where did you take her after you returned?"

Jealous anger surged anew, but Gideon fought it this time. He shouldn't care that another man had touched her skin, had seen her naked breasts, but the memory brought violent urges ever closer to the surface. And his sexual frustration only compounded his need for violence. "She twisted her ankle fleeing your tender ministrations," he snapped.

"She threw herself from my horse," Crispin objected, then asked more quietly, "Is she in the infirmary or did you return her to the dormitory?"

"I took her to the dormitory, but you must be sure Gabriel checks her condition in the morning."

"And how will she explain her injury to Gabriel?"

"That is not my concern. She can tell him whatever she likes."

"Do you consider this a success? Will this help her trust you or was—"

Crispin's question was cut short by Gideon's fist. He managed to temper his strength, but he could contain his wrath no longer. Crispin grunted, the impact of Gideon's punch snapping his head to the side. Gideon welcomed the pain that shot up his arm as bone connected with bone.

A seasoned warrior, Crispin reacted immediately. He returned each blow measure for measure and then launched himself at Gideon with a string of shouted obscenities.

The two men tumbled out into the clearing in front of the barracks.

"I should break your hands," Gideon snarled, landing a punishing jab to Crispin's stomach.

Crispin fell to one knee, but shot himself forward, ramming his head into Gideon's midsection. "You are jealous!" Crispin laughed.

Gideon could kill Crispin with effortless ease, but he didn't want his friend's death. He wanted to rid his mind of *her* image, and Crispin seemed to understand. They pummeled each other and rolled across the dirt yard. One would gain the advantage for a moment only to fall beneath an especially vicious blow.

Neither of them cared that a small crowd gathered to watch the spectacle. Four men lounged in the open doorway to the barracks. Work had stopped completely in the armory and several others loitered near the stable, trying to be less obvious about their interest in the fight.

"You will *never* touch her again," Gideon shouted a few minutes later.

Crispin staggered to his feet and wiped the blood from his nose with the back of his sleeve. His chest heaved with each breath and several bruises were already darkening portions of his face, but amusement had taken over his expression.

"Be careful, my friend," Crispin warned with a reckless smirk. "This girl may teach you a lesson you're not prepared to learn."

Gideon cursed at him, but made no move to stop him when he walked off toward the barracks. With the excitement over, the crowd dispersed and work resumed.

Damn her! How had she managed to penetrate his defenses? She certainly hadn't done so intentionally. She didn't even like him. He had aroused her physical desire, but she kept her emotions protected, insulated by mistrust and fear.

He needed to think. He needed to understand what was happening to him, to analyze the insidious changes this mortal woman had triggered. Checking every angle to make sure he was alone, Gideon released his form and disintegrated into mist. The night breeze carried him beyond the castle compound and out into the darkness. When he reached the crest of a hill overlooking the vast Orontes valley, he materialized again.

Even from a distance, the fortress was imposing. It effortlessly dominated everything surrounding it. Torchlight glowed from inside the various structures, creating a shadowy silhouette of crenellated walls and stout watchtowers against the blue/black sky.

The warm night wind caressed his face and fluttered through his hair. He embraced the darkness and forced the tension from his body. A three-quarter moon and legions of stars silvered the scene with tranquil light, so different from the harsh, burning rays of the daytime sun; the burning, torturous rays that had become his enemy.

Gideon sat and closed his eyes, lifting his face to the moonlight. He had come to the Krak to confront Gabriel. In return for Gabriel's betrayal, he had planned to disrupt his life and destroy his reputation. He had hoped to force Gabriel to abandon his masquerade and return to Heaven.

But Naomi had been working in the scriptorium, not Gabriel. He grinned into the darkness as vivid memories flashed to life within his mind. She was fire and ice, passion and innocence, courage and fear.

She was human!

His eyes snapped open and golden fire illuminated the night. She was a means to an end, nothing more. The moment he touched her and felt her devotion to Gabriel, he knew exactly what he would do. He would seduce her and then disappear without a trace. He would unleash all the passion he sensed within her and then tell her to ask Gabriel *why* she had been used.

It didn't matter that she had done nothing wrong. Gabriel had betrayed him! He refused to remember the longings released within his soul by his brief exposure to her purity.

She was human!

That alone was reason enough to justify his actions. Gabriel didn't understand his resentment of humans. Neither did Michael. But they were mindless sheep, willing to serve and obey without thought or question.

This is your last hope, Gideon. You must find peace within the madness or you will be consumed completely by your own rage.

Michael's words echoed back through Gideon's mind and he spat a curse into the night. There was no peace in this madness, yet something within him still fought against the rage. He was trapped between two worlds, neither good nor evil, neither angel nor demon, neither light nor darkness.

With an angry snarl, Gideon stood. There would be no comfort in the silence tonight. He was simply too distraught. Focusing his energy on the image of a falcon, he spread his arms, crouched down, and launched himself upward from the hill.

For a long moment, he hung suspended above the earth with no substance or form. He could feel the currents of air flowing through his being. Then he concentrated, focused his energy, and took on the outward shape of the bird.

His wings flapped strongly. His bright golden eyes were all that remained of his human shape. He soared. High above the Krak he flew in lazy circles, at home in the sky, at one with the night.

Chapter Six

"Thankfully, you sent Gideon to find me. If I'd walked back to the Krak on—"

"I did not send Gideon to you." Gabriel interrupted her, his gaze narrowed and intense. "Did he tell you this?"

Fear's icy fingers stroked Naomi's spine. She sat on one of the infirmary's beds, as she had for the past five days. Her ankle was still swollen and discolored, but with her foot bound firmly for support, she was able to walk with only a bit of discomfort.

"Aye, he said you sent him to look for me."

Brother Gabriel glanced away and Naomi felt even more uncomfortable. He fiddled with the wooden cross suspended from his neck, sure proof of his anxiety.

"Why does your brother mean me harm?"

It took a long time for him to answer. "Gideon is angry with me, and he knows harming you will hurt me more deeply than any direct assault."

His compassionate gaze moved slowly across her face. Warmth seeped through her. He'd always been able to calm her fears and set her mind to rest.

"What does he believe you did? Why is he so angry?"

"I'll speak with Gideon." Gabriel evaded her question. "But you must stay away from him."

Naomi laughed, the thin, nervous sound harsh even in her own ears. "I've tried to avoid him. He seeks me out. I knew he followed me that night, but he said you sent him."

Brother Gabriel knelt beside her bed, capturing her icy fingers in the warm cradle of his hands. Naomi savored the familiar beauty of his face.

"Fear not, Naomi. I will not allow anything to harm you."

She managed a smile, but for the first time in her life she doubted his assurance. "I think perhaps this time 'tis I who must protect you." He looked so crestfallen at her words that Naomi immediately regretted them. "Or perhaps we must work to protect each other."

"Forces are at work here that you don't understand," he said. "I'm not sure if you're even more powerless than I or if you're the only glimmer of light left in his darkness. I do not know how to advise you."

"Especially when you love us both?" She guessed from the pain in his eyes.

He nodded stiffly.

"I am not afraid of Gideon."

His gaze flew to hers and his expression hardened. "Nay. You must fear him. You must not trust him. You must suspect everything he tells you and everything he does."

"I'm not a fool. I know what he's about. His weapon is seduction and he wields it masterfully. He cares nothing for me; he wants only to torment you."

Again he nodded, but his expression remained troubled.

"Go now," she urged with a quick smile. "You'll be late for Sext."

Reluctance showed in every step he took, but he finally left her side. Naomi pushed her hair off her forehead and tried to relax.

The thought of being completely overwhelmed by Gideon's passion was not altogether unappealing. He stirred feelings in her that she had never experienced before and part of her was eager to explore them more completely. But she knew it was wrong. It was sinful. She must resist him.

Gabriel would torture himself with guilt if he thought she'd been compromised because of him. Even if *she* didn't find the possibility of being compromised nearly as distasteful as she should.

But what if he never found out?

A secret thrill raced through her at the wicked thought. Nay, if she ever surrendered to temptation, Gideon would make sure Gabriel found out. Surrender was not an option.

With a frustrated sigh, Naomi turned her attention to her ankle. She carefully tested its tolerance by moving it very slowly, first up and down and then from side to side. It was only as she bent it up at a similar angle to the one that had caused the injury that she felt a painful protest.

"How does it feel?"

She glanced up from her foot to find Gideon standing beside her bed. She gasped. How had he moved so soundlessly? Had he somehow sensed her improper thoughts? It was utterly impossible, and yet looking into his golden gaze it seemed almost probable.

Forces are at work here that you don't understand.

Ignoring the echo of Brother Gabriel's warning, she smiled at Gideon. "Better, but your brother still insists that I lie in bed like an invalid."

His grim mouth parted in a spontaneous smile and Naomi felt her heart flutter. Why did she find him so appealing? With his long black hair pulled back from his angular features he appeared—well, mean. She should be frightened of him, but she found him fascinating.

"What would you be doing were it not for my brother's decree?"

"Working." She flashed a conspirator's smile. *"Cleaning* the scriptorium."

He studied her for a long, silent moment. His strangely penetrating gaze caressed each of her features in turn.

"Gabriel told me to stay away from you. He's concerned that my interest in you is not in your best interest."

"And is it?" she ventured.

He chuckled and his expression relaxed. "Probably not."

"Then, why do you continue to seek me out and why did you lie to me?"

"I enjoy your company and what did I lie about?"

She licked her lips; his eyes dropped to her mouth. It had not been her intention to draw his attention there, but an unexpected tingle crossed her lips as if he had touched them. "You told me Brother Gabriel sent you to find me. He told me he did not, so why were you following me?"

"Did I misinterpret what I interrupted? I thought you were relieved that I'd been following you." His voice was deceptively calm.

"I want you to stop."

"Following you?"

"Aye." She shifted restlessly. "Following me, pursuing me. I want you to leave me alone."

He shook his head, his gaze hot upon her face. "Nay, you do not. But this is neither the time nor the place to settle that particular debate. I want you to know that I spoke with Crispin."

"Crispin?" She didn't recognize the name.

"The man who accosted you. He offers his most sincere apologies and is willing to make them in person, if that is your want."

"I have no desire to ever see that man again." She shuddered as his sneering face flashed through her memory. "How did he explain his behavior? Is it Crispin's practice to force his attentions on whatever female happens to cross his path?"

"He will never lay a hand on you again."

"And are all of the other women at the Krak to be offered the same assurance? There are women who welcome the attentions of men. It's not necessary to force the ones who don't."

"We discussed the matter at great length, damsel. Crispin has seen the error of his ways."

There was a certain humor in his tone, a hard sort of amusement that made Naomi curious. "Was this discussion, perchance, physical in nature?"

He grinned. "It did not begin so, but Crispin was slow to admit the magnitude of his mistake, so I felt compelled to enlighten him."

"I see." The idea of Gideon thrashing that horrible creature had a certain appeal, but Naomi found nothing about the subject amusing. She'd been terrified and humiliated, and Gideon had witnessed it all. Still, if he hadn't been following her, she would have been far more than terrified and humiliated.

"I should go," he said, but he was obviously reluctant to depart.

"How much longer will you be staying at the Krak?"

"Are you anxious to be rid of me?" he teased. "Or are you missing me already?"

* * *

Gideon prowled a darkened corner of the upper bailey near the high crenellated wall. Glancing down at the missive crumpled within his fist, he mentally scrambled for a way to turn this situation to his advantage. It was too soon for an outright confrontation! He was not yet ready. Naomi was not yet sufficiently embroiled in the battle. But Gabriel's summons forced his hand.

Lifting his face to the moonlight, Gideon closed his eyes and carefully constructed Naomi's image within his mind. His body responded with pulsing desire. Gideon groaned. This was ridiculous. She shouldn't have such power over him. Refocusing his mind, he sent out a summons of his own, compelling Naomi to his side.

"I was not sure you would come," Gabriel said.

Gideon opened his eyes. Gabriel stood before him, nearly concealed by the darkness. A smile parted Gideon's lips at the irony. "What do you want?"

"I want you to stay away from Naomi," Gabriel responded impatiently. "I know you visited her in the infirmary today."

He could see little more than the darkened silhouette of his brother's form, but Gabriel's voice cracked with anger and determination.

"Did you honestly believe I would not?"

Gabriel stepped forward. A moonbeam silvered his features, revealing how they twisted with rage. Pleasure surged through Gideon. Where was the serene, ever-perfect "brother" so many had come to know?

His hand shook as he pointed a finger at Gideon. "You *will* leave her alone. I will not allow you to harm her."

Gideon braced his legs apart and tested the spring in his knees. He flipped back his hair with a sharp toss of his head, clenching his hands into fists. "How do you intend to stop me?"

The golden shards in Gabriel's eyes came alive. Gideon felt a responding rush within himself. If Gabriel wanted a fight, he'd be happy to oblige—but she wasn't here yet. He could sense her moving through the night, but she had yet to reach them.

"Has Naomi come to any harm because of me?" he asked, prolonging the conversation.

"I'm not sure. I cannot manipulate minds as you do." Gabriel's gaze remained bright, but he made no move to attack. "How was her ankle twisted, Gideon? Was she running away from you?"

There she was! He could sense her presence, feel her unique energy pulse through him. But he kept his eyes fixed on Gabriel. "What did she tell you? How did she say she was injured?"

"I asked *you.* Have you touched her? What do you hope to gain by dishonoring her?"

Gideon had no intention of discussing his motivation with Naomi listening in the shadows. "Oh, I touched her and I tasted her. The sweetness still lingers on my tongue. I can hardly wait to taste more of her."

Heaven's light shot from Gabriel's eyes, enveloping Gideon's body. He staggered back, emitting a sound that was half hiss, half groan as pain shot along his nerve endings. He struggled within the light, fighting against the pain and the restraining pressure. Gabriel's strength rivaled his own.

Gathering power into the center of his chest, Gideon concentrated and focused. Forming a dense, dark pulse in the palm of his hand, Gideon threw it at his brother. Gabriel flew backward like a leaf tossed upon the wind and collided with the castle wall.

"I will protect her," Gabriel shouted as he struggled to his feet. "You cannot have her!"

Light shot from Gabriel's fingertips, ripping through Gideon. Ten individual blades stabbed his flesh, searing his senses. Embracing the pain, drawing strength from his fury, Gideon strode to Gabriel and twisted his hands in his thick monastic robes. He lifted him and slammed him against the wall. "You are powerless to—"

Gabriel shoved his wooden cross against Gideon's chest.

Gideon screamed. He let go and stumbled back, panting harshly. A violent surge in his dark nature drove him to one knee. The beast within him wanted to tear out Gabriel's throat and gorge on his blood, but Naomi was watching. He couldn't end this performance by savaging his brother!

"Stop it! Please, stop it."

Springing to his feet, Gideon made sure Gabriel could see Naomi. Gideon's fingernails dug painfully into his palms as he looked at her. Even in the moonlight, her face looked drawn and colorless. She clutched her skirts, her eyes wide and frightened.

"Naomi," Gabriel said, a wealth of tenderness and regret in the single word. "Fear not. We will not harm you."

Gideon shot Gabriel a challenging smirk. "Do not make promises on my behalf, brother." He grabbed for Naomi's arm, but she shrieked and jerked away.

Huddled in the corner of the castle wall, her disbelieving gaze moved from him to Gabriel and back again. "What...how did you... What *are* you?"

Gabriel took a cautious step toward her, but she shrank away from him as well. Her whole body shook visibly and her eyes grew wild.

The desire to comfort her took Gideon by surprise. What was wrong with him? She was supposed to be frightened. He needed her to be afraid. This is why he had summoned her.

"Be still," he commanded and stepped up to catch her body as she slipped into unconsciousness.

"What are we going to do?" Gabriel's customary composure had deserted him entirely. He was actually wringing his hands.

Gideon shifted Naomi higher against his chest. Her weight was insignificant to him, but her softness and her scent were playing havoc with his senses. "I know many things I would like to do."

Golden light flashed in warning. "You must convince her she had a vivid dream or that it was a trick of the moonlight," Gabriel said. "Or erase the memory altogether. I know that is within your power."

"Do you have any idea what I could do if I entered her mind?"

Gabriel began to pace like a caged animal and Gideon laughed. He had hoped for a more worthy opponent.

"Then convince her it was a dream, or—"

"You underestimate Naomi," Gideon said. "She'll never believe it was a dream. Any denial I might offer will only make her more determined to learn the truth."

"I *cannot* lie, Gideon." He came closer, frustration and fear radiating off him. "You know that. If she asks me to explain what she witnessed, I will have to tell her."

"You cannot lie and, in this at least, I will not. So I guess she is destined to learn the truth."

"Give her to me. I will return her to the infirmary." Gabriel held out his arms expectantly.

Gideon turned away. "I will return her to the infirmary when I am good and ready."

"You are good and ready now!"

Gideon laughed again. He had accomplished more than enough for one night. Clasping Naomi's warm body against his chest, Gideon walked beside his brother toward the infirmary. They said nothing, but he could sense Gabriel's anger and his fear. He wasn't afraid for himself; he was afraid for Naomi. Gideon didn't care, so long as he suffered.

After arranging her comfortably on a narrow cot, Gideon induced a sleep from which she would awaken naturally.

When they stepped out into the bailey, Gabriel grabbed his arm. "Did you take the memory from her?"

"Nay. I told you I would not."

Glancing around quickly, Gabriel asked, "Why do you want her to know what we are?" He paused. "Did you *summon* her?"

Gideon grinned, giving his brother a glimpse of pointed fangs.

"You did! Why? How does her knowing advance your twisted scheme?"

"You will just have to wait—and watch."

Gabriel stepped closer, the golden shards in his eyes beginning to glow. Did he even realize his control had slipped again?

"This cannot go on forever, Gideon. I begged Michael—"

"Do not speak that name to me!" he snarled, then continued in a softer, if no less threatening, tone. "And you answered your own question. I am interested in Naomi because I have not forgotten the part you played in the existence I now endure."

"You're enduring an existence of your own making. You're an angel, and yet you—"

"I am *not* an angel. Michael saw to that."

"Nay, *you* saw to that. Michael did not create your thirst for blood. He just allowed it to become literal." Gabriel took a deep breath and the intensity of his gaze began to lessen. "I ensured that your punishment would not be permanent. You can still find redemption if you try. But you must want redemption. You must learn from this, Gideon, or all is lost."

He scoffed. "What makes you think that all is not lost already? Would you have me believe that He will have me back after all I have seen—all I have done?"

"Not while this battle rages within you. You have been running in circles for a century. It's time to take a stand. You must embrace the darkness or step back into the light."

"Perhaps I'm so comfortable in the darkness that I've forgotten the light."

Gabriel slowly shook his head. "I don't even know you when you speak like this. I can't stop you if you're bent on destroying yourself. But why take an innocent with you? Why must Naomi pay the price for your rebellion?"

"She isn't paying the price for my rebellion, brother. She's paying the price for your love."

Chapter Seven

Gideon made his way silently though the darkness, his mind troubled, his heart torn. He should feel exalted that he had come so far so quickly, but he found no joy in his victory.

Naomi's face appeared in vivid clarity. He pictured her as she had been moments before, angry and defiant, despite her fear. Then, he saw her as Crispin had left her, vulnerable and terrified.

A potent combination of lust and rage shot through him again. It was staggering that just the memory of the incident could produce so powerful a reaction. He had wanted to kill Crispin for playing his part so well.

Be careful, my friend, Crispin had said. *This girl may teach you a lesson you're not prepared to learn.*

Gideon hadn't responded then, but the warning came back to him now. Why had he reacted so violently when he knew Naomi had been in no real danger? Why would her image not leave his mind? Why did her hesitant smile and easy laughter tear at a heart he did his best to ignore?

She was more dangerous than he ever would have guessed.

Closing his eyes, Gideon surrendered to the night, allowing his form to melt away into the darkness. He needed to feed. All of the emotional upheaval had left him depleted and weak.

He had fought his need for blood in the beginning, not fully understanding what he had become. But hunger came upon him with violent spasms of pain and his body rejected everything except human blood. He had long since come to terms with the conditions of his survival. He was a predator; he relished the hunt. And he never forgot the reason—an existence of his own making, Gabriel had called it.

A guard was dozing on a secluded section of the parapets. Gideon materialized in front of him and kicked the man's sword out of reach. "Your captain would be displeased to find you so," he said in a rough whisper.

Snatched from his sleep by the scraping of metal across stone, the guard jerked to attention and looked up at Gideon with both anger and confusion in his blurry eyes.

"Who are you?" the guard asked.

"Rise," Gideon directed, allowing the radiance of his golden eyes to enthrall the guard. The man wore no chain mail or metal helm. Obviously, he didn't take his assignment seriously. Gideon grasped his hair and jerked his head to one side, exposing his throat.

Deepening his mental control, Gideon ensured the guard's silence as he sank his fangs into the human's neck. Rich, warm blood filled his mouth and soothed his ravaged composure. He drank deeply, but halted before any real harm was done to the mortal. He never killed to feed, though he often fed from the victims of his sword. Finding fresh blood on a battlefield was never difficult. Protecting his ultra sensitive skin from the sunlight had always been more of a challenge.

A creature of light, forced to hide from the sun—it was despicable...

He sealed the wound with the careful sweep of his tongue and dematerialized before releasing his hold on the guard's mind. The human would remember nothing and would attribute his weakness to lack of sleep or something he had eaten.

Gideon chuckled as he passed through the darkness, becoming part of the night. As Gabriel had said, it would have been simple for him to rid Naomi's mind of what she had seen. With each passing year, his ability to control humans grew. He could erase or manipulate memories with little effort.

He didn't consciously choose his destination, but suddenly he floated above Naomi's narrow cot. She lay on her side, curled like a child. He sank toward her and gently penetrated her mind. Instead of taking the memory as Gabriel suggested, Gideon infused her dreams with sensual images and burning desire. She moaned, rolling onto her back.

Gideon burned with the need to materialize and touch her. He shifted restlessly, pulling back from her mind before the desire to take her overwhelmed him completely.

He was playing with fire.

Passing through the thatched roof, Gideon soared straight up and joined with the night sky.

Soon!

The word was whispered on the wind before it dissipated into the darkness.

* * *

Gideon's mouth descended along her throat, across her shoulder, onto her breast. Why was she naked? She never slept without a modest garment. But his eager lips closed around her nipple, drawing firmly on the sensitive peak. She moaned, arching her back, pushing herself more deeply into his mouth. He caught her nipple between his teeth and laved it with his tongue. Tingling heat swirled through her chest, spiraling deep into her body, igniting her woman's core.

Oh, this was wrong. He should not be taking such liberties and she should not be enjoying his carnality!

Her body melted, liquid heat easing the way for his penetration. She spread her legs, accepting his presence between them shamelessly. She wanted him, needed him, burned for him.

Caressing her legs, her hips, his hands never stopped moving, all the while his mouth adored her breasts, suckling firmly.

He took her hand and closed her fingers around his thick shaft. She trembled. He would thrust this inside her. This would fill her, complete her. She tried to guide him closer, to move him to her entrance, but the image wavered, fading...

Naomi sprang up in bed, barely managing to stifle a moan. She pressed her hand to her chest and felt the frantic pounding of her heart. Where was she? Distorted images and fragments of memory combined, melding until she wasn't sure what was real and what she had only imagined.

Shifting on the narrow cot, she took several deep breaths and looked around. The first rays of dawn colored the room in pinks and gold. She was back in the infirmary, but she had no idea how she had gotten here.

Her mind was muddled. Sensual images shifted and rolled, confusing her, disturbing her. Gideon's face loomed, his eyes bright with desire. His body tangled with hers, pressing and sliding, his hands stroking, moving—always moving... That much couldn't be real. Regardless of how tempting she found him, Gideon had never shared her bed.

The last thing she clearly remembered was sensing that something was wrong and slipping from the infirmary to investigate.

Thinking back on it now, even that seemed odd. Why had she gone wandering around in the dark? Why did she leave the safety of the infirmary? And how had she known just where to go?

Naomi threw back the covers and began to dress. She wanted to believe the rest had been some bizarre dream, but unlike the other images, she knew what followed had been real. She'd heard their angry voices. Golden light had flown from Brother Gabriel's eyes and Gideon had flung him about without actually touching him.

She paused, shaking as possibilities inundated her mind.

Forces are at work here that you don't understand.

Brother Gabriel had tried to warn her, but she had no idea he meant the words so literally. Were they sorcerers? Practitioners of the Dark Arts? Did the Holy Order of St. John realize they harbored...harbored what? What were they?

She paused and drew a long, calming breath into her lungs. She was loath to bring danger to Zarrah's door, but Naomi had nowhere else to go. She had no intention of remaining at the

Krak to see what they intended now that she knew they were not human.

She could no longer trust Brother Gabriel. Pain lanced through her at the thought. He was the only father she'd ever known, her trusted friend and mentor. Until last night.

The bell tolled announcing Prime and Naomi muttered a curse. It was later than she realized. Hurrying to the dormitory, she gathered her possessions into a bundle and thought of her sketches, charcoals and pens. Did she dare risk a trip to the scriptorium?

Someone cleared their throat in an obvious attempt to gain attention. Naomi looked up and caught her bottom lip between her teeth. Brother Seth stood in the open doorway. Fear prickled across her skin, but she tried not to panic. True, he was Brother Aaron's assistant, but he could be looking for someone else.

"What can I do for you, Brother Seth?" Naomi asked, careful to keep her tone casual and calm.

"Brother Aaron wishes to speak with you."

Her hope sputtered out. "Did he mention what it was regarding?"

"He didn't say."

"I'll be there directly," she responded, needing him to leave.

If Brother Aaron was one of these creatures, it was more imperative than ever that she escape. And if he didn't realize there was something *unusual* about Brother Gabriel, then she had no hope of convincing him of what she had seen. Who would believe such a wild tale if Brother Gabriel chose to deny it?

"He requested that I escort you," Brother Seth informed her.

Tension banded her abdomen. What should she do? She couldn't run with her injured ankle. Would they try to stop her if she simply ignored Brother Seth and left the Krak?

"Shall we go?" he asked.

This might not have anything to do with the night before, but Naomi could think of no other reason for the summons.

It was unlikely she could make it to Zarrah's village without assistance and she really didn't want to endanger her friend. Perhaps it was best to find out what the castellan wanted.

With a reluctant nod, she fell into step behind Brother Seth. When they reached the southwest tower, he knocked briefly, then opened the massive door.

Before she could change her mind and find a place to hide, Naomi stepped past him and into the castellan's chamber. The ceiling was dramatically vaulted, drawing Naomi's eyes upward. The subtle scent of costly beeswax candles drifted in the air even though the shutters framing the wide windows had been thrown open to welcome the sunlight.

"Thank you for coming, Naomi."

Dragging her gaze away from the sculpted masonry high above her, Naomi settled her attention on the man seated behind a heavy oak table. Writing instruments, a large ledger and several well-read tomes were scattered across the surface. Brother Aaron was dressed in monastic robes, but the white cross centered upon his chest was elaborately embroidered.

Brother Aaron's gaze shifted to some point behind her. Glancing over her shoulder, she found Brother Gabriel standing in the open doorway. Fear rippled through her in a numbing wave. He smiled, but Naomi just stared. She had only to close her eyes to see the strange golden light emanating from him.

"Come," Brother Aaron said. "Sit. I have interesting news."

Brother Aaron seemed casual, almost jovial. This couldn't have to do with the night before. Did he know what Brother Gabriel was? And what exactly was Brother Gabriel? Naomi settled herself in the chair beside him, but she was uncomfortable even looking at him.

"I received a message from Antioch this morning," Brother Aaron began, apparently oblivious to the tension crackling between the other two.

"Who sent the message?" Brother Gabriel asked.

"King Louis of France." He paused for a rather cheeky grin. "Perhaps you have heard of him."

Brother Gabriel smiled and shot Naomi a speculative glance. "Perhaps," he muttered. "What was the message regarding?"

"It seems that King Louis is making inquiries on behalf of one of his noblemen."

"Inquiries into what and on behalf of whom?" Brother Gabriel prompted.

"The message is not detailed. King Louis says only that one, Leon of Le Puy needs to speak with the Knight Hospitaller who was entrusted with an infant girl in Jerusalem eighteen years past. To my knowledge, that can only be you."

He rested his hands on the tabletop and gazed at them silently as if there was no more to explain.

Naomi folded her hands in her lap. What did it mean? Was someone looking for her? This was every orphan's dream, but why now after so many years?

She was about to speak when Brother Gabriel asked, "What is his interest in the incident?"

"That is what you shall find out two days hence. That is when Monsieur Le Puy is due to arrive," Brother Aaron informed them with a casual smile.

"This man is coming here?" Her voice cracked with disbelief. Seeing the displeasure in Brother Aaron's eyes, she quickly bowed her head, offering a belated show of deference. "I beg your pardon. I'm confounded by these tidings. What will be expected of me?"

"The message was to make us aware of his impending arrival and to encourage our full cooperation with his investigation. It would seem that our guest is on rather familiar terms with the French royalty."

"And if his investigation proves I have some connection to this person, you will no doubt be pleased." Naomi continued to stare at her folded hands, knowing her gaze would reveal her frustration.

"I have reserved my conclusions. I suggest you do the same." Hearing the calm authority in Brother Aaron's tone, she glanced his way. "I intend to extend Monsieur Le Puy every hospitality, and I expect you to be polite and cooperative. These are characteristics that do not always come naturally to you, hence the reason for this meeting."

"Naomi." Brother Gabriel's beseeching tone drew her gaze to his. "Why do you feel threatened by this man when you have yet to meet him?"

The threat closing in on her had nothing to do with the unexpected Frenchman, but she couldn't explain that in front of Brother Aaron. "I treasure my life the way it is. I have worked very hard to find contentment in circumstances that are unusual, to say the least. I want nothing to disrupt the order I have managed to create."

"If the order of our lives was never disrupted, we would never change, never grow, never become more than we had been before," Brother Aaron said.

Naomi silently inclined her head, unwilling to debate the issue when she was unable to explain the true cause of her turmoil.

"I will have Sister Renee find something more suitable for you to wear when you are presented to Monsieur Le Puy." He held up his hand when she started to object. "You may go."

Brother Gabriel nodded and motioned Naomi toward the door. Brother Aaron pulled the ledger back in front of him and carefully opened it across the table. Brother Seth closed the door after they stepped out into the corridor.

Anger joined the anxiety knotting Naomi's stomach as they headed for the stone stairwell. She understood a woman's role in the world. The world had been designed by men for men, but in the quiet sanctuary of her scriptorium, she sometimes forgot that she too must follow the rules. She worked on her drawings and the world agreed to pass her by.

Well, her sanctuary was well and truly breached, and she wasn't sure where to turn for solace.

Naomi preceded Gabriel down the steps.

"Naomi," he said softly, halting her just before they reached the bottom. "Why are you afraid of me? I have never seen this fear in your eyes before."

She turned around. He stood two steps up from her, so she tilted her head to see his face. "I have never seen lightning bolts shooting from your eyes before."

He smiled, his expression uncertain. "Surely not lightning bolts," he teased. "Sunbeams, perhaps, or Heaven's light."

"Heaven's light? Then, what does that make you? A god? An angel? A ghost? What happened last night? How were you able to do those things?"

"I will never hurt you, Naomi. You must believe that. I could not, even if that were my want. It is impossible for me to cause you harm."

He hadn't answered her questions, Naomi realized, and her eyes narrowed. "Who are you?" she asked directly.

"I am Gabriel, and I love you more than life itself."

A tingle ran down her spine and Naomi felt tears burn her eyes. How she wanted to believe it, but he still danced around the issue. *"What* are you?"

Gabriel hung his head, his posture defeated.

Why did *she* feel guilty? He was the one harboring secrets. "I should be thrilled by Brother Aaron's news. I never dared to dream that something like this might happen. I accepted that my mother was dead and whatever family I might have was lost to me. But all I can think of is escape. I want to run away from *you.* My father, my dearest friend. How can I trust you? How do I know—"

"You can trust me with your life." Conviction rang in his tone. "No harm will come to you while you are in my care."

"How can I believe that, when you will not even tell me what you are?" He reached out to her, but she jerked away. "Do not touch me. My entire life I believed in a person who does not exist. I will mourn for my friend and mentor, but I do not know what to make of you."

Ignoring his pain-filled call, she rushed out into the bailey and headed in the opposite direction from Brother Gabriel.

When had the world gone mad?

She didn't want to meet this Frenchman and yet she wanted nothing more. She wanted to scream and she wanted to weep, but she no longer had a shoulder to cry upon. Ignoring the twinges of pain in her ankle, she hobbled back toward the dormitory.

Many lonely nights she had tossed in her bed, wondering about her parents. How had her mother come to be in Jerusalem alone, lost or deserted, at the mercy of strangers? Did her father know she existed? Was he still alive somewhere, wondering what had become of her?

The questions were unending once they began, so Naomi forced them all aside. She longed to confide in Zarrah, but she was not yet sure what she would say. Would she simply explain that a man was making inquiries into her past or dare she share what she had seen the night before?

If Brother Gabriel wouldn't tell her what she had witnessed, how would Gideon respond? Was she brave enough to search him out and demand a clear, concise explanation?

Tingling heat chased shivers down her spine. Gideon did nothing without a reason. If he gave her the answers she desired, what would he demand in return?

Chapter Eight

Church bells rang, announcing Compline, but Naomi was too upset to pray. She sat in a secluded corner of the upper bailey informally dubbed the meditation garden. Stone benches scattered throughout the area invited others, but Naomi was glad to be alone.

She toyed with the figs and nuts contained in the woven basket on her lap, but very few actually reached her mouth. Having long since abandoned her sandals, she wiggled her toes in the prickly grass and angled her face to better catch the gentle evening breeze.

What was she going to do?

No one seemed to know where she could find Gideon. Half of the people she asked didn't even know who he was. Even Brother Gabriel hadn't been in any of his usual places. Were they together somewhere plotting their next move? She chuckled at the ridiculous thought and tossed a nut against the wall. They might share extraordinary abilities, but they were still adversaries.

"I was told you were searching for me."

His voice was so much a part of her thoughts that it took Naomi a moment to realize Gideon had really spoken. She looked to her right and found him standing indolently beneath one of the trees. His shoulder rested against the slender trunk, arms crossed over his chest.

"Brother Aaron received a message from King Louis of France," Naomi began. "A man named Leon of Le Puy is making inquiries regarding an infant girl, who was born in Jerusalem eighteen years ago."

"And you believe this infant girl is you?"

"I don't know what I believe. Brother Gabriel seemed…this is not why I was looking for you."

He grinned, a slow salacious smile. Her nipples tightened against her undertunic and she fought the urge to cross her arms, hiding the distinct bumps. "Brother Gabriel won't answer my questions. I was hoping you would—" In three long strides he stood before her, his fingers cupping her cheek. She turned her face away. "Please don't touch me. That is not why I came looking for you."

"Little liar," he taunted, drawing her to her feet. "We were parted for less than a day and already you crave my touch. Did you dream about me again? Is that why you were searching for me? So I could show you what it feels like in reality?"

In a flurry of angry movements, she snatched up a shallow bowl and threw the figs at him. Gideon only laughed and batted each aside.

"You arrogant beast. I want nothing from you but information. When will you accept that fact?"

A fig bounced off his cheek and Gideon reacted instinctively. He slapped the bowl from her hand and shoved her against the curtain wall. His hands pressed against the stones on either side of her while he glared into her eyes.

Fear exploded all around him, the rancid smell, the icy tension, the unwanted stimulation. "Do not push me too far, Naomi. I will retaliate."

He knew she was terrified—his senses didn't lie—but her expression revealed none of her fear. Her wide blue eyes sparked with defiance and her shoulders remained stubbornly squared.

"You don't mean me harm," she said emphatically. "Not physically, at least. It wouldn't serve your purpose."

"You have not begun to comprehend my purpose. Only a fool would believe otherwise." He didn't touch her, but a heated current flowed between them. He didn't need to touch her to feel her.

"If hurting me would accomplish what you have set out to do, you would have ended my life last night."

He moved closer, his craving for her a sweet agony. His clothing brushed hers. Her scent filled his head and all he could see was her eyes. "Shall we speak of last night? What has Gabriel told you? Did he explain what you saw?"

"He would not speak of it." Her lips parted and her tongue darted out. "But you want me to know. *That's* why I was looking for you. Why do you want me to know...what is it you want me to know?"

The stones were cool beneath his palms, but desire raged through him. He wanted to kiss her, to touch her and taste her.

He wanted to feel her silken heat close around his shaft while his fangs sank slowly into her throat. Channeling the urgency of his need into his hands, he drove his fingernails into the wall.

"You drew me there last night. I know you did. I would not have left the infirmary otherwise." She prompted him when he didn't speak. "So, explain what I saw."

"You saw an angel lose control."

She laughed. The sound grated along Gideon's frayed nerves.

"You expect me to believe that you're an angel?"

"I didn't say I was an angel," he said.

"Brother Gabriel is an... *Gabriel,* as in the Holy Scriptures?"

"Angels are not well represented in the Scriptures, but aye, some of what Gabriel has done is recorded there."

She swallowed and Gideon watched the movement of her throat. Her lips parted, then pressed together. He could almost hear the questions racing inside her mind.

"How can you be his brother if you aren't an angel? Are angels born? I don't understand any of this."

"Angels are not born, they are created. Gabriel and I were created together. Brother is simply the easiest way of explaining the bond that lies between us."

Her gaze shot to his as he spoke the last. "A bond so strong that you seek to destroy him? Gabriel told me you hope to punish him by..."

When she couldn't find the words, Gideon assisted her. "Possessing you."

"If you're not an angel, then what are you?"

"There are words for what I am," he told her. "But I don't think they would mean anything to you."

"Are you a fallen angel, like Lucifer?"

The question tore through his senses. Rage flared as his mind filled with unwanted memories. "When an angel Falls, he forfeits his immortal soul. If Gabriel is to be believed, my soul is still intact."

As his explanation grew more specific, her fear rose again. He watched the pulse pound along her throat and felt each of her anxious breaths against his skin.

"Why are you angry with Gabriel?"

He could no longer ignore his need to touch her. Retracting his nails from the stone, he framed her face with his hands. "He betrayed me. He has chosen to participate in my punishment."

"Punishment? Why are you being punished?"

Gideon lost interest in the conversation. "I have a bad attitude."

Naomi's head throbbed as she tried to assemble all of the fragments of information. The warmth of his palms against her cheeks distracted her, muddled her thinking.

His face descended slowly. She knew he meant to kiss her, but she didn't turn away. The harder she fought, the better he liked it. The faster she ran, the more persistently he pursued.

The first brush of his lips was soft, teasing. She inhaled his unique, spicy scent and allowed her mouth to relax, neither responding nor resisting.

"Your skin is so soft," he whispered. His fingertips danced along her jaw to stroke the arch of her neck. "I want to touch you, Naomi. I want to touch all of you."

She shivered. Already liquid heat and tingling anticipation stirred within her body. He had to be a sorcerer. How could she hope to resist such skill? "You can make me want you, but it will never be more than physical desire."

His arm slipped around her waist, molding her against his body. "What makes you think I want more?"

His mouth sealed over hers before Naomi could respond. The taunting tenderness was gone. She did her best to hold her emotions back, to feel no more than the slide of his mouth against hers and the slow stroke of his tongue. But heat and friction gradually wore her down. She felt tingling sparks shoot down her spine and her toes curled into the grass.

His fingers raked through her hair and splayed across the back of her head. Forceful now, his mouth urged her to accept the penetration of his tongue. A sharp, hollow ache erupted in response to the intimacy. She groaned and arched her body into his, needing to feel the unyielding contours of his form. Everything about him was hard and hot.

He tore his mouth away from hers and Naomi murmured a breathless protest. How was he able to command her senses so effortlessly? Her head spun and all she could think about was getting closer to him, having more of him.

He tilted her head and stroked his tongue along her throat. She had never realized her neck was so sensitive. Her breasts began to ache and the material of her chemise irritated her nipples. He scraped his teeth across her skin and Naomi moaned.

Gently, his hand cupped her aching breast. Even through her clothing the pressure felt wonderful. She wanted to strip naked and offer herself to the moonlight, the night wind and this man. Wild, primal urges, frightening in their intensity, made her arch into his hand.

"Touch me, Naomi. Put your hands on me."

She didn't question the command, but burrowed through layers of clothing until she found heated skin. He groaned. His fingers plucked her nipple and she parted her legs, allowing his muscular thigh to rub against her aching sex.

"Here. Touch me here." He brought her hand down along his body and Naomi gasped. She could scarcely close her fingers around him. Hot and hard within the circle of her fingers, his shaft jerked and pulsed with a life of its own. Molding his fingers over hers, he showed her how to move, how to stroke him.

Fascinated by the mystery that was this man, Naomi moved her hand up and down along his shaft. He rocked his hips while he explored her body with his hands.

He found her knee and pulled her leg up, angling her calf across his hip. Feeling the cool brush of the night wind against her heated flesh, Naomi murmured a protest.

"Our first time will not be against a cold stone wall. Trust me, sweeting. I'll not hurt you."

His fingers parted her passion-slick folds and she whimpered, clutching his shoulders for support.

"Keep your leg up," he said.

Then she felt him rub something hot and blunt against her. "You said—"

He silenced her with his mouth. His tongue thrust deeply, while he traced her feminine slit, over and over, around, but not into her.

Her leg shook, her arms wrapped around his neck, as he carefully worked between her thighs. He pushed against her, venturing as far as he dared. Her folds stretched to accommodate him, then his fingertips stroked that secret knot of nerves and her core exploded with sensation. She arched forward, her head thrown back as each spasm of pleasure rippled her body tightly around his. Jerking his hips backward, he spilled his seed into the dirt.

Stunned by what they'd just done, Naomi lowered her leg and glanced around guiltily. She'd been so lost in passion, half the order could have strolled by and she'd not have noticed.

He framed her face with his hands and kissed her gently. "When we do this, really do this, it will be so much better."

He pulled her into the circle of his arms, molding her to his tall, warm body. She pressed her face against his chest, embarrassed, yet unafraid.

Suddenly, his head snapped up and he spun around. "Who goes there?" His voice cracked with authority.

She covered her mouth with one hand. Had someone seen them? What was wrong with him? She saw no one.

He spread his arms, his stance protective. "Show yourself!"

"There is no one here," Naomi whispered, but even as she said the words the hairs on her arms and at the nape of her neck prickled. She could sense something.

"Show yourself or be gone. I have no time for games."

Naomi wanted to laugh at that statement, but tension gripped her muscles and made her pulse leap. Something was here, unseen, yet present.

"Who are you?" Gideon stepped away from her.

Had he determined she wasn't in danger or just forgotten about her? She remained against the wall, crossing her arms to hide their shaking.

Gideon turned in a slow circle, arms spread, eyes closed. "There," he said, striding toward the space between a palm and the castle wall. "If you have no purpose here, be gone."

Naomi heard a distant, eerie laugh. It could have been a trick of the wind, but suddenly the tension knotting her belly released.

They were alone.

"What was that?" she whispered, as his posture began to relax. Her heart still pounded and every nerve in her body hummed with an awareness so acute it hurt.

"I'm not certain."

Gideon took a step toward her, but Naomi held out her arm to ward him off. Angels and unseen spirits. It was suddenly just too much. She needed to be away from him, far, far away.

"No more," she whispered. "Just leave me alone."

Naomi snatched up her sandals, hobbled past him and hurried along the path as quickly as her ankle would allow.

Chapter Nine

Naomi folded her arms and rested them atop the thick battlement. From her vantage point high on the southeastern tower, above the scriptorium, she could see the immensity of the castle compound. As one wandered through its numerous passageways and wards, it was easy to forget the imposing grandeur of the Krak des Chevaliers. But standing here now, with the wind kissing her face, Naomi was awed again by its majesty.

This was her home, her fortress, her sanctuary, and never before had she felt so besieged.

The very foundation on which she had built her life had been shaken—was quaking still. How could she make rational decisions when the world no longer made sense?

"You are being needlessly dramatic," she spoke to the wind. "Surely, other women have learned that their fathers are really angels and the only man they have ever been attracted to is not a man at all."

She laughed, needing the release, but feeling only desperation.

"You are not a stupid person. It is within your power to determine what is best for you. Gabriel is an angel, so how does that change your life?"

Warmth caressed her back, though she faced the sun. She dragged in a deep breath, ignored the fist squeezing her heart, and slowly turned around.

Gabriel stood there, as she knew he would. His beautiful features expressed uncertainty and his hope that somehow she could still accept him.

"What brings you here?" she asked, doing her best to sound casual.

"A heavy heart." He laced his fingers together, his gaze earnest and sad. "Naomi, I cannot bear it if you despise me."

Her skin prickled and the fist around her heart loosened just a bit. She searched his face, looking for the angel, but seeing only Gabriel: her friend, her mentor, her confidant.

"Tell me truthfully, are you an angel?"

His warm gaze met hers directly. "I am."

"Why did you keep this from me?" Tears burned the back of her throat.

"There was no reason for you to know. It does not change who I am or how I feel about you."

The deception still stung, but it could not be changed, so Naomi left it alone. "What is Gideon? He said he was once an angel, but he is being punished. How is he being punished? What did he mean?" She whispered the questions, needing the answers, but fearing them.

He fiddled with the cross around his neck. "What do you know of angels? How do you perceive us?"

Naomi hesitated. Was this simply another way for him to avoid the issue? "I know what is recorded in the Scriptures: heavenly host proclaiming the birth of Christ and delivering messages from God."

"And how much do you know about Lucifer?"

The wind carried a strand of hair across her face. Naomi tucked it behind her ear and said, "He coordinates all things evil."

"Aye. But he began as an angel," Gabriel reminded her.

Goosebumps broke out on her arms. "I have never understood why God created his own enemy," Naomi confessed. "If God created Lucifer, then did not God create evil?"

Gabriel smiled patiently. "There must be balance in all creation, Naomi. Good and evil, light and darkness, right and wrong, life and death. Lucifer knew it and I suppose he felt it more powerfully than anyone else."

Fascination and revulsion washed over Naomi in alternating waves. She was speaking with an angel about the devil. Her heart did a little flip within her chest. "Gideon knew Lucifer?"

"We all knew Lucifer," Gabriel said. "When he began his campaign, we were forced to choose sides. We either joined the rebellion or defended Almighty God."

"And those that joined the rebellion were cast out of Heaven with Lucifer." Naomi thought of the passages she had read and the stories she had heard, but until now none of it seemed real. How could such conflict exist in Heaven, the wellspring of ultimate peace?

"Gideon chose to remain loyal to God, but he was bitterly torn. He knew that Lucifer was wrong—that he was paying the price for his pride and arrogance—but they had been friends, Naomi, close friends."

"What did Gideon do?" His image came to her, the angry press of his lips, the tension in his expression and the flash of rage so often in his eyes.

"Gideon took his place in Michael's army and systematically destroyed the ones he loved. He obeyed, but he resented what he was commanded to do."

"It made him bitter," she said softly.

"It filled him with resentment and rage. It stirred something dark, something violent within his nature." Gabriel paused, glancing away. "Once the rebellion was over, he no longer had an outlet for his frustration, so he looked for someone to blame."

"I don't understand."

"He couldn't blame Lucifer, for he loved the angel Lucifer had been before the Fall. So, Gideon focused his resentment on the most important of all God's creation: man. He began to crave violent assignments, to revel in them. He saw the love and devotion God poured out on mankind as a sort of betrayal, another injustice."

She fought against the compassion unfurling within her. Gideon ruthlessly manipulated anyone and anything to get what he wanted. She would not feel sorry for him!

"God cast him down to Earth as He did Lucifer?"

"Nay, Gideon was not cast out." Gabriel took Naomi's hands between his own. "Michael, the archangel, told Gideon he must reform."

She sighed as the warmth of his touch soothed her. "Michael has authority over the other angels?"

Gabriel nodded. "Michael directs the angels at God's command."

"But Gideon did not reform. He told me that he has a bad attitude."

Again, he nodded. Releasing her hands, Gabriel walked about the walled enclosure. Each movement revealed his anxiety.

"Michael was ready to let him Fall. He felt that Gideon had already chosen; that his lust for blood and his resentment of humans had corrupted his angelic nature. I couldn't spare Gideon completely. His rebellion had to be punished—even I understood that—but I was able to convince Michael to make the punishment temporary."

"But what is his punishment?"

Gabriel took a long time to answer. "Angels are creatures of light. Gideon is now a creature of darkness."

Naomi shifted against the rough stones at her back. How could she be attracted to a creature of darkness? How could his touch melt her inhibitions and make her senses burn? "He is evil?"

"It is not that simple. There is evil in Gideon, but there is goodness as well. I meant the phrase literally. He cannot be in the light. The rays of the sun burn his skin and drain his strength. He must avoid the light of day."

Anxiously searching her memory, she verified that each time she had seen Gideon it had been near sunset or fully night. "How does he travel if he cannot tolerate sunlight? How has he survived as a mercenary? Not many battles are fought during the night."

"Gideon must explain it to you. It is really not my place to reveal his secrets."

Naomi wasn't about to argue. He'd explained far more already than she'd hoped to hear. "You said his punishment is temporary. How much longer must he remain in darkness?"

"Again, there is no easy answer. It isn't a matter of time. Michael didn't create in Gideon anything that wasn't there already, he simple expanded his freedom."

"Are you speaking of free will? The ability to choose good over evil?" Naomi shifted her weight, finding a more comfortable position. Gabriel continued to pace.

"Angels are not created with the same freedom of spirit that God has given to man. We are designed to be obedient and faithful. Michael released the constraints on Gideon's spirit, allowing him to experience fully the extremes of his own nature, much as mankind does."

"And how is this supposed to lead him to redemption?" Naomi asked. She wasn't at all sure she liked Michael's idea of rehabilitation.

"It isn't meant as a cure for his rebellion, Naomi. It's a trial, a final time of testing that will decide Gideon's eternity."

Naomi shivered and crossed her arms over her chest. An anxious fluttering, like the wings of a butterfly, tumbled about in her stomach. "What must he do to end the trial?"

"He must work through his anger. He must learn to love and understand humans, or at least desire the understanding, then—"

"His only hope lies with the creatures he hates most?" she cried. "That is so unfair."

His warm brown gaze came to rest upon her face. She saw a subtle pleading there and suddenly wanted to run.

"He doesn't hate you, Naomi. You're the first human with whom he has made any sort of a connection. I don't fully understand why he wanted you to know what we are, but it was important to him."

Unable to stand still any longer, Naomi reached for the end of her braid and pulled loose the ribbon. "He knew I would feel betrayed by your omission."

"That was part of it, but I can't help hoping that something within him still longs for the light."

She didn't know what to say. Turning to face the bright sunshine, she raked the thickness of her hair with her fingers and let the wind play through it.

He stepped up beside her. "I know you're afraid of him, and you should continue to be wary, but if you could..." He shook his head and looked away. "I can't ask this of you. It is just that he is my brother and I love him."

She had so many questions. But the more she learned, the more frightened she became. "If I could do what?"

"If you could point him back to the light. He needs to see the goodness in mankind, the tenderness, the loyalty and bravery. You are all of these, Naomi. I know what Michael expects of Gideon, but I don't know how to change him. He will not listen to me."

"You cannot change him; no one can. He must want to change himself."

Gabriel nodded, his expression suddenly sad. "That's what frightens me most. But whether he realizes it or not, he's reaching out to you."

The wind blew her hair all around her and Naomi felt as tousled as the strands. "What if I'm not strong enough to lead him? What if he leads me?"

"I'll not let it go that far. If you begin to succumb to his darkness, I'll pull you back. I love Gideon, but I'll not lose you both. If he doesn't respond to the light within you, then Gideon will Fall."

* * *

Naomi spent the rest of the day researching angels in the order's extensive library. The Holy Scriptures contained very few details about the Fall of Lucifer, but the number and variety of activities attributed to angels surprised Naomi. From wrestling with Jacob all night and dislocating his hip, to annihilating Sodom and Gomorra, angels were certainly said to have done more than deliver messages.

Gideon would have had ample opportunity to spill the blood of men in his role as an angel.

She stopped by the dormitory on her way to the scriptorium and found three "secular" outfits neatly folded on her bed. Doubtlessly the clothing Brother Aaron had mentioned. It wouldn't do to have her meet a nobleman looking like a pauper. She exchanged her plain brown tunic for an ensemble of vivid blue wool. Even the undergarments were soft, much finer than hers. Making a mental note to thank Sister Renee for her generosity, Naomi continued her trek toward the scriptorium.

Her mind was so occupied with everything she had learned in the library that she didn't immediately notice Gideon lounging on the stone steps leading up to her workroom.

His mouth parted in a beckoning smile and he whispered, "I've been waiting for you."

Chapter Ten

With the predatory grace that accompanied all of his movements, Gideon stood and casually blocked the stairwell. The supple material of her garment molded to the fullness of her breasts, silently inviting his gaze and his touch. "Where have you been? I missed you."

She cocked her head and laughed softly. "Did you now? What did you miss? My charming wit, my challenging intellect or the fact that I have no intention of succumbing to your practiced seduction?"

"My seduction is not nearly so practiced as you presume."

"You just have a natural aptitude for such activities?"

"Nay." He hesitated. The truth would make her angry, but perhaps it was safer for them both if that soft, approachable warmth left her eyes. "Seduction has seldom been necessary."

Sure enough, anger flared within her gaze. "How foolish of me. Women must trample each other to share your bed."

"Oh, I seldom bother with a bed."

He watched those enticing breasts rise and fall as she indulged a deep sigh. "What do you want?"

"I want to see if your breasts taste as delightful as..." His words dissolved into laughter as she turned around and walked away.

Her gait was a bit uneven, he noticed. Her ankle must still pain her. "I was only being honest," he defended himself, falling into step beside her.

"You were being outrageous. You enjoy being outrageous."

"I enjoy many things."

"None of which interest me." She stopped and faced him. "Do you intend to follow me back to the dormitory? Men are not allowed within, so it's a waste of time."

"I have all the time in the world." A pang of some unnamed emotion responded to the boast.

"Are you certain of that?"

Her velvety gaze moved over his face and Gideon bristled. He didn't want her pity. How much had Gabriel told her? Why would she look upon him with anything but fear or desire? "Walk with me."

"Why?"

"Because the scriptorium is hot and you don't really want to hide within the dormitory."

She finally smiled. "Hiding from you is the wisest course. I've known from the first moment I saw you that I couldn't trust you, but I find I can't even trust myself where you're concerned."

Why would she admit this to him? Did she not realize the power it gave him?

"You know my body responds to you. So, what point is there in pretending?"

Stepping toward her, he asked, "What point is there in resisting?"

Her hand came to rest in the middle of his chest, holding him back. "I mean nothing to you. I'll not lie with a man who has no feelings beyond desire."

He shrugged off her hand, not understanding how she'd turned the situation around. She ran, he pursued; that was how the game was played.

"If I walk with you, will you answer my questions?"

"If I answer your questions, will you let me touch you?" he countered.

"Perhaps," she said, shocking him. "We both know I enjoy your touch."

Heated desire tore through him and he felt his fangs distend. The little minx. She wasn't supposed to enjoy the game. She was supposed to struggle and resist.

"There's something I wish to show you," she said softly. "Will you agree to behave, if we go to the scriptorium?"

"I'd be pleased to see anything you're willing to show me."

He couldn't read her expression, he realized, as they retraced their footsteps. She learned quickly and she was not nearly as helpless as he had first supposed. Or perhaps he was just less dangerous. That thought disturbed him greatly.

"Where did you pass the day? Gabriel didn't know, or wouldn't tell me," he said.

Her musical laughter floated around him like the warmth of a summer breeze. "Gabriel was in the chapel when I left the scriptorium, so he wasn't hiding my location."

"Which was?" he asked impatiently.

"Most recently the dormitory. Brother Aaron didn't want me appearing before the Frenchman looking like a beggar, so he persuaded Sister Renee to donate her clothing to me."

"Thus the new gown." Her cheeks blossomed with color and Gideon smiled. Was she pleased that he had noticed, or embarrassed? "It is most fetching. Though I find myself quite envious of the material." She was definitely embarrassed now.

They reached the top of the curved stone steps and Naomi paused. "Do you always say exactly what you please?"

"Aye. I find no reason to do otherwise."

"Tact and politeness?" She made the suggestion with just a hint of challenge in her smile.

"Boring concepts created by hypocritical old men."

She laughed again and his whole body clenched. Did she not realize how she stirred his hunger? Nay, how could she? She didn't know what he was, unless Gabriel told her—and that was unlikely.

"So did my brother finally admit that he is an angel?" he asked casually, but what he really wanted to know was how much Gabriel had told her about him.

"Aye. Is it physically impossible for him to lie?"

She was struggling to light an oil lamp, so Gideon waved his hand and the wick ignited. Gasping, she took a quick step back, then looked at him.

"Angels can speak only truth." He lit two additional lamps before he asked, "What did he tell you about me?"

"A mere fragment of what there is to know, I suspect."

She moved the lamp to the small stand near her angled table. The golden glow upon her face made her skin appear impossibly smooth and soft. He wanted to touch her flesh and slowly remove her new garments until lamplight caressed her entire body.

"What did you want to show me?" His voice sounded thick and rough. He couldn't help but smile. Hiding his emotions from humans generally came effortlessly to him, but she made him feel everything so strongly he could conceal nothing.

"I would prefer to answer your question first. Gabriel explained why you are being punished."

"Because I'm not content to be a mindless servant?"

Pulling her stool away from the table, she sat and looked directly into his eyes. "I spent the day in the library learning what I could about angels. I'll not pretend to understand how you feel, but I'm attempting to—"

"Why?" He cut off her words with his sudden movements. Grasping the table on either side of her, he framed her with his body. "Why would you try to understand me?"

He expected her to shrink back, to cower against the table or push him away. When her hand rose to his cheek and warmth filled her bright blue eyes, it was all he could do not to retreat. Her fingers were so warm and her touch so gentle that the beast within him tossed restlessly.

"There is more to what you feel for me than the desire to hurt your brother," she said softly, carefully. She brushed her thumb over his bottom lip, her gaze following the movement.

Gideon set his teeth, but refused to flinch.

"I'm not a fool. I know you don't love me, but this is no longer about revenge."

Deftly catching the pad of her thumb between his teeth, he punished her honesty with a firm nip. She gasped and then laughed, but her hand trembled as she pulled away.

He leaned in closer, inhaling her scent, absorbing her heat. "It is about lust." He whispered the taunting words directly above her ear.

"Lust is cold," she whispered in return. "Easily sated and quickly forgotten. What burns between us is far more complicated than lust."

She pivoted on the stool and he was forced to step back. Dislodging one of his hands, she reached under the table and retrieved a scroll and an intricately carved wooden box.

"Is this what you wanted to show me?" He exaggerated the disappointment in his voice.

She chuckled and nodded her head. "If you cannot expose yourself to sunlight, how have you survived as a mercenary?" She glanced back over her shoulder. "Are you a mercenary? You arrived with a group of them, so I presumed you were one."

"I have no association with those men, but I do offer my sword for various forms of compensation."

Her fingers encircled his wrist and she pulled him around to stand in front of the table. Did she feel safer with an obstacle between them or was it simply easier to converse facing him? No matter, he certainly enjoyed looking at her.

"Most battles occur during daylight hours. How are you able to fight?"

"The trappings of war have served me well. A coif and hauberk, mail gauntlets and a helm—I am covered from head to toe."

"Then it is only your skin that reacts to the sunlight?"

"Nay. I am a nocturnal creature now. I cannot fight my nature. I also search out valuable information. Certain of my abilities make this nearly effortless."

She put her elbows on the table and rested her chin on her folded hands. "You're a spy."

He chuckled at the mischief twinkling in her eyes. "I am many things."

Her attention turned back to the items she had set on the table. First she opened the box and withdrew ragged scraps of vellum in various shapes and sizes. "I drew most of these when I was quite young, so you must not laugh or you will hurt my feelings."

Though her technique had improved greatly over the years, her talent showed in even the first drawings. Gideon looked at each sketch she handed him, determined to remain unmoved by her work. The first group depicted boys and girls, most of them about five or six.

"Where were you when you drew these?" he asked.

"Jerusalem. Brother Gabriel had not yet been transferred here. Some of these were my friends; some were other orphans that I cared for. I was twelve when we came to the Krak."

"This is primarily a military outpost. Why did you not remain in Jerusalem? Surely, you were less isolated there."

She returned the loose sketches to the box and put it back on the shelf beneath the table. "I didn't want to be separated from Brother Gabriel. Besides, he had allowed me to assist him with his work by then and I became nearly obsessed with improving my craft. I began with simple borders and progressed until we were working side by side."

Motioning him back to her side of the table, she was relieved when Gideon obliged. She slowly unrolled the first section of the scroll and Gideon's breath caught in his throat.

"I began this two years past," she said softly. "It is rather self-indulgent, but it chronicles life from my perspective."

The first person she had drawn was the castellan, Gideon saw. She had perfectly captured his subtle arrogance and the sharp intelligence in his eyes. There were many people Gideon didn't recognize, but he paused when he came to the depiction of a young woman.

"Who is this? What caused the sadness in her eyes?"

"The sadness is often in her eyes. She lost her husband and now her son has no father. Her name is Zarrah."

He offered a stiff nod and shifted the scroll. She had drawn Zarrah again, but this time she was with a dark-haired boy. Pride and affection radiated from her expression.

"That is Benjamin, her son."

Next she had drawn a grouping of people. An elderly man had joined Zarrah and Benjamin. Gideon studied their expressions, denying the knot of emotion forming deep in his chest.

War had exposed him to brutality and ruthlessness. These sketches radiated all of the emotions Gabriel had named: loyalty, joy, tenderness and—love.

He quickly worked his way through the scroll until the drawings stopped and the surface was blank, ready for her next entry.

"You have not drawn Gabriel," he said, handing it back to her.

She carefully tightened the scroll and secured it with smooth leather thongs. "I have tried. I cannot capture his..." She paused, searching for the right word. "Illumination."

Gideon made a derisive sound and walked to the window. Bright stars dotted the vast darkness of the sky. He felt restless. He felt empty.

He could hear her shuffling things, moving around, but he didn't turn and look at her. Her innocent beauty was more than he could endure right now. Why had she shown him those sketches? Why did she want him to *feel?* Why should she care...

Her scent interrupted his discontent. She stepped up beside him but said nothing.

They stared out into the night. He didn't touch her. She didn't speak. She simply shared his isolation, and for the first time in nearly a century Gideon was not alone.

Chapter Eleven

Naomi paused outside the castellan's chamber to gather her composure. Smoothing the plush velvet surcoat down over her hips, she adjusted the angle of her chain link girdle and took a deep breath.

Leon of Le Puy waited on the other side of the door. Every instinct she possessed warned that he held her future in his hands. The past few days had given Naomi a confidence she had never known before. If she could face down the likes of Gideon, what had she to fear from a mere mortal?

Amused by the thought, she knocked firmly on the door and offered Brother Seth a quick smile as he pulled open the barrier. Brother Aaron stood beside Brother Gabriel; they faced a third man, whose back was to the door.

"Here is Naomi, my lord," Brother Aaron said as she moved farther into the room.

The stranger turned and her steps faltered. Breath lodged in her lungs, refusing to be expelled. His rich garments and sparkling jewelry bespoke his station in life, but she squared her shoulders and reinforced her determination.

I'll not be intimidated by his regal bearing. He has come looking for me.

"My lord." She greeted him softly, even managing a small curtsy.

She noticed his eyes next. They were a bright, true green, fringed by thick dark lashes. His straight brown hair had been neatly trimmed over his ears, with the back only slightly longer. Devoid of beard or mustache, the clean planes of his cheeks and jaw made him look almost boyish, but his skin was creased at the corners of his eyes and deep brackets framed his mouth.

"I am Leon." He introduced himself informally. "And I have reason to believe that you are my niece."

"Shall we sit?" Brother Aaron suggested. "I believe we'll all be more comfortable." He moved behind his desk. Three high-backed chairs had been arranged in front.

Naomi waited until everyone was settled before she asked, "What led you to believe that I am your niece, sir?" She watched his expression closely.

"I had suspicions before, but you are Esther's image." His gaze moved over her face, then gradually focused in on her eyes. "Your hair, your features, everything except your eyes—and they are doubtlessly a gift from your grandfather."

His eagerness to claim her sent suspicion tumbling through Naomi. "If I have living family, then why has it taken you eighteen years to find me?"

"Let me explain."

"Please do," she said.

"Roderick of Monthamn is your grandfather."

"Only if I am indeed your niece."

"Let him speak, Naomi." There was warning in Brother Aaron's eyes.

"My father and Roderick went on crusade together." Apparently undaunted by her objections, Leon continued. "They spent four years here and became fast friends. When Roderick returned to England, he decided to foster his son with my family."

"You have holdings in England as well as France?"

"Nay. Malcolm was sent to France. We grew up together. Malcolm was as much a brother to me as a friend."

She noticed that he used the past tense. "Please, go on."

"Esther was my youngest sister. She fancied herself in love with Malcolm long before he saw her as anything more than an annoying child. But as she matured, we all noticed the change in Malcolm's attitude toward her."

"He began to return her affection?" Brother Gabriel guessed.

"To say the least. Malcolm was a zealot. He dedicated himself wholeheartedly to whatever caught his attention. So, when Esther caught his attention, no power on earth could have kept them apart."

He paused and Naomi fidgeted. "I still do not understand."

He smiled. "You will. My father welcomed a match between our families but felt Esther was too young and Malcolm too immature to allow more than a betrothal. Then, he sent us here, to the Holy Land. My family was granted a fiefdom in the county of Tripoli and my uncle was overseeing the construction of a castle. Father thought that some time apart would serve to slow the attraction between Esther and Malcolm."

"How did Esther come to be here?" Naomi asked.

"We had been gone for several weeks before she began to suspect that she was increasing. None of us realized that their relationship had progressed so far, of course. Esther was headstrong and determined to be with the man she loved. Without my parents' permission, she made her way to Tripoli."

Naomi folded her hands in her lap and looked at him askance. "How did she accomplish such a voyage without the support of her parents?"

"Our family owns a small fleet of ships, my dear. She simply boarded a vessel bound for Tripoli. All of our captains are well used to transporting family members."

Such a thing seemed inconceivable to Naomi, but she didn't question him further. Instead, she asked, "How did Malcolm react to her arrival?"

He sighed and his mouth pressed into a grim line. "Malcolm met a member of the Knights Templar and, as was his wont, he dived into his new passion with his whole heart. He took vows of poverty, chastity and unrelenting dedication to the order. He had moved to Jerusalem by the time Esther arrived in Tripoli.

"I sent word to Malcolm and his response was shocking to say the least. He sent a missive documenting his marriage by proxy to Esther and naming her child his sole heir, but he said his calling was genuine and his past life no longer existed for him. He refused to leave the order."

Shocked by her father's selfishness, she could barely speak. "What if my mother had survived? What if she had wanted to marry?"

"An annulment was out of the question with offspring, but divorce—"

"Is an abomination," Brother Aaron muttered.

Sparing the pious castellan only a quick glare, Leon continued the tale. "Needless to say, she was devastated. I arranged an escort and scheduled passage back to France, but again without telling anyone, Esther changed the itinerary."

"Why would you send her away after such demoralizing news?"

Naomi could picture her mother, frightened and alone, abandoned by those she loved most. Her heart ached and she closed her hands into fists.

"I'm a soldier, Naomi. Esther needed the support and understanding of our mother and other women. Besides, my orders took me into battle within a fortnight of her arrival. It was not safe to leave her unprotected."

She nodded, but pity still tugged at her heart. "How did you learn what she had done? And what become of this missive?"

"I sent a message home inquiring after her wellbeing, but instead of receiving a written reply, my parents arrived in Tripoli. We went immediately to Jerusalem, figuring she had gone after Malcolm, but he had not seen her, so we worked our way backward from Jerusalem to Tripoli. The closest we ever came to locating her was finding out that she had made arrangements with one of our captains in Jaffa. She never arrived to make the voyage, and no one knew what had become of her."

Naomi looked at Brother Gabriel. The pieces of the puzzle were beginning to fit, but parts of the story were still jumbled. "Did you not send word about the woman who had come to you?"

"Aye," Brother Gabriel said. "But we had no idea who she was. We couldn't begin to guess who to notify."

"When Malcolm told us she hadn't contacted him, we believed she had never made it as far as Jerusalem," Leon continued. "We organized our efforts believing she was headed home from some port before Jerusalem."

Naomi scooted to the edge of the chair, tucking her hands beneath her skirts to hide their trembling. Was it possible? Could all this be true? "And this document still exists?"

"The document never left my mother's keeping. But at the time, we all believed Esther and her child were lost to us."

"And what brought you here now? After all these years, what led you to Brother Gabriel?"

"A minstrel." Leon chuckled softly before he explained. "A minstrel came to Monthamn Keep and sang about a mysterious flame-haired damsel who came upon a gallant Knight Hospitaller in the Church of the Holy Sepulchre. She pressed her newborn babe into his arms and then died from a broken heart. When Roderick questioned the minstrel, he explained that his brother was a Knight Templar and had witnessed the events himself. Esther's hair was more brown than red, but the ballad originated in the Year of Our Lord, 1130, the same year she disappeared.

"The coincidence was too intriguing to ignore. Roderick sent for me. He asked that I return to Jerusalem and continue the investigation we had abandoned eighteen years ago."

"You have been to Jerusalem?"

"Nay. I encountered King Louis' entourage as I traveled and he agreed to use his influence to assist me in my quest. He contacted someone within the Order of St. John and they sent word to the Krak des Chevaliers, and here we are."

Naomi felt control over her life slipping away. With nobility came responsibilities and obligations. She was free to do as she pleased, free to pursue her work and...she didn't want to reshape her life according to this stranger's expectations.

"Surely, I was not the only child orphaned in Jerusalem that year," she objected. "What proof do you have that my mother was Esther of Le Puy?"

"Beyond your physical appearance?" he asked with a patient smile. "There is one way to be sure." He turned to Brother Gabriel. "When Esther was seven, she was scalded while helping my mother make soap. She had a scar on her hip and thigh. Did the woman you tend have such a mark upon her person?"

"Aye," Brother Gabriel said. "She had a rather large scar on her right hip and thigh. It was faded, but it could well have been the scar left behind by a burn."

Leon simply nodded.

Naomi knew that Brother Gabriel would never lie to her. Leon had no reason to establish a relationship if none existed, but still she held herself back.

"You're overwhelmed," he said softly. "That was not my intention. I'll leave you now. Think over what I have said and we will speak again on the morrow."

"What do you want from me?" she asked as he reached the door.

"I want nothing from you, Naomi. I want only to restore to you what is rightfully yours."

He bowed and took his leave.

Time stood still. So many thoughts and emotions inundated her mind that she could absorb none of them.

"Are you all right?"

She glanced up, drawn from her shocked stupor by Brother Gabriel's voice. He stood in front of her, his hands folded together, his expression compassionate and concerned.

"I do not know," she answered honestly.

"He has no reason to concoct such a tale," Brother Aaron said, echoing her thoughts. "You are clearly this man's niece."

Pressing a hand over her pounding heart, Naomi cleared her throat. "Will he expect me to return with him to France? Or was it England?"

Brother Aaron shrugged. "It sounds as if you have ties to both. Why does this dishearten you? Anyone else I know would be thrilled."

Naomi did not miss the snap of annoyance in the castellan's tone. "I am..."

"Overwhelmed, as Leon said," Brother Gabriel repeated.

"Have I no choice but to do this man's bidding?" Worry awakened her numbed senses. "What if I do not wish to leave? I have a life here. I have friends and a purpose. Do I still have a place within the Order of St. John?"

"Are you ready to join the Order of St. John?" Brother Aaron challenged. "You have avoided the commitment for too long already. If you choose to remain, Naomi, we will expect you to take your vows."

She felt her jaw go slack and snapped it shut.

Men! Why must she be controlled by these men?

Slowly pushing to her feet, she glanced at Brother Gabriel. Turmoil churned within his gaze, but he held his peace.

"I understand," Naomi said stiffly, and left the room.

Chapter Twelve

"Naomi, I can pass through the door," Brother Gabriel said. "Bolting it against me serves no purpose."

Naomi glared at the locked portal and turned back to the scroll she had just secured to the surface of her drawing table. "If it were your intention to intrude upon my privacy, you would have done so by now."

"You have hidden away since you left us this morning. You need food and you need to speak with someone about your feelings."

"I have no appetite and my feelings are obviously irrelevant. I will see you on the morrow."

She heard nothing more for a long moment. Had he finally abandoned his post? Good. The more she thought about Brother Aaron's ultimatum, the angrier she became.

Turning back to the scroll, she puffed out a frustrated breath. Anything she drew in her present state of mind was bound to be macabre. She interlaced her fingers, put her elbows on the table and rested her chin on her hands.

"If you do not wish to speak to me, I cannot force you. But you need to eat."

She pivoted on the stool and found Brother Gabriel standing a step back from her table. He proffered a shallow woven bowl.

"Can you walk through walls or is it only wooden doors that prove no barrier?"

"I am able to go where I am needed," he said.

"You are not needed here."

"I may not be welcomed, but I am needed."

She took the basket, more because he looked uncomfortable than from any real interest in the food. "What can you do? What can I do? I must make a choice; it is as simple as that."

"You do not find the choice simple or you would not be upset. Let us move to the supply table. You could spill something on the scroll."

She laughed at the parental suggestion but followed him across the room. He'd cleared a small space for her basket by the time she reached the table. He quickly brought two stools and in moments they sat facing each other.

Naomi blew a loose lock of hair out of her eyes and looked dispassionately at the contents of the basket. A roasted chicken leg, two thick slices of brown bread and a chunk of yellow cheese.

"Did you bring wine?" she asked.

"Cider." He nodded toward an earthen pitcher she hadn't noticed before.

She poured the murky beverage into a cup and waited for his lecture to begin.

"I have no speech prepared. I just know you're in pain."

Raising her gaze to his, she asked, "Can you read my thoughts? Can Gideon?"

"I am able to sense basic impressions of your emotional state. Gideon's abilities are more complicated."

Her brow arched at his evasion. "Is avoiding direct answers any different than telling outright lies?"

He chuckled. "Apparently. I am able to be evasive, but lies cannot pass my lips."

"Can Gideon read my mind?"

"If he wants to, he can hear your thoughts. As I understand it, he must make some sort of mental connection before the thoughts begin to flow. The thoughts of each person around him do not enter his mind."

"I see." She took a quick sip of the cider. The spicy taste rolled across her tongue, cool and surprisingly welcome.

"Is questioning me about Gideon your way of avoiding what is really troubling you?"

She laughed and took a deeper drink. "Gideon troubles me, make no mistake about that."

His forehead furrowed and the shards of gold within his eyes grew brighter. "What has he done?"

"Nothing. That is the problem. I showed him my private scroll and I know he was moved by the drawings. He seemed more conflicted than ever, and now he's avoiding me."

Gabriel grinned. He all but bounced with his pleasure. "This is wonderful. Do you not see? You stirred his goodness. You touched that place in him that has been hidden for so long. I knew you could do it. I knew you were the—"

"He will retaliate. I sense it. He will come after me as he never has before."

For a long moment Gabriel just stared at her, searched her features and her gaze. "What do you feel for my brother? What emotions does he stir within you?"

Naomi picked up one of the bread slices and ripped it in half. "All of them." She expelled a sharp little laugh. "I feel compassion and tenderness, sympathy and pity. Yet, he makes me angry and frustrated. I want to understand him, and yet the thought of fully understanding him is more frightening than anything I have ever imagined."

"You desire him."

It was not a question. "He knows I'm attracted to him in the carnal way. I have stopped trying to hide the fact that he fascinates me. That confused him. He expected me to continue to resist."

Gabriel took the mangled bread and gently squeezed her hands. "You move him in ways no other could. But you're right. The more successfully you challenge him, the more apt he is to retaliate. Be careful."

"Brother Gabriel."

"Aye."

Could she speak the words? Could she admit her deepest fear? "I... I..." Even with her gaze averted she couldn't confess the dark cravings Gideon had unleashed within her. "I'll be careful."

He kissed her brow. "Shall we speak of Leon now?"

"Nay. I meant what I said about that. It is a choice I alone must make. You really cannot help me decide."

"If you change your mind, call out to me and I will come."

She expected him to vanish into thin air, but he walked to the door and unlocked it. Disappointed by his conventionality, she quickly slid the bolt back into place after he had departed.

"What did you really want to say to him?" Gideon asked from somewhere behind her.

Naomi closed her eyes and leaned her forehead against the door. Why would they not leave her alone?

"`I will be careful' is not what you meant to say. I no longer wish to participate in this game? I want you and your brother to leave me alone? I—"

"You're not as perceptive as you think," she said and turned to face him.

Gideon sat on the stool she'd just vacated, one foot propped on the cross rung of the other stool. The evening breeze stirred strands of his loose hair, drawing her attention to his angular features and flashing golden eyes.

One dark brow arched at her statement. "Then, what were you going to say?"

"How long were you lurking in the shadows, listening to our conversation?"

"Not as long as I should have been, if the last few comments are any indication. The more you challenge me, the more likely I am to retaliate? That makes your actions sound just as calculated as mine. Are you trying to challenge me, little girl?"

His golden gaze swept over her, a silent provocation. Naomi's skin tingled as if he stroked her with more than the heat of his gaze. Tension gathered low in her abdomen and her breasts ached.

She couldn't deny his charge. The change in her attitude had been intentional. "I challenge you to look beyond the darkness, to see yourself as I see you."

He crossed the chamber in three angry strides. Her back bumped against the door. She'd never seen him like this, so obviously tormented.

Bracing his hands against the door, he leaned in until the heat of his body saturated her clothing, but he didn't touch her.

"And how do you see me?" he asked, his gaze on her mouth.

"With my heart," she whispered.

He growled and his arms closed around her. Naomi cried out as the room swirled and the floorboards disintegrated. She wrapped her arms around his back, desperately clinging to him. They fell through space, passing through walls and a dense section of earth before emerging in complete darkness.

They landed with a muted thud and Naomi gasped. Her back pressed against something soft as Gideon came down on top of her. She cried out again, blinking frantically.

She could see nothing.

The dense, cloying void pressed in on her, suffocating her. "Gideon," she whimpered. "Light a lamp."

He straddled her hips, his body arched over hers, but she couldn't see him. Reaching out blindly, she found his chest and the loose strands of his long hair.

"Please," she said urgently. "I'm frightened."

"This is what I see, Naomi," he snarled. "This is the world in which I live."

His mouth found hers effortlessly in the darkness. She squirmed, clutching his shoulders and closing her eyes against the oppressive lack of light.

He wanted her to be frightened—because she had frightened him. The realization soothed her, allowed her to think.

She pushed her fingers into his hair and responded to his kiss. Desire could only be a punishment, if she allowed it.

Stroking her tongue over his, she heard his throaty groan. She arched, pressing her breasts against his chest. She touched his cheek with her fingertips and traced his jaw, slowing the kiss, making it gentle.

"Stop it," he said, pushing her away.

A torch flared to life high on the stone wall.

"Where are we?" she asked, trying to see beyond him. She lay on a pile of furs, but there was nothing else in the windowless room.

"In the undercrofts of the castle." He took her hands and pressed them into the furs above her head. "This is where I sleep, while sunlight rules the earth."

"Why have you brought me here?" she asked softly, meeting his gaze with manufactured calm.

"I thought it would be more comfortable than one of the tables in the scriptorium."

He wouldn't hurt her. This was a game to him. If she didn't want him, he wouldn't force... She licked her lips.

But she did want him. How could she possibly resist him, when she wanted him as badly as he wanted her?

"You made me look into the light, to feel the pain of all that I have lost. Now it's your turn, Naomi. Are you ready for the darkness?"

Gideon sealed his mouth over hers before she could respond. His hands tightened around her wrists as he slowly sank his tongue into her mouth. She stiffened beneath him, but gradually she accepted the bold thrust and tilted her head, fitting their mouths together more securely.

Damn her! She was supposed to resist, to be appalled by his black soul. Where was her terror? Why did she sigh so sweetly and accept his aggression, arch into his touch?

Tearing his mouth away from hers, he stared down into her flushed face. "Do you doubt that I will take you?" The words ground out, raw and anguished.

"I doubt that you will hurt me." Her eyes were wide and luminous in the torchlight.

"Then you are a fool." He needed his anger. Without his rage, there was nothing.

He dragged her to her knees, unclasped her metal girdle, and yanked her clothing off over her head. She gasped and said his name in a soft plaintive whisper, but she made no move to cover her body.

She knelt there, naked but for her sandals. Her thick braid trailed over one shoulder and down into the valley between her high, rounded breasts. Her arms remained at her sides, leaving her feminine curls visible. Torchlight danced across her silken skin, taunting him, tormenting him.

He shed his own tunic with the same urgency and watched her eyes widen. Ah, there it was. He finally smelled fear. Now she would grab her garments and race from the room.

But she didn't move. She stared at him, her expression uncertain, yet tender.

"You aren't the monster you would have me believe," she said softly, her lips trembling. "Or if you are, you need not remain so."

He should shove her to her back, thrust to the hilt and feed from her breast. That would show her what sort of monster resided within him.

Panting for breath, he pulled her to him and molded her body to his. He circled her waist with his arm, cupped her cheek with his other hand and dragged her scent deeply into his lungs.

"I *am* a monster, Naomi. Never doubt it."

She started to argue, but he silenced her with his mouth. She needed to understand the scope of his darkness, see clearly how dangerous it was to trust him.

He lifted her slightly and turned her away from him. Still on their knees, he pulled her hands behind her back and held them there in one fist while his other hand cupped her breast.

"I want to touch you," he said, moving his hand to her other breast. "So, I will touch you."

Her head dropped back onto his shoulder and she moaned. "You're not a monster," she whispered stubbornly.

He rolled her nipple, plucking one and then the other until they were hard, distinct peaks. Each sharp little gasp, each jump and quiver of her flesh sent heated thrills darting through his body.

"How do you like the darkness so far?" He taunted her, sucking a patch of skin at the base of her throat so forcefully he knew she'd bear his mark.

She shifted against him restlessly. He threaded his fingers through her feminine curls and pulled her backward, pressing his throbbing shaft against her buttocks.

Gideon groaned. "Shall I take you now, Naomi? Shall I bend you forward and sink into—"

"Stop it." She jerked away from him, but he still held her hands at the small of her back. Her sudden movement rocked her forward, nearly into the position he had described. "You will not hurt me." She no longer sounded certain.

Good.

"You are a virgin, sweeting. Pain is unavoidable the first time—but the second and the third..."

"You will not take me against my will. You are not a monster."

She sounded desperate, not defiant.

Gideon nearly let her go, but his middle finger slipped between her folds and he felt the moist heat awaiting him. "Oh, Naomi," he murmured.

He released her hands and rotated her body, quickly laying her back against the furs. She struggled madly, but in an instant he had his legs wedged between hers and her arms pinned above her head.

"Still doubt that I'll hurt you, little girl?"

Her wide unblinking eyes stared up at him as he arched over her body. All he had to do was thrust home. He knew she was afraid, but he could not define the other emotions twisting in her tear-bright gaze. Shifting both her wrists to one hand, he touched her face. Her breath escaped in a ragged whimper.

His fingers curled around her neck and his mouth settled over hers. She didn't respond to his kiss, remaining passive and distant beneath him. It became a challenge. He traced her trembling lips with his tongue and only ventured deeper when he knew she wouldn't bite him.

"Kiss me, Naomi," he said coaxingly. "Know my taste."

Tentatively, she touched her tongue to his. He released her hands and slipped his arm under her neck, supporting himself on his forearm and his knees. He deepened the kiss. She raised her arms, slipping one hand into his hair and exploring his shoulder with the other. She responded, eagerly stroking him, feeling him, tasting him.

Her uninhibited touch thrilled him, encouraged him. He cupped her breast, framing her nipple between his thumb and forefinger. She made a soft, urgent sound as he dragged his mouth from hers and his body clenched in response, throbbing painfully. He dipped lower and captured her waiting nipple. She cried out.

Distracting her with his mouth, he moved his hand between her spread thighs. He had to touch the heart of her, penetrate her, if only with his fingers.

He pushed his middle finger slowly into her body and groaned as her slick flesh closed around him. She trembled. He slid out. She grabbed his wrist.

He nipped her breast in silent warning. "Let me," he whispered.

"I should not."

"But you will."

Her hand moved to the back of his head, anchoring him against her breast. Gideon focused on the slick heat of her feminine core, pushing into her again and again. Carefully, he added a second finger and heard her moan. She tossed her head against the furs, her legs shaking. The scent of her arousal, and the heat, was nearly more than he could bear.

He lifted his head to watch her face. Her eyes were closed, her lips parted. She arched her back, thrusting her breasts upward. He couldn't resist the invitation. Lowering his head again, he suckled firmly, circling her nipple with his tongue.

She clung to him, her neck bowed, offering more of her silky skin for his mouth to explore.

Pushing his fingers deeper, he butted up against the thin membrane humans valued so highly. The urge to thrust through it slammed into him, making him shake.

Instead, he searched with his thumb until he found the swollen nub that made her whole body jerk. He circled it gently, feeling the pulsing of her body around his fingers take on a distinct rhythm.

Her fingernails bit into his shoulder and her back arched.

"Don't fight it," he coaxed. "Let it come."

He changed the motion of his hand, combining the circular stroking of his thumb with the steady slide of his fingers.

Dark hunger stirred ruthlessly within him. Her scent wrapped around him like incense, and he felt his fangs distend.

No! He could not do this.

You are not a monster. Her soft voice called to him through the darkness.

Her body clenched his fingers as her climax washed over her. Gideon squeezed his eyes shut, fighting back his need.

He battled the dark hunger, raged against the nature consuming him. He raised his face, absorbing the torchlight. A raw cry tore from his throat, and he sank his fangs into her throat.

Chapter Thirteen

Gideon's heart thundered in his chest as Naomi slumped to the furs in front of him.

What have I done?

His body hummed with pleasure so intense it was nearly painful. And the taste of her blood still coated his tongue. He covered his face with his hands and cried out, howling in anguish and fury.

What have I done!

Not trusting himself to touch her, he tossed his hair out of his eyes and bent over her. He waited for the stirring of her breath against his cheek, his own breath trapped within his lungs.

A faint, warm puff finally came and relief shook his entire body. He hadn't killed her.

He angrily batted at the tear hovering at the corner of his eye. Lifting her into his arms, he sealed the wound he had made in her neck and cradled her against his chest. Her skin was cold, her lips blue.

The dichotomy within him stretched and pulled until he felt as if his physical body would be torn asunder. He clutched her to his chest, buried his face in her hair and rocked her gently like a child.

How could he have lost control?

You're not a monster.

The echo of her stubborn assurance brought a new wave of guilt crashing over him. He stared down at her pale features, aching with the need to protect her—from him. His hand trembled as he brushed hair off her brow, and he loathed the creature he had become.

Or if you are, you need not remain so…

He couldn't allow her to remember this abomination. Where should he take her? She would be weak and confused when she awakened.

He could take her to Gabriel.

And confess what he had done?

Never.

The scriptorium, then. He gently supported her against his chest as he pulled her clothing on over her head. Donning his own tunic was nearly as awkward, but somehow he managed.

He lingered a moment longer, caressing her cheek with the back of his fingers. This must never happen again. As much as the thought tormented him, it must end tonight.

He had to let her go.

Surrounding her with mist as he surrendered his corporeal form, he swept her along with him. Through the darkness, through the night, to the scriptorium in the southeastern tower.

He lit a single lamp and glanced about the small chamber. The only area not cluttered with tables was near the window. Sitting her against the wall, he carefully leaned her into the corner, and went to work. Retrieving her cloak from its peg by the door, he spread it on the floor and arranged her upon it.

He pressed his lips to her temple and carefully removed the memory of their encounter, replacing it with other images. She would remember falling ill soon after Gabriel left and feeling too weak to return to the dormitory or summon assistance.

Tucking the cloak around her legs, he stared at her for a long moment.

Cold objectivity protected him from the world, but he couldn't be objective with Naomi. He couldn't think of her as irrelevant, expendable—human.

Even now, he ached with the need to hold her, to shelter her, to lose himself in her goodness. It couldn't go on. The only way to protect her—and rid himself of these desires—was to stay away from her.

He glared at the lamplight and it sputtered out. Inhaling her scent as the darkness embraced him, Gideon leapt from the window to the courtyard below.

Unfamiliar emotions expanded within him as he moved through the shadows. The subtle warmth of passion shifted and intensified, but he couldn't identify what he was feeling. It had been so long. This was tenderness, he realized suddenly and—he was happy!

Why would the thought of leaving Naomi make him happy?

Because it is the first selfless thought you have had in nearly a hundred years.

A smile parted his lips.

If Naomi could accept what he was, if she could look beyond the resentment and the rage... Hope tore through him and Gideon groaned.

No. He couldn't allow himself to think like that. She must never learn the true nature of his punishment. He couldn't bear to see the inevitable horror in her eyes.

Sharp, burning pain stabbed through his abdomen, driving the breath from his lungs. He bent over, clutching his stomach and collapsed to his knees. Like a wind-fueled wildfire, the sensations expanded, radiating outward from his belly to his chest and down his arms.

Panic seized him. He couldn't breathe!

He had to do something—anything—to ease the violent cramping. Rocking forward, he wretched into the dirt. He heaved in long, draining spasms until every drop of Naomi's blood was purged from his body.

Rolling away from the mess, Gideon lay flat on his back, trembling uncontrollably. He bent his legs and threw his forearm over his eyes.

What did it mean?

He drew slow, deep breaths into his body and exhaled them even more slowly.

Why had his body rejected her blood?

Or had her blood rejected his body?

This didn't make sense. He'd never reacted this way with anyone else. He *had* to feed to live.

Struggling to sit up, he shoved his hair out of his eyes and groaned.

"You've looked better, my friend."

Gideon's head snapped to the side and a violent shudder shook him. He could sense the entity, but it was not visible. "Show yourself, you coward, or is spying from the shadows all you know?"

"I didn't want to frighten Naomi or I would have revealed myself sooner." As the creature spoke, his form solidified.

"Domieno?" Gideon whispered incredulously.

He hadn't seen his friend since before the Fall. The transformation was subtle, but unmistakable. Domieno's long, pale hair hung to his shoulders in lank strands, where before it had flowed in golden waves. The shape of his body, tall and lithe, seemed unchanged, but his eyes—his demonic nature burned with malevolent intensity within his soulless eyes.

"It's been a long time, my friend," Domieno said.

Gideon stared at his onetime companion and the conflict within him raged. His fingers dug into the dirt and his muscles tightened and rippled. "Why are you here?"

Domieno strolled toward him. "To help you find peace."

Each step he took made Gideon more restless. Clamoring and clawing, the evil in Gideon reached out for Domieno. Yet revulsion and abhorrence intensified with equal fervor until Gideon had to turn his face away.

He fought down the bile rising again to his throat, sucking in great gulps of air.

"You're being torn apart and it does not have to be like this." Domieno spoke in a soft, silky tone. His words slid across Gideon's senses, drugging him, coercing him. "It's only painful because you fight it. You're one of us already, but you must accept it, surrender to it."

Gideon enjoyed the intoxication for a moment, allowed it to ease the conflict, to soothe him. It was so tempting.

"Get thee behind me, demon! You have no place here!" Gabriel's sharp command snapped Gideon out of his stupor.

Domieno hissed and his features fluctuated grotesquely as his demonic nature surged. "That is for Gideon to say, messenger!"

Gabriel helped Gideon to his feet. Gideon felt a warm, comforting tingle flow out from the seemingly casual touch and realized that Gabriel was strengthening him.

"I will not Fall, Domieno." Gideon shook away the last of the demon's spell. "My choice was made long ago."

"We want you back, brother," Domieno said. "We've missed your company. Lucifer has so much more to offer someone with your abilities."

Gabriel took a threatening step forward. "He gave you his decision. Now be gone! I find your stench revolting."

"You have always been content as a mindless slave, but some of us have the ability to think for ourselves. Lucifer will not give up on Gideon. We want him back! This is far from over, errand boy." Domieno sneered, then he turned to Gideon. "We'll meet again."

Gideon waited until the demon disintegrated before revealing his weakness. He stumbled and then fell to one knee, bracing himself against the ground.

Pulling him back to his feet, Gabriel stretched Gideon's arm across his shoulders. "What ails you?"

Gideon laughed, but didn't speak. *I drank from Naomi and the purity of her blood didn't agree with me.* Gabriel would leave him in the darkness to rot if he made such a confession.

Crispin hurried across the upper bailey, drawn instinctively by Gideon's peril. "Is he ill?" he asked. "What happened?"

Gabriel supported much of Gideon's weight while Crispin pulled his other arm across his shoulders. Gideon trembled between them, his head sagging forward. His vision spun sickeningly.

"What do you need? What is amiss?" his brother asked.

"Take me...below," he managed to say, though his mouth tasted of ash.

"Did Domieno do this to you?" Anger hardened Gabriel's musical voice.

He didn't have the strength to shake his head. Violent tremors wracked his body and the toes of his cross-gartered boots dug furrows in the dirt. They dragged him toward the stairwell leading to the undercrofts of the castle.

Gideon moaned as they lowered him to the furs in his secret chamber. Heat rippled through him, then cold. His muscles continued to spasm, milder cramps, more diffused, but undeniably painful.

"What do you need?" Gabriel asked again.

Crispin knelt, putting his wrist within easy reach. Revolted, Gideon turned his face away.

"Rest." He forced the word past his parched lips. "I need to sleep."

Gideon's eyes began to close when Gabriel's sudden motion drew his attention. His brother reached past Crispin and dragged something metallic from beneath Gideon's shoulder.

Naomi's girdle.

His eyes flew to Gabriel's.

"Where is she?" he demanded, his voice tight, his expression not quite concealing his fury.

"In the scriptorium," Gideon whispered and closed his eyes.

* * *

Naomi felt arms slip beneath her and gently lift her into the air. "Gideon," she murmured and forced her eyes open.

"Nay, `tis I," Brother Gabriel whispered. "Why are you sleeping on the floor, child? What do you remember?"

She looped her arms around his neck and rested her head on his shoulder. "I'm not sure. Everything is…confused."

"Can you sit or shall I take you to the infirmary?"

"I am fine," she said, but why were her thoughts so muddled?

Brother Gabriel sat her on the stool in front of the supply table. The image of Gideon sitting there with his foot propped on the cross rung of the other stool flashed through her mind.

"Was Gideon here?"

"Do you remember his being here?"

She shook her head and rubbed her eyes with her fingertips. "I'm not sure. Was he here when you arrived?"

"Nay," he said firmly. "You were alone. The door was bolted from the inside."

"That would not have stopped Gideon."

"True. Think back. What do you remember?"

She poured herself a cup of cider and took several sips before answering. "You brought me this basket and insisted I eat." She paused for another sip. "I think something made me ill. My head is pounding."

"You look unusually pale. Are you sure you don't want to go to the infirmary?"

"Nay. I will be fine."

Her knees wobbled unsteadily as she pushed to her feet. She grasped the edge of the table, waiting for the weakness to pass. The muscles along her neck and shoulders felt especially stiff, so she rolled her head and shrugged her shoulders.

Brother Gabriel gasped. Her eyes darted to him, but his gaze was fixed on her throat. He reached out, his fingers trembling, and gently touched her skin.

"What?" she asked. "What is it?"

His warm brown eyes locked with hers, but he didn't answer. "Are you sure you feel well enough to walk?"

Her gaze narrowed on his face. She knew this game all to well. "What is wrong with my neck? Tell me now."

She watched his throat work as he struggled to swallow. The golden shards in his eyes glistened, but he answered her. "Your skin bears his mark."

Naomi felt her neck, but she could detect nothing with her fingertips. "What mark? What do you mean?"

"Come. Let us get you to the dormitory."

He reached for her arm, but she jerked away. "What did he do to me? What mark?"

"He bruised your skin with his mouth. It will fade in a few days." He offered no more information.

"Then, he was here. And he did something to muddle my memory of what took place. Where is he now?"

"He is ill. Crispin is with him."

His short, succinct answers frightened Naomi. If this was what his angelic nature forced him to share, did she really want to know more? "What made him ill?"

"I don't know."

"Will he recover?"

"I don't know."

Her mouth gaped at his words. "You don't know?" she cried. "If he is that ill we must summon a leech."

"Crispin is tending him and I will return as soon as I have seen to your—"

"Take me to him."

"Nay! We will tend to Gideon."

"Where is he?"

"You can do nothing for him. I will see you to the—"

"Where is Gideon? I will just keep asking until you tell me the truth, so tell me now."

Chapter Fourteen

Naomi nervously clutched at her tunic as she followed Brother Gabriel through the undercrofts of the castle. He held a torch aloft, but dense shadows still concealed much of the massive room. Sturdy shelves and covered bins contained supplies of every imaginable variety. Foodstuffs, thick bolts of cloth, bandages and blankets, even basic building materials could all be found in the cavernous chambers.

Brother Gabriel turned down an aisle between the storage shelves and paused at the entrance to another room.

Naomi couldn't see beyond him. Why had he stopped?

She stepped up beside him and peered into the small chamber. Gideon thrashed about on a pile of furs, moaning and striking out at Crispin. The younger man silently battled Gideon's flailing limbs, trying to keep him from injuring either of them.

Compassion for Gideon eclipsed her dislike for the other man. She slipped past Gabriel and pushed Crispin out of her way.

"Damsel, he will hurt you," Crispin protested.

She spared him only a scathing glance.

"Gideon," she said softly, kneeling beside him. "Gideon, be still."

He muttered something in a language she didn't understand. Brother Gabriel stepped into the room, obviously ready to intervene, but she held up her hand, staving him off.

"Gideon. Listen to my voice. You're not alone. I'm here with you."

Suddenly his arms closed around her, dragging her down to the furs beside him. She cried out softly at the aggression in his movements, but he laid his head against her breast and gradually relaxed.

She couldn't ignore the intimacy of their position. The heat of his breath penetrated her garments. His arms circled her waist and one of his legs rested possessively over her thighs.

Naomi stroked his tangled hair and continued to murmur into his ear, soothing him, reassuring him.

Brother Gabriel knelt beside them, folding his hands, his lips moving rhythmically in a silent prayer.

Drawn by a weariness she didn't fully understand, Naomi closed her eyes and surrendered to sleep.

* * *

Naomi awoke to darkness. Gideon's body pressed against hers, his arms firmly wrapped around her waist. Fear tingled along her nerve endings, but there was something else as well. This felt...familiar.

Where had Brother Gabriel gone? How long had she slept? It was impossible to tell if it was night or day in this windowless tomb.

Glancing to her right, she was able to discern the outline of the doorway and somewhere in the distance torchlight flickered. If it was day, she needed to change her clothes and make ready for her meeting with Leon of Le Puy. Her uncle.

He expected her decision, but she had found very little time to contemplate her choice.

She felt no Divine Calling. Could she really take sacred vows for the express purpose of continuing her work? The possibility seemed dishonest.

Scooting away from him slightly, Naomi managed to sit. But before she could stand, Gideon clasped one arm around her leg, the other around her hips and nestled his head intimately against her lap.

Heat and jumbled images swirled through Naomi. She could almost feel his hands and his mouth moving over her body. He held her down, kissing her with consuming passion. Her nipples gathered into tight little buds and tension gathered low in her belly.

His head tossed restlessly, his face rubbing against the juncture of her thighs.

She rested her head against the wall, trying to ignore her pounding heart and the teasing heat of his breath. The images seemed so real, more like memories than dreams. She shivered and pushed her fingers into his hair.

It didn't make sense. Gideon had kissed her and even touched her breasts, but she would never allow him such intimacies… She squirmed a bit at the thought. What was the point in lying to herself? Her body wanted those things. Part of Gideon still craved the light, but something dark and primitive stirred within her each time they touched.

She was finding it harder and harder to resist.

A soft golden light drew her attention to the doorway. Good, Brother Gabriel had returned. Her hand stilled in Gideon's hair. What if it was Crispin? She didn't want to be in the same room with that man, especially while Gideon was unconscious.

The light intensified and Naomi's breath lodged in her throat.

"Fear not, Naomi," the entity said, his voice flowing over and around her.

Light emanated from his garments and the waves of his glistening hair created a glowing nimbus.

"Who are you?" she whispered. How many angels were there at the Krak des Chevaliers?

He folded his arms across his chest and Naomi noticed the sword strapped to his side. No soft golden light shone from this blade; the entire length burned like fire.

"My true name is impossible for humans to pronounce. Just call me Michael."

He moved a step closer and Naomi shrank back against the wall. The radiance of his face made his features hard to distinguish, but Naomi was left with two impressions: beauty and brutality.

"What do you want?" she asked.

"Gabriel told me that Gideon is improving. I came to see for myself."

She stroked Gideon's hair, averting her gaze from Michael's brilliance. "Why would you care? Are you not the one who did this to him?"

He chuckled. The warmth in the sound surprised her.

"No wonder Gideon is drawn to you. All I did when I dispersed their little band of rebels was to give each of them *exactly* what they wanted."

What did he mean? What had he given them? Little band of rebels? "Are there more like Gideon? Other angels banished from the light?"

He tilted his head as if to study her from a different angle. "You need only concern yourself with *that* rebel." He nodded toward Gideon. "But Gabriel is another matter."

"Gabriel is not a rebel," she protested. "He is the kindest, most—"

"I find no fault with Gabriel, but I have operated without him long enough. His assignment was to observe Gideon without interfering—which he has failed to do."

"You said you found no fault with him."

Again he laughed, his nimbus momentarily brightening. "Are you hoping to become Heaven's champion? We're on the same side of this war, Naomi."

"Then, what do you mean to do?" He hadn't come merely to check on Gideon. Gabriel could speak only truth; why would Michael doubt his report?

"There comes a point in each person's life when they must turn a corner and carry on. Often portions of one's past do not travel on into the future. It is part of the cycle. It is natural and ordained."

She stared at him silently, seeing only the brutality in his beautiful face.

"It is time," he said. "You're stronger than you know, Naomi. Much stronger than Gabriel likes to believe."

Her mouth trembled and tears gathered in her eyes. "Is he still here? You must at least allow us to say goodbye."

"I must, must I?" He shook his head.

The golden haze around his face wavered and she could clearly see his smile. Her heart lurched at its beauty and tingling warmth enveloped her being even after Michael had gone.

* * *

Naomi stepped away from her drawing table, unable to see through her tears.

He was gone.

Michael had taken Gabriel from her without allowing them to say goodbye. She cursed her rash tongue. Who was she to challenge an archangel?

Her meeting with Leon had taken place in the upper bailey. She had been searching for Brother Gabriel when she spotted Leon and some of his men.

She approached him boldly and performed her best curtsy. "I have made my decision," she said.

He waved his men away before asking, "And what did you decide?"

"I would be honored to accompany you to… Where will we be going?"

A beaming smile parted his thin lips and he spontaneously pulled her into his arms for a sound hug. "England, demoiselle.

My parents are anxious to meet you, but Roderick must take precedence."

"Roderick is my grandfather."

It was not really a question, but he nodded. "Aye. There will be plenty of time on the journey for you and I to become better acquainted. How soon can you be ready to depart?"

"Two days hence?" she suggested.

"Perfect." He kissed her cheek and hurried after his men.

Their impromptu meeting had spared her the irritation of seeing Brother Aaron.

After several fruitless hours of searching for Brother Gabriel, she retreated to the scriptorium, surly and depressed. Unrolling her private scroll she quickly sketched Brother Aaron. To be perfectly fair, his chin did not tilt quite so arrogantly and she had never seen such open scorn in his narrowed gaze, but her interpretation made her smile.

Summoning all of her skill and fueling her creativity with longing, she tried to draw Brother Gabriel. His features appeared on the parchment, the likeness unmistakable, but as always, she failed to capture his inner glow—his illumination.

Tears blinded her and she stepped back from the table before flinging the pen at the wall. She wrapped her arms around herself and squeezed her eyes shut.

She did not want to `turn a corner and carry on'.

Arms enfolded her and she started violently. She cried out and opened her eyes. Her eyes focused on Gabriel's smiling face and Naomi fell apart.

She clung to him, mashing the back of his robe in her fists. She wept, releasing her frustration, her anger and her fear. His hand patiently stroked her hair, while he spoke softly into her ear.

"We can never be truly parted, Naomi. My love surrounds you. It goes wherever life may take you."

She eased away from him so she could bask in the warmth of his eyes. "You are so dear to me," she sobbed. "Have I ever told you how grateful I am for all you have taught me?"

He smiled. "You have many lessons yet to learn." He brushed his knuckles along her jaw. "But you are brave and intelligent, and I am so proud of the woman you have become."

She pressed her lips together to still their trembling. "I will miss you every day."

"Nay," he said firmly. "You will remember me fondly every day."

A ragged sob tore from her throat.

"Why can I not draw you?" It was such an incidental thing, but she could not let him leave without understanding. He was her mentor. Could he teach her one last skill before Heaven reclaimed him?

Kissing her cheek, he took her hand and led her to her drawing table.

He studied the sketch for only a moment before he explained, "The image is too perfect. I see only devotion and joy. Where is the sadness of our parting? Where is my fear that something might hurt you? Where is the exasperation Gideon unleashes in me? These are all part of my character as well."

Even in the brightest soul there is a speck of darkness. She shivered, but chose not to share her conclusion, knowing it would upset him.

He framed her face with his palms and kissed her tenderly on the brow. "Love comes with the risk of pain, and the more deeply you love, the greater the pain. But you must never be afraid of the risk. It is what makes love so exciting."

"Will I ever see you again?"

He smiled and mischief glimmered in his eyes. "Most definitely."

Naomi accepted the sadness as he walked from the room. His reluctance to flaunt his angelic abilities made her smile. The aching of her heart was a testimony to how deeply she loved him and how much they had shared.

She found a freshly sharpened pen and paused to study her drawing. Accessing the pain still burning within her, she added a touch of sadness to his gaze and a hint of stubbornness to his jaw. She drew a few strands of mussed hair and tiny lines at the corners of his eyes.

Tears streamed down Naomi's face as she watched his image come to life—illuminated by the imperfection of her love.

Chapter Fifteen

Gideon sat alone in the underground chamber, restless and confused. Naomi's scent permeated his tunic, sinking into his very pores. Yanking the garment off, he tossed it across the room and pressed his naked back against the cold stone wall.

She'd sat with him through the entire crisis, soothing him with her embrace and the soft cadence of her voice. Why had she done it? How could she feel anything for him after...she didn't remember what he'd *done.* That was the only possible explanation. He'd successfully purged her mind. She still believed in the illusion that he was not a monster.

He remembered Michael's voice, the intensity of his presence, but that made no sense either. Why would Michael bother?

The musical chinking of metal distracted Gideon from his contemplations. With a flick of his wrist, he ignited the torch secured to the wall in an iron sconce. He'd extinguished it a short time before when he sent Crispin off on his errand. The darkness better suited his mood.

Crispin approached, heavily laden with the remainder of Gideon's belongings.

Gideon felt an unexpected pang in his chest. Naomi wouldn't be the only one turning a corner and carrying on.

"Why do you want all of this down here?" Crispin asked. He draped Gideon's chain mail hauberk over the chest containing the rest of his armor.

"It's time I reacquaint myself with a little band of rebels." He couldn't contain his sardonic smile as he remembered the exasperated edge to Michael words. "You've served me faithfully, Crispin. But where I go, you cannot follow. I spoke with Algernon, captain of the French mercenaries. You will be accompanying them to Antioch to join King Louis' troops."

"As you wish," Crispin said stiffly. He clasped his arms behind his back and averted his gaze. He looked almost wounded. He was a soldier. What difference did it make who he served?

These humans could be so irrational.

Gideon rose and commanded. "Look at me."

Their gazes locked and Gideon cast his thrall. "When you awaken on the morrow you will have no remembrance of my true nature. You will remember only a fellow soldier with whom you fought." He framed the younger man's face with his hands and delved deeper into his mind, meticulously purging every image, every memory that might incriminate him.

The longer he worked the more saddened he became. The human penchant for irrationality must be contagious. Crispin was a servant, not a friend. But so many of the images contained Crispin's easy laughter and his calm resolve, his bravery and loyalty.

Gideon would miss him.

Breaking away with a soft hiss, he released Crispin and reached into the trunk for a clean tunic. When he straightened again, Crispin was gone.

* * *

Gideon felt a heated tingle scurry down his spine and knew Naomi was near. Striding between the cluttered storage shelves, he paused on the threshold of his chamber.

She knelt on the furs, a vision in the wavering torchlight. Her sandals rested beside the bed and the fine material of her gown molded gently to her curves. The garment must have been part of her new wardrobe. The sleeves were slashed to reveal the elaborate embroidery on the undertunic.

How long had she been here?

Why had she come?

She lifted an item from the fur beside her and he realized it was his jeweled dagger. She'd been rummaging through his chest! He couldn't figure out what she was doing as she turned it this way and that.

"There are less painful means, if you want to take your life," he said lightly.

Her gaze flew toward him and she proffered the dagger, hilt first. "It's a beautiful blade."

He took the knife from her, but his gaze remained on her flushed face. "What were you doing just now?"

"This is a monastery, so I suppose I shouldn't have been surprised, but I have been unable to find a looking glass."

"What need have you for a looking glass?" *Why do you continue to tempt me, when I want you so badly I cannot control the demon in me?*

"I have been told I bear a mark on my neck," she said quietly. "A mark, no doubt, put there by you."

He lifted her chin and turned her face to the side. The purple bruise was obvious at a glance, but even the two puncture wounds were still visible, if one knew what to look for.

"Aye, it's still there," he told her. "Is that all you needed?"

She jerked her chin out of his grasp and stood. "I see images of...I know I was here in this room before you became ill. I know that we shared—intimacies—and you did something to muddle the memory."

Gideon struggled to conceal his shock. Never before had his powers failed. Why was she able to remember? He idly fiddled with the dagger, not knowing what to say.

"Do you deny what I have just said?"

"Nay." He closely watched her reaction to the single word. She nervously rubbed one hand with the other. Her tongue darted out to wet her lower lip.

"Why?"

One dark brow shot up at her question. "Why did I bring you here or why did I attempt to take the memory from you?"

She pulled her braided hair forward, concealing his mark. He wanted to push it back over her shoulder. He wanted the world to know she was his.

That she was his? His insides twisted at the thought.

"Why did you bring me here?"

"To punish you for forcing me to feel things I did not want to feel," he answered honestly. Her gaze softened. Her hands unclasped, one reaching out toward him. He pointed the dagger at her. "Do not touch me, unless you want to finish what we started the other night."

Naomi smiled and raised her hands to shoulder level. "I am such a threat you must hold me off at knifepoint?"

He glowered at her and she drank in the sight of him. His hair hung in damp waves to his shoulders, his golden eyes glistening in the torchlight. Had he just returned from the baths? What a decadent thought. The front of his tunic gaped, revealing a teasing glimpse of his chest beneath the loose lacing.

"You keep looking at me like that, little girl and I—"

"Why do you keep calling me that?" She took a step toward him. "I'm a woman grown. Most women have been wed and have several children by the time they reach my age."

"It reminds me how innocent you are," he said, his voice growing husky and thoughtful.

"How innocent am I? Is there any possibility I could bear your child?"

His features contorted with rage and he threw the dagger. She screamed and ducked. The knife imbedded in the stone wall far to one side of where she huddled, the metallic protest making her flinch and shiver.

"Even had I taken your virginity, Naomi, I am incapable of planting a babe in your womb. Creating life is a gift God withdrew from us before He flooded your world."

Anger radiated off him in tangible waves. Naomi felt the hairs on her arms bristle, but she did not understand his reaction. "Before the flood, angels could produce offspring?"

"How do you think your world was populated after Adam and Eve left Eden? Have you never heard of the Nephilim? It's recorded in the Holy Scriptures, `The Nephilim were on the earth in those days—when the sons of God went to the daughters of men and had children by them.'"

"Why did he take the ability away?" She didn't want to provoke him further, but she needed to understand.

"The children were often extraordinary—giants, born with unusual abilities. That's in the Scriptures as well, `They were the heroes of old, men of renown'. But many were also evil, so He put an end to the interaction. He constrained the emotions of angels and rendered us all infertile."

Naomi wanted to touch him, but she suspected he would find no comfort in her touch. She wanted to help him, but he had never seemed so far away.

"Is that why you came here? To ask me if you are still a virgin?"

She nodded.

"Believe me, Naomi. When I make love to you, you will remember it."

"I leave for England with the dawn," she said, her voice shaking.

"I know."

If he knew she was leaving, then when did he expect they would make love? She had so many questions. Where was he going? Was his war with Gabriel over? Was he any closer to making peace with God? Had she drawn him any closer to the light?

Or had he only taught her not to crave the darkness?

She swallowed, greatly disturbed by the thought.

Will I ever see you again? Her heart ached with the question, but she kept silent.

Dragging this out would only make it more painful. She took a deep, fortifying breath and stepped passed him. She made it to the doorway, when he grasped her upper arm and spun her around.

They held each other tightly, kissing deeply, fervently. She molded herself against him, loving the hard shape of his back and his shoulders beneath her hungry hands. He nudged her lips and she opened to him, thrilled by the slow penetration of his tongue.

Just when she began to feel the sweet ache unfurl within her, he pulled back. His mouth didn't leave hers completely, but the kiss changed. He was tender now, slow—and sad.

He was saying goodbye.

She clutched him tighter. She didn't want to let him go, but she knew there was no rational alternative.

He eased away, his fingers lingering on her face.

For a long, silent moment they stared into each other's eyes. She saw the true scope of his bitterness, the vast desolation, a century of pain.

Tears choked her. She didn't know how to reach him, how to heal him. What to say.

"This is the closest I've been to Heaven in a hundred years," he whispered, and disintegrated into mist.

Chapter Sixteen

Jerusalem
A fortnight later

Gideon heard the knock on the door, but didn't turn from the window. Night had fallen hard upon the city, driving the inhabitants into their small, stacked houses and sprawling villas. Darkness didn't differentiate between rich and poor, shepherd and king. Everyone was equally susceptible to the dangers hidden in the shadows.

"Gideon."

He heard his name and closed his eyes. It had been a mistake to come here. He'd expected to find solace with Alyssa, expected her to understand.

She was one of "his little band of rebels," as Michael had so aptly put it.

Rebels, they were, but they didn't belong to him. Gideon was a participant, not their leader. Most would balk at the idea of having a leader; still, one in their midst had incited their discontent, inspired their rebellion.

But Gideon was not that one.

"Gideon, may I enter?" She persisted when he made no move to open the door. "I have a surprise for you."

"Is it your intention to pester me until I allow you in?" he asked.

"But of course," she responded cheerfully, stepping into the small, airless room.

Opening the window hadn't dispelled the stale atmosphere slowly smothering Gideon. He needed to be away from this place, away from everything and everyone.

He needed to think.

He needed to rid his mind of *her!*

"Did you dream of Naomi again?" Alyssa joined him at the open window.

He knew Alyssa couldn't read his mind, so apparently his thoughts were written on his face. "I thought being away from her would help, but the restlessness grows stronger every day."

Her soft, warm hand came to rest on his arm and Gideon looked at his friend. She had chosen blue eyes today and bright red hair. Her delicate features and pleasing shape always remained the same, but she found it amusing to change her coloring.

"I have a surprise for you." Her mouth curved in a tempting smile.

"I'm in no mood for your games."

Indignation sparked within her wide blue eyes. She stepped back, tossing her mass of fiery curls. "You came to my home, seeking shelter and solitude. I have protected you and honored your request. Well, it ends tonight. You will participate in `my games' or you will find some other place to sulk."

Annoyed by her ultimatum, Gideon closed the shutters and silently debated his options.

"Daniel is downstairs," she said stiffly. "Join us or not, I no longer care."

Daniel.

The name made Gideon smile. How had she located him? Gideon had tried and failed.

"Alyssa." She paused at the sound of her name. "I will be down directly."

"Good." She offered him a bright smile. "Daniel is anxious to see you. I would hate to disappoint him."

Another toss of her bright curls told Gideon that it was *only* Daniel she didn't wish to disappoint. He laughed. Alyssa could be so temperamental.

* * *

They stood together before the hearth. Gideon paused in the doorway and watched his friends. Firelight danced in Alyssa's hair and cast Daniel's face into high relief. Dark brown hair fell to his shoulders in distinct waves, softening the harsh angles of his face. Alyssa laughed at something Daniel said and Gideon let the sound roll across his senses, calming him, relaxing him.

Daniel's long mantle was thrown back over one broad shoulder, revealing a plain woolen tunic and cross-gartered boots. From head to toe, he was dressed in black. He had tucked a dagger in one boot and doubtless had others concealed within his garments. A long, lethal sword was strapped about his waist, but he wore no armor.

"When I seek you out, you are like a phantom in the night, but Alyssa crooks her finger and you obediently appear?" Gideon challenged his friend.

They turned to face him and Daniel smiled. Gideon felt impaled by the intensity of his ink-black gaze.

"Alyssa has always been hard to resist. While you…"

Daniel didn't bother completing the comparison. Gideon chuckled. "How have you been?" He joined them in front of the fire.

"Bored, my friend. Utterly bored," Daniel admitted. "These endless campaigns have grown tedious. I'm ready for a change."

"As am I," Alyssa piped in. "Let us go somewhere together. Somewhere new and different."

Michael hadn't specifically forbidden their interaction, but it had been implied when he dispersed them to different locations.

"Surely, you're not afraid of bending the rules?" Daniel asked.

Gideon laughed. "The thought never crossed my mind." He lied. Thanks to Naomi, thoughts like that never left his mind.

He needed this—badly. A distraction. Something to divert his treacherous mind. To free him from the disturbing tendency to evaluate each thought, each action, by what would please her the most.

Chapter Seventeen

Monthamn Castle
Sussex, England
May, 1148

Naomi fidgeted on her palfrey as Leon of Le Puy called out the expected greeting to the guards in the watchtower. A drawbridge lowered and the iron portcullis rose, allowing the party into the lower bailey. Naomi could see the keep now, situated on an earthen motte, rectangular in shape, with crenellated towers at each corner. The outer curtain wall was stone, but the fortification surrounding the keep was constructed of wood.

"The Monthamn fief dates back to the days of the Conqueror," Leon said as he helped Naomi down from her horse. "The first Baron Monthamn crossed the channel with William of Normandy, and the holdings have grown and prospered ever since. Monthamns are known for their strategic marriages. Roderick's own marriage doubled the size of the estate."

"I see." Naomi responded politely, but *strategic marriages* sounded so manipulative, so hollow. Why could her family not be known for their charity and compassion?

"It all belongs to you now."

"Nay, it belongs to my grandfather," Naomi insisted. She was in no hurry to inherit so vast a responsibility. She had much to learn before she was ready to step into that role.

A tall, lanky lad ambled out of the stables to take their horses. Naomi glanced around the spacious clearing, her heart in her throat. It was all rather intimidating. A series of small stone workshops marched along the curtain wall and several rambunctious children chased each other through the grassy commons.

To one side, Naomi spied an orchard and a large garden. Eager plants had just pushed through the fertile earth to celebrate the promise of spring.

"Come, my lady," Leon said, casually cupping her elbow.

She fell into step beside him as they crossed the domestic range. Naomi couldn't help but compare it to the mighty Krak. Monthamn Castle, in its entirety, would easily fit within the lower bailey of Krak des Chevaliers.

Leon used the huge brass knocker to announce their arrival. Two lads heaved the door open, but a dour-faced man, standing back from the threshold, offered the greeting.

"Please, come this way. We have been expecting you."

None of it seemed real to Naomi. She had moved through the past nine weeks as if in a dream. Countries and seas now separated her from anyone who had ever cared about her.

Still grieving the loss of Brother Gabriel, Naomi had foolishly allowed Gideon to slip away. Nay, that had *not* been foolish. Every day she tried to convince herself of that fact. It didn't matter that she missed his wicked smile and longed for the molten heat of his strange gold eyes. He was part of her past, and she was determined to concentrate on the future.

The servant motioned to his right. "This way."

He led them to the small counting room in the back corner of the great hall. Rapping his knuckles against the door, he pushed the portal open and then departed without saying another word.

"You'll have to forgive Kruthers. He's a masterful bailiff, but not much for socializing."

Naomi couldn't see the speaker until Leon stepped out of her way. Leon turned slightly and offered her an encouraging smile before she stepped fully into the room.

A man stood behind the wooden table, staring at her curiously. His thick hair just reached his shoulders in snow-white waves. Creases and wrinkles concealed his expression, so Naomi focused in on his eyes. They were wide and clear, accented by surprisingly dark lashes, and they were the same bright blue as her own.

She dropped into a nervous curtsy and forced her gaze down. When she dared to raise her face again, the man stood directly in front of her.

"You look very much like your mother, girl. But there is some of Malcolm there, too. And by God, you've got my eyes!"

He seemed pleased by the discovery, so Naomi tried to relax. "My name is Naomi." She spoke softly, surprised by the emotion constricting her throat.

Roderick's gaze shot to Leon. "Who gave her that name? Did the monk who raised her name her? Is it possible that he knew?"

Leon just shrugged, so Roderick turned back to Naomi. "Who named you?"

"My mother. She told Brother Gabriel my name and pressed me into his arms before she lost consciousness." Her throat began to burn and she felt her lower lip tremble. "It's all I've ever had of her."

He brushed his wrinkled fingers gently across her cheek, his gaze intent upon her face. "My wife was also named Naomi. Malcolm promised her that his first daughter would carry on her name."

His big blue eyes filled up with tears and Naomi lost the battle with hers. "I wish I could have known them," she sobbed.

Roderick pulled her against his big, barrel chest and Naomi melted into his embrace. She rested her forehead against his shoulder and allowed herself to cry. She cried for the mother she'd lost and the father she'd never know. She cried for all of the lonely nights she spent parted from her family.

"Welcome home, Naomi," he said, easing her to arm's length and smiling into her eyes. "I have prayed every day for this event."

"I never dared to hope…" Naomi's voice broke and her chin quivered. "I dreamed as any orphan dreams, but I never really allowed myself to believe that they were anything more than silly dreams."

He touched her face again, as if to assure himself that she was real. "Well, this is no dream, Naomi." He hesitated over the name, then smiled broadly.

Stepping back from her, he turned to face Leon. "To you I will be eternally grateful. I sent you away on a fool's errand and you returned with the answer to my prayers."

"Yours were not the only prayers. My family was just as anxious to find her as were you."

Roderick slapped Leon on the back and said, "Your family is going to have to wait. I intend to be completely selfish with this young lady. At least for a while."

"I expected as much."

Moving with obvious effort, Roderick made his way to the hearth. "There is so much here to understand. Come, sit by my fire. Let us talk."

Naomi sat on one of the benches flanking the fire.

Leon recounted the tale of how Esther came to be at the Church. Naomi interjected comments now and then to clarify.

"And this monk saw to your care for all the years that followed?" Roderick leaned forward, resting his forearms across his knees.

"I was a ward of the Order of St. John, but Brother Gabriel was never far from my side," Naomi explained.

"Where is he now?"

"Brother Gabriel had obligations that made it impossible for him to accompany me." The emptiness within Naomi pulsed in response to the words.

"Then, you were raised entirely in the company of monks?"

Naomi managed to smile. He made it sound so unappealing. "For the majority of my childhood we remained in Jerusalem. There were other orphans for me to play with and I spent many hours helping out in the hospital. Brother Gabriel and others of his order schooled me. My days were filled with the excitement of learning and the satisfaction of helping others."

"What were you taught by these brothers?" Roderick asked.

"Everything. History and theology, languages and ciphering. He even let me try my hand at illuminating manuscript pages."

Roderick's jaw dropped and his eyes widened to amusing proportions. "You can read and write?"

"God has blessed me with incredible opportunities, sir. I speak five languages, but I am only literate in English, French and Latin."

"Unbelievable," Roderick muttered. "My granddaughter is a scribe."

Naomi smiled again. "How well those skills will serve me here has yet to be seen. I fear I've much to learn."

Leaning forward to rest his elbows on his knees, Roderick returned her smile. "Well, you appear to be quite adept at learning."

"There is further proof that I am Esther's daughter," she told him. She felt it important that they completely solidify her identity.

Roderick chuckled. "All the proof I need is written on your face, Naomi."

"I thank you for your confidence, but others may not share your certainty. I want all of the facts known. As Brother Gabriel tended my mother he noticed the scars of a long-healed burn on her skin. Uncle Leon has confirmed that his sister also possessed such marks."

Nodding solemnly, Roderick absorbed this new information. "We shall organize a feast, send invitations far and wide, but tell no one the reason for the celebration. Then at the height of the festivities, I shall introduce my granddaughter and heir."

"I'll stay until the feast," Leon said. "That way I'll be here to offer my endorsement and demonstrate my acceptance of Naomi as well."

"What say you, girl? Are you up for a celebration?" Roderick asked with a cheerful grin.

"Not today," she admitted and both men laughed. "I'm overwhelmed by all of this. Please, slow things down just a bit. Give me a few days to adjust."

Roderick rose and took her hands between his. "I apologize. I've been waiting so long for this day. I keep forgetting how it must be affecting you. Relax. Settle in. We will make plans once you have found your bearings."

He drew her to her feet, his eyes searching her face.

"I want you to be happy here," he said softly. A sudden sadness clouded his gaze. "I only wish your grandmother had lived to see this day. She would have adored you. And she would know what to do to ease your fears and make you feel at home."

Hope blossomed within her breast, pushing back the darkness and making her feel strong. Gazing deeply into eyes so like her own, Naomi said, "I am not afraid."

Chapter Eighteen

After a hot meal, a long leisurely bath and a good night's sleep, Naomi awakened refreshed and ready for the day. Roderick took her on a quick tour of the domestic range, but not long into the outing his skin grew pale and his legs began to tremble.

"Damn and blast," he muttered. "Can hardly walk to the privy without needing a nap."

Naomi squeezed his arm and smiled. "There's no hurry. I'm not going anywhere."

With obvious reluctance, he recruited Leon to show her the rest of the castle and the village beyond. Leon made a courteous and informative guide, but Naomi's thoughts remained with Roderick.

"How long has he been ill?" she asked softly as they passed beyond the outer curtain wall.

"He had a bout with lung fever this summer past that nearly claimed his life. He's never fully recovered. Since Michaelmas his strength has gradually faded. No one expected him to last the winter, but Roderick is a tough old buzzard."

Naomi only nodded. If she was only to have a short time with her grandfather, then she needed to make every moment count.

Monthamn Major, the larger of the two villages, lay closer to the castle than Monthamn Minor. Naomi strolled through the village on her uncle's arm silently taking in the quiet charm.

Leon's steps faltered slightly and Naomi followed his gaze, curious what had caused the reaction. Two men stood in front of a stone church. Black robes and a large golden cross identified the priest, but there didn't seem to be anything unusual about the man speaking with him.

"Who are they?" Naomi asked.

"Father John and Frederick of Westerville."

Before Leon could offer a more detailed explanation, the priest noticed their interest. He walked toward them, the other man half a step behind.

"Good day, kind sir." The priest greeted them. "What brings you to my humble village?"

Something within Naomi recoiled from the priest. His dark hair was shorn close to his scalp and his rounded cheeks had a ruddy cast. Nothing unusual there, but cold calculation gleamed from his dark eyes.

"Roderick asked me to show Lady Naomi the sights," Leon said simply.

Father John stepped nearer and Naomi stomped down the urge to back away.

"Lady Naomi?" The priest inclined his head ever so slightly, but his gaze never left her face. "I don't believe I've had the pleasure."

"She has only recently arrived," Leon told him.

The other man stepped forward and took Naomi's hand. She had not raised it and his presumptuousness made her stomach knot.

"Frederick of Westerville," he said, not waiting for Leon to introduce him. "From whence have you come to grace our provincial village?"

Leon stepped closer, eyes alert as he studied the tall stranger. "Lady Naomi is Roderick's guest and that is all you need know until such time as Roderick himself announces more."

At first glance, Naomi found Frederick handsome. His thick auburn hair just reached his shoulders and the bright blue of his eyes was not unlike...Roderick's, or hers, for that matter.

"What could that old goat possibly announce?" Frederick's well-formed lips twisted into a sneer and his gaze slid over Naomi with sudden insolence. "Even if he bought himself a fertile field, he would need some seed to sow."

Naomi gasped, shocked by the insulting implication. Anger burned through her shock and her hand flew, connecting forcefully with his cheek.

"You little bitch!"

He grabbed for her, but Naomi ducked under his arm. His hand caught her thick braid through the fabric of her wimple and jerked her to a stop. She cried out, kicking wildly and clawing at his hand.

Leon grabbed Frederick's arm with both hands. "Release her, you fool, or you'll find yourself—"

The sharp cry of a bird cut short his threat. A falcon swooped out of the sky and dove directly toward Frederick's face. The man screamed and stumbled backward, releasing Naomi's hair in his haste to avoid the bird's sharp talons.

Frederick landed on his back in the dirt and Naomi kicked a rock at him. "Touch me again, you bastard, and I'll have you publicly flogged! There is nothing licentious in my relationship with Lord Monthamn, but I assure you he will not tolerate my abuse."

"You need not explain anything to the likes of him," Leon insisted, pulling her firmly away from the prostrate man.

She glanced suspiciously at the sky. Could that have been...?

"Did he hurt you?" Leon asked, falling into step beside her.

Not trusting herself to speak, Naomi shook her head. For endless days she'd tried to accept that Gideon belonged to her past. Their short acquaintance shouldn't have affected her so powerfully, but she ached for his touch and craved his infrequent smiles. One odd occurrence and the wound bled again. She wanted him, needed him—missed him.

Where was he? Was he well? A violent shiver shook her body. She prayed each day that he did not Fall.

Leon stopped walking and turned her to face him. "Do not let Fredrick upset you. There is reason for his resentment. If I had not located you, he would have had some hope of claiming Monthamn Castle."

"Claiming?" she asked, focusing her attention on the issue at hand. "Who is this man?"

Leon tucked her arm into the bend of his elbow and resumed their trek. "Frederick is the son of Roderick's cousin. Until I found you, he was the only person left with blood ties to Monthamn Castle. Roderick had signed documents returning control of his holdings to the crown, until I sent him word that you were still alive."

"Grandfather would return his holdings to the crown rather than allow them to pass to Frederick?"

"Aye," Leon said grimly. "He is a vile man, both cruel and corrupt."

"Then why does Grandfather allow him on Monthamn lands?"

Leon patted her hand, his expression troubled. "What Roderick allows and what he can enforce are two different things. Frederick knows he's not welcome here, but Westerville is not far and Roderick seldom leaves the castle."

"Father John seemed at ease with him. Are they in league?"

Leon chucked. "You are perceptive. Roderick has suspected such an alliance but has yet to find anything specific to connect them."

"What will he do if it comes to light that Father John is assisting Frederick?"

"That is up to Roderick. I would imagine it would depend on the nature of the connection and the strength of his proof."

It was nearly nightfall by the time they returned to the castle. The main meal of the day had been served and cleared away long hours before.

Kruthers explained that Roderick had gone to bed, but it was his desire that plans progress without him.

"What plans does he mean?" Naomi asked. Kruthers moved away without addressing her directly. Did the man not like women or had she somehow offended him?

"Roderick has asked that I outline the scope of your responsibilities," Leon said softly. The sadness had returned to his warm green eyes. "As you said yourself, there is much for you to learn. Roderick knows we're running out of time. I cannot stay indefinitely and he is unsure how much longer he can hold on."

Fear and sadness gripped Naomi's heart. She couldn't lose him so soon! She'd only just found him. "Is he that ill?"

Gently squeezing her hands, Leon nodded. "Aye. I must be honest, Naomi. He is dying." Taking a deep breath, he seemed to force away the gloom. "He'll not want us to mope. He has lived a long, full life and his last wish is that you be established and secure before he leaves you."

"May I take a few moments to attend to my needs before we begin?" Naomi asked.

"Of course. Roderick has arranged for a waiting woman. Her name is Elspeth. She should be in your chambers. If she is not, have Kruthers find her."

Naomi found a young woman in her chamber working to unpack her clothing. Her long, strawberry blonde hair was simply braided, her head uncovered. She offered Naomi a friendly smile, but did not speak.

"Are you Elspeth?" Naomi asked.

"Aye, milady."

A fresh ensemble lay across the bed and a battered kettle simmered near the fire. Elspeth appeared to know her duties well. She moved immediately to Naomi's side.

"Shall I help you change?"

Naomi felt hot and gritty after her long stroll through the village. "Aye, that would be wonderful." Naomi stripped to her chemise and Elspeth poured hot water into a large earthen basin. Naomi washed away the travel grime. "What do you know of Frederick of Westerville?"

"Only what the others say, mistress. I've not been at Monthamn long."

"And what do the others say?"

"That he's an evil beast with an eye for Monthamn Castle. 'Tis a good thing Lord Roderick has arranged for your protection," Elspeth replied.

Naomi moved to the low stool near the fire and Elspeth worked the tangles from her hair with a silver comb.

"What do you mean he's arranged for my protection?" Naomi glanced over her shoulder.

Elspeth's cheeks flamed and her round dark eyes darted away. "Did I speak out of turn, milady?"

"I don't believe so." Naomi gentled her tone and offered the girl a smile. "Just tell me what you mean."

"I heard some of the grooms talking about your personal guard. They said Lord Roderick was so concerned about your safety he'd hired men to watch you from sunup to sundown. I thought it was rather strange, but mayhap he was right to worry."

"He has hired a guard whose sole purpose is to protect me?" Naomi tried to make light of the concept, but her belly knotted. Was Frederick really so dangerous or were there other risks as well? "Will this guard not become fatigued if he is never allowed to sleep?"

Elspeth chuckled. Naomi turned back to the fire and Elspeth quickly braided her hair.

"He will lose no sleep, milady. There are six members of the guard as well as their captain."

Naomi's eyes widened. She was no longer amused. "It will take seven soldiers to keep me safe? What sort of place is this?" She stood and turned to face Elspeth.

"I did not mean to frighten you, mistress."

"I'm not frightened. But my dislike for Frederick of Westerville grows deeper with each word uttered."

Silently allowing the girl to dress her, Naomi felt her insides flutter. This was not the peaceful homecoming she had imagined.

"Milady," Elspeth said as she fastened the end of the golden girdle around Naomi's hips. "Have I displeased you?"

"Nay. I appreciate your candor. So much has happened so quickly, my head still spins."

The girl accepted her explanation with a quick smile and went to fetch a fresh wimple. Naomi crossed her arms over her chest and shook her head.

Would nothing in her life ever be simple?

Chapter Nineteen

Just before she stepped into the counting room, Naomi heard his laughter. The rich, smoky sound washed over her entire body in a heated caress. He said something. She couldn't make out his words, but she knew the sound of his voice.

It could not be Gideon. How could it possibly be him? But she knew it was. He was here.

Gideon was here!

Trembling so badly she feared her knees would knock, Naomi tapped on the open door to announce her presence. They stood facing the fire, Uncle Leon and Gideon.

The men turned and Naomi's heart flipped over in her chest. This was ridiculous! Why was she trembling?

"Good eventide," Leon greeted. "Come in. Let me make the introductions. May I present Sir Gideon de le Ombres."

Naomi inclined her head as much to hide her smile as to acknowledge the introduction. *Sir* Gideon of the Shadows? "I am pleased to meet you." She endeavored to keep her voice calm.

"As you learned this afternoon, there are those here in Monthamn who feel threatened by your reappearance. So, Roderick felt it wise..."

She didn't hear the rest of what Leon said. Gideon's gaze captured and devoured hers. He was *here.* He was really here!

The corner of his mouth quirked and images inundated her mind. She saw him draw her near and bend her backward over his arm. His mouth possessed hers and Naomi felt tingling heat unfold in time with the image.

"Please, find your ease. I will have Kruthers bring us wine." Leon departed.

"You are here to *protect* me?" she asked, once they were alone.

"You do not think me capable of the task?"

Naomi's breath lodged in her throat. He sounded angry, yet his gaze was warm. Nervous energy set her in motion. She moved to one of the chairs facing the fire and sat, arranging her skirts before she spoke.

"It's not a matter of your capabilities, but of your motivation. How long have you been here? Why would Roderick entrust *you* with my safekeeping?"

He grinned and his golden eyes sparkled. "I arrived before you left the Holy Land and your grandfather has known me for years. I'm a faithful and trusted friend. He was thrilled to learn that I am available for this important task."

"You managed in just over a fortnight what it took us nearly three cycles of the moon to accomplish? In what form did you travel? What did..." Her words trailed away as the full import of his words sank in. "You're able to implant memories as well as steal them."

Moving to the fireplace, he rested his forearm along the mantel piece and whispered, "Did you miss me?"

Leon returned with a pitcher of wine and three silver goblets, saving Naomi from the question. He handed a goblet to her and one to Gideon.

"Let us drink to Lady Monthamn," Leon suggested. "May she find happiness in her new home." He raised his cup and they drank.

The sweet, fruity wine eased Naomi's tight throat and she tried to relax. Her conversation with Gideon would have to wait until they were alone again, so she focused on Leon.

"Gideon has recruited the best of Monthamn's knights to protect you, but it is important that you follow his instructions without question."

Naomi shot a challenging glance at Gideon. Had that stipulation been insinuated into Leon's mind? "I'm not an invalid. I understand there are dangers, but I'm capable of taking care of myself."

"Nay, you are not," Gideon said emphatically.

Taking exception to his condescending tone, Naomi set her goblet aside and scooted to the edge of the chair. "If Frederick of Westerville is such a danger to me, why not apprehend him rather than treating me like a prisoner?"

"We have no proof, only suspicions. Still, it is not our intention to treat you like a prisoner," Leon assured her. "Most noble ladies travel with a private guard. Your activities need not be curtailed unless Gideon deems them unsafe."

She wanted to laugh. He had no idea he was sending out a wolf to guard a lamb. "And what are my activities likely to be? What will be expected of me?"

"If you would excuse me," Gideon said, before Leon could respond to Naomi's question. "I have duties awaiting me."

"Of course," Leon responded respectfully.

"I shall return and explain my expectations to Lady Naomi."

Naomi felt like a fraud. She did her best to stay attentive as Leon listed the people she would meet and the responsibilities she needed to become familiar with, but Gideon wouldn't leave her thoughts. She knew of his deceit. Did that not make her guilty of it as well?

"We have a surprise for you."

The sudden gleam in Leon's eyes drew her full attention. "We?" she questioned. "What sort of surprise?"

"Roderick and I, and the sort we hope will please you."

He offered no more of an explanation. Proffering his hand, Leon led her from the counting room and across the great hall. In the back corner, a staircase spiraled up to one of the tower rooms.

He paused on the small landing and smiled. "Your upbringing was rather unconventional. It is not our intention to change who you are, simply to support you as you find your place in our world. We hope this will illustrate our sincerity."

Naomi felt as if a fist clench around her heart, while he opened the door and motioned her into the room. A familiar tang sharpened the air. Naomi's pulse leapt. Ink; it smelled like ink.

Half afraid that her imagination had run amuck, she took a tentative step. Leon opened the shutters and twilight spilled across the floor. He quickly lit lamps and candles until a warm golden glow illuminated the entire room. A sloped desk sat near the windows and neat rows of shelves lined the walls. Naomi moved along the shelves, emotion choking her, tears blurring her eyes. Stacks of neatly folded parchment, quills and numerous brushes, gold leaf and gold powder, and pots and pots of ink.

With a trembling hand, she lifted one pot and looked inside. Velvety black carbon ink waited for the loving dip of a pointed quill pen.

"How was this done so quickly? I've not yet been here three days." Naomi put the inkpot back on the shelf and lifted the stopper of another. "Vermilion." She whispered the word with reverence, as she saw the vivid red.

Leon rocked on the balls of his feet, his hands clasped behind his back. He looked positively smug in his pleasure. "'Twas done before you arrived."

Naomi spotted a pot set slightly apart from the others. Instead of a simple stopper, it had a top that screwed into the pot. Carefully, Naomi rotated the lid and lifted it free. She gasped. "This is ultramarine. This is so precious they scrape it off and reuse it. It can only be made with lapis lazuli. How? Why?"

Leon took the pot from her trembling hands and carefully returned it to the shelf. "Roderick spared no expense. He wanted you to have everything you would need to continue your work."

Naomi covered her mouth with a trembling hand, moved beyond words.

"Are you pleased?" Leon brushed her cheek with the back of his knuckles.

"She seems rather overwhelmed," Gideon said from the doorway.

Eyes the same vivid blue as the costly ink turned his way and Gideon's entire body reacted. His eyes narrowed and his nostrils flared. His lips tingled and his fingers itched. Tension gripped his muscles, making him restless and hungry.

"I will let Roderick know that your suggestion was sound," Leon told him. He looked at Naomi and then back at Gideon, his expression revealing his concern. "Shall we return to the hall below?"

Gideon chuckled. "I've been charged with her protection, Leon. You need not protect her from me."

Still, he hesitated. "Naomi if you are not comfortable—"

"I am well. Sir Gideon does not frighten me."

Gideon smiled at the subtle challenge. Would she never learn?

After another moment of indecision, Leon departed.

It was all Gideon could do not to crush her in his arms and plunder her mouth. Her radiant smile was nearly as painful as the memory of her passion.

"He said this was your doing."

Emotion caused her voice to catch, but Gideon couldn't decipher what she was feeling. "I had to do something."

She took a step toward him. Gideon folded his hands into fists to keep from touching her.

"Why?" Her wide blue eyes swam with tears. "Why did you do this?"

He turned away before she saw how powerfully her gratitude moved him. "Leon mentioned in one of his messages that Gabriel taught you the art of illumination. Roderick wanted to do something special, something to make you feel welcomed. I simply suggested this as the means."

Her warm hand touched his arm and Gideon groaned. If she had any idea how close he was to feasting on her tender flesh, she would run screaming from the room. But she stood beside him, touching him gently, her eyes limpid pools of blue temptation.

"You are lying."

He shrugged off her hand and moved toward the window. Cool evening wind fanned out his hair and chilled his heated skin. "Why would I lie?"

"I never told Leon about my art. You and Brother Gabriel are the only ones who know."

Grinning into the twilight, Gideon embraced the coming night. "You are mistaken. Just ask your uncle. He sent a message informing Roderick of your unusual abilities."

Her soft chuckle wrapped around his senses like fur. If he didn't have her soon, he'd go mad. He'd tried to stay away, to ignore the bone deep ache. But it was useless. He needed her too badly.

"*My* unusual abilities?"

She was right behind him. He could smell her tantalizing scent and feel the heat radiating off her body. Without conscious thought, he spun and pulled her into his arms. They sighed together and she wrapped her arms around his back, molding her body against him.

Dark hunger flared within him, driving the breath from his lungs. His fangs extended and his muscles cramped. Pulling her face into his chest, he gasped and trembled.

Damn it, not now!

"What's wrong?" she whispered against his skin, sending tingles up and down his spine.

"Nothing," he said into her hair. "It has just been too long since I held you."

A shiver shook her body and echoed through his. She would be the death of him; there was no doubt. He closed his eyes and allowed the languid pleasure of her embrace to push away the darkness—at least for now.

She eased away from his chest and looked up into his eyes. "Are the customs so different here? Will I be allowed to illuminate openly?"

Tracing the edge of her wimple with his fingertip, Gideon said, "Nay. But you are capable of much more than illuminating manuscripts. The scroll you showed me is proof of that. Have you ever attempted something larger? A canvas? A wall?" He proposed the last with a chuckle.

She stepped out of his arms and moved to the desk. Finding the lever on each side that adjusted the angle of the workspace, she shifted the position to her liking. "I'm still confused. How did you know what I would need and from whence did the supplies come? These are not compounds found in an average castle's scullery."

"There is a large monastery two days ride from here. With a sizable donation from Roderick, they were persuaded to part with my list of supplies."

She faced him, her steady gaze searching his face. "And how did you compile this list? How did you know what I would need?"

Unwilling to reveal the full scope of his sacrifice, Gideon scrambled for a feasible explanation. She didn't need to know what it had cost him to bring this about.

"I asked Gabriel," he said simply and hurried from the room.

Chapter Twenty

Midnight came and went and still Naomi could not sleep. The shock of seeing Gideon had receded, leaving her restless and unsure. Why was he here? What did he want? Why was he being kind to her?

Seduction could no longer be his purpose. He had been the one to stop before they shared the final intimacy.

"This cannot go on," she whispered.

She had to understand what purpose drove him. The tension within her was tearing her apart. It would be tonight. Tonight they would be lovers, or he would leave her life forever.

Not bothering to dress, Naomi pulled her hooded mantle from a peg by the door and swung it around her shoulders. He had been given a tiny cottage within the castle walls. Elspeth had learned this from one of his men.

Her guards were nowhere in sight when she slipped from the solar and tiptoed across the great hall. Either Gideon had yet to implement their rotation or there would be hell to pay come morning.

The gatekeeper merely tugged his forelock as she passed into the lower bailey. With her identity concealed by her hood, he didn't spare her a second glance.

Moisture seeped through her slippers and Naomi hurried her pace. The faint scent of horses and wood smoke drifted on the breeze. It wasn't really cold, but Naomi drew her cloak more tightly around her.

There were three small wattle and daub buildings adjacent to the barracks, which was how Elspeth had described the location of Gideon's cottage. Naomi studied each for a moment and then approached the only one with firelight escaping around the shutters.

After a single tap, the door jerked open and Naomi ducked inside. Gideon quickly barred the door and turned to face her.

The fire was at her back and she hadn't lowered the hood, so she knew he couldn't see her features. Secure in that advantage, Naomi studied him. Tension hardened his features to the point of ferocity. He wore nothing but woolen hose. She watched his muscles ripple and flex as he moved beyond her to stoke the fire.

"Why are you here?" he asked.

Naomi laughed. "I came to ask you that very question."

"I live here."

She had tired of word games and half-truths. Tossing back her hood, she shook out her hair. "Why did you follow me?"

"I arrived before you. How could I have followed?"

Planting her hands on her hips, she glared at him. "What do you want? Why are you here?"

He stalked toward her with the loose-limbed grace of a wild animal. "All I understand is that I burn for you night and day. I tried to stay away from you, Naomi. I honestly tried."

"I came to you that night, and you did not take me. You kissed me goodbye—and—"

"A mistake I will not make again!" He grasped her upper arms and dragged her forward until she pressed against his naked chest. "I will never be satisfied without you. You are mine, Naomi, and I am yours."

She didn't stop him when he unfastened her cloak and tossed it over the back of a chair. If she hadn't wanted this, she wouldn't have come.

His fingers threaded through her unbound hair. Naomi tilted her face and closed her eyes. The fire popped, but nothing happened.

"Open your eyes." His voice sounded harsh and strangled. Naomi did as he asked. His gaze glowed with otherworldly light, but Naomi was not afraid.

"There can be no regrets. You must come to me freely, without reservation, or not at all."

Annoyed by the ultimatum, yet understanding his hesitation, Naomi paused but a moment. "I am yours," she whispered, "and you are mine."

His eyes squeezed shut and his lips compressed as if he were in agony. She stepped closer, but he shook his head. After several deep, ragged breaths, he opened his eyes. The otherworldly light was gone, but he looked so forlorn that Naomi wanted to weep.

"What is it? Why do you—?"

"I promised Michael I would not seduce you," he lamented.

She smiled into his eyes and raised her hands to the laces at the front of her chemise. "You are not seducing me, Gideon. I am seducing you."

The chemise slid to pool at her feet and Naomi held her breath, waiting for his reaction.

Gideon feared his heart would burst through the wall of his chest. Firelight danced across the surface of her skin, creating hypnotic patterns that did nothing to distract from the beauty of her shape. Her long slender arms remained at her sides, though he saw a flicker of uncertainty in her eyes.

"You make me ache just looking at you," he said.

She smiled and glanced away. His gaze immediately descended to more intimate treasures while her eyes were averted. Lush and round, her breasts beckoned his touch and his mouth. The rose-hued nipples had already distended and tightened.

He had just begun his visual investigation of her feminine mound when she took two quick steps forward and wrapped her arms around his neck. The velvet heat of her skin on his made him groan, but he wanted to see her and touch her and taste her, before he joined his body with hers.

"Please, Gideon." She rubbed her cheek against his chest and her moist breath fanned his skin. "We have waited so long."

"We have waited too long not to enjoy everything there is to enjoy."

So saying, he grabbed her bottom and dragged her up along his body until her mouth was even with his. Her lips were parted and pliant, waiting for him. Gideon savored the texture and the softness of her lips before venturing into her mouth with his tongue. She angled her head and swirled her tongue around his, clutching his shoulders. She tasted of wine and woman and Gideon drank deeply.

"Wrap your legs around my waist," he murmured against her damp lips.

Without argument, she drew up her long legs and wrapped them around him. He came to rest at the entrance to her body and she tensed. Did she expect him to ram into her like a beast, a monster...a creature of the night?

Gideon stroked her back and buttocks and kissed her slowly, deeply. His fingers delved into the crevice between her bottom cheeks and he felt her start. "Easy."

The damp heat of her sex enveloped his fingertips. He could thrust into her now and she would take him, but he wanted so much more.

Setting her down on the edge of his narrow bed, Gideon quickly parted her thighs and knelt on the floor between them. He moved her arms behind her and pushed gently until she rested back on her elbows.

"Watch me, Naomi. See my hands on your flesh and my mouth touching you. Know that it is me and only me who gives you this pleasure."

He thought she would respond, but his mouth closed around her nipple and she only murmured. He filled his palm with one soft breast while his mouth adored the other. Her nipple pebbled against his tongue and he drew it deeply into his mouth. Restlessly, she moved, her head rolling back on her shoulders.

"Nay," he said. "Watch me."

Naomi forced her heavy lids to rise and look down at Gideon. His dark head bent over her heaving breasts, his mouth suckling one, his hand covering the other. The caresses stirred her senses, but seeing the contrast in their skin tone and the strength in his sword hand gentled to tease her made her arch and moan.

He raised his head and kissed her until the room spun. She returned the kiss with eagerness and trust. It was not until she felt the gentle prodding of his fingers that she realized he had been distracting her with his kiss.

Ever so gently, he parted her folds and pushed his finger into the core of her sex. Naomi moaned into his open mouth. The simple penetration accelerated her desire as nothing had before. Her inner muscles clenched, her breasts throbbed, and tension gathered deep in her abdomen.

She heard him mutter that obscene word then he moved away slightly. Following the direction of his stare, Naomi repeated his obscenity. His finger moved slowly into her sheath and then pulled back out. It was the most beautiful thing she had ever seen and yet so graphically carnal that it made her tremble.

With a slow twist of his wrist, he added a second finger, and a ripple of pleasure spread out through her body. "Oh my," she murmured.

"Oh, *mine.*" He pushed in as far as he could.

Naomi could stand it no longer. She collapsed back across the bed and raised her hips against his finger. "Please, Gideon, I need you now."

"Nay. I will not hurt you."

She hurt already. The tense burning in her core had long since turned to pain. Each breath and movement only intensified the throbbing.

Gideon held himself back with iron control. He stubbornly prepared her body, keeping her on the edge of the precipice for as long as he could, while he stretched her with his fingers. Her sheath clung to him almost painfully, but her liquid response assured him she was nearly there.

Slipping one hand beneath her, he anchored her with a firm grip on her rounded bottom. He needed her to stay still, but he knew she would not. The scent of her arousal filled his head and stirred his hunger. Never again would he take her blood, but as often as she would allow it, he intended to taste her.

Keeping his fingers butted up against her maidenhead, he searched with his tongue until he found the spot that made her entire body jump. *Oh, aye!* He circled the spot and flicked his tongue across it over and over. She whimpered and tried to move, but he held her firmly. Her inner muscles rippled rhythmically, announcing her coming crisis.

Concentrating carefully, he closed his lips around her pulsating nub and allowed his fingernails to grow and sharpen, slicing through her maidenhead.

He sucked gently and she cried out, driving her hips up against his fingers. Each blessed contraction of her muscles and each sobbing breath assured him she had felt only pleasure. He waited until the last, faintest ripple ended before he slipped his finger from her body and kissed her one last time with a slow thorough swirl of his tongue.

Naomi lay sprawled and replete, stunned by the intensity of her pleasure. Still he had not joined his body to hers. Surely he didn't intend to end this way.

She sat up and reached for him. "Please do not deny me—"

He chuckled and pressed his mouth to hers. "Not tonight. Not ever again."

He shed his hose and started to join her on the bed, but Naomi stopped him. "Do I not get the opportunity to torment you?"

"Not tonight."

"Not ever?" She pouted and batted her eyelashes.

"Oh, I will let you torment me to your heart's content, but if I do not come inside you now, I will lose my mind."

Her gaze descended along his body as he eased her back across the bed. A tremble of fear skipped through her, but she tried not to let him see.

"I will not hurt you, Naomi. There will be only pleasure."

Dragging her gaze back to his, she said, "But Zarrah told me—"

"I took your maidenhead with my fingers. There will be only pleasure."

She wasn't about to argue with him. He crawled onto the bed and kissed her gently, tenderly, until she relaxed beneath him.

"Part your legs. Invite me in."

His sensual whisper unleashed countless tingles and Naomi opened for him.

"Draw up your knees and kiss me with your whole body."

She had no idea what he meant, but she pulled her knees up along his sides and found his mouth with hers. Moving and molding his lips with hers, she heard his ragged groan and felt him press against her opening. She tangled her hands in his hair and kissed him wildly.

With firm, gradual pressure he sank into her, joining with her, filling her. Naomi tore her mouth away, panting harshly. Her body stretched to take him, pulsing around him, but there was no pain.

Just the incredible fullness of having his body inside her.

"Oh, Gideon." She moaned.

"Aye, love, feel me. Know me."

He kissed her and kissed her, while Naomi adjusted to his penetration. Gently stroking her breasts and caressing her legs, he waited for her to accept him.

Naomi released his hair and ran her hands across the slick muscles of his back.

"What happens now?" she whispered, knowing he must have to move somehow.

He chuckled, a deep, sinfully wicked sound. Naomi's nipples tighten. His hands moved between their bodies, on the inside of her thighs, then under her buttocks. He lifted her as he rocked back onto his knees. Naomi gasped and clutched the bedding. Her legs were looped over his arms, keeping her open and accessible. He pulled back, nearly out of her and then thrust in quickly, deeply—completely.

She arched her back, tightening her inner muscles around him. The friction of his movements accented the aching burn. She thrashed beneath him and lifted toward him. With each thrust, he became more forceful, more demanding. It thrilled her to realize just how much he had been holding back.

He strained, his muscles rippling with each forceful lunge. Naomi wanted to touch him, but she couldn't reach him.

Instead, she closed her eyes and concentrated on the sensations building within her. Each rhythmic pulsation tightened her sheath around him and she understood what had been missing before.

His fingers gripped her bottom with urgent force. He was losing control. She opened her eyes, basking in the intense, golden glow that was his gaze.

"Now, Gideon, now," she murmured and he slammed into her with a sound, part growl and part groan.

She felt him loose his seed deep within her and the heat triggered her release. Ripples of tingling pleasure washed over her and twisted through her. She cried out, shaking and throbbing as her climax unfurled.

Chapter Twenty-One

Awareness returned slowly. She felt his fingers against her lips and realized he had released her legs. He was still buried deeply within her body, but she didn't feel quite so full.

"What happens now?" he asked, echoing her earlier question.

His gaze was intent, but no longer glowing, and his long dark hair tickled her face.

"Give me a few moments to catch my breath and I shall show you," she said teasingly.

He shook his head. "Nay. What role shall you set for me now?"

"What role?" She didn't want to think about the morrow. She wanted to bask in this moment forever.

He shifted so his arms kept his weight from crushing her. "I want you with me, Naomi. I want to awaken to your smile and know you will be there when I reach for you in the night."

Naomi licked her lips and stared up into his gilded eyes. "What are you suggesting? That we marry?"

She tried to keep the tension from her voice, but he must have felt her hesitation. He pushed away and sat on the end of the bed facing her. Naomi sat as well, drawing her legs up and wrapping her arms around her knees. Her body still hummed with the incredible pleasure he had given her and already he was discontent.

"Is the idea so intolerable?" he asked.

"The idea is not intolerable, Gideon, it's impossible. How can I wed with you? You are not...human."

That set him in motion. He bounded off the bed and reached for his hose. "You can share your body with a creature who is not human, but you cannot share your life?"

"I cannot share my life with you until you have ended your war with God."

He planted his fist on his hips and glared at her. "I am not at war with God, I am at war—"

"With humans," she finished for him. "And I am human."

Raking his fingers through his hair he turned from her and stared into the dying fire. "I am weary of war."

His words surprised and pleased her. Naomi quickly donned her chemise, while she debated what to say.

"What keeps you from ending the war?" She wanted to approach him, to press herself against his broad back and wrap her arms around his waist. But she stayed on the bed, afraid of distracting him.

"All that I have seen. All that I have done. I do not see how..."

She had to touch him. It was simply unthinkable to leave him alone in his misery. She crossed the cottage and slipped her hands up under his damp hair. The muscles in his shoulders flexed and flinched, but he didn't pull away. She rubbed him with firm pressure, leaning in to smell his hair.

"You said that Gabriel told you what supplies I would need." She spoke only after he began to relax beneath her hands. "How were you able to contact him?"

He braced his hands against the mantelpiece, allowing her to massage more forcefully. "I think you are inciting me with your touch to reveal all my secrets." He groaned. "That feels so good."

She pressed a kiss to one shoulder blade. "I thought I knew all your secrets."

Tension bunched his muscles and Naomi's heart plummeted. She had meant the comment in jest, but apparently she had struck a nerve.

"I made a deal with Michael," he said, bringing them back to her original question. "I told him I'd treat you honorably if he would allow me to speak with Gabriel."

He volunteered this information, so there must have been more to it. "If Michael was worried about my honor, would he not have kept you away from me?"

"He could have tried."

Smiling despite the arrogance in this tone, Naomi moved his hair aside and cuddled up to his back. The fire had warmed his chest and her hands moved across the heated contours eagerly. It was thrilling to know she could touch him whenever she wanted, however she wanted.

"What else did you promise Michael?" She spoke the words against the warm hollow where his shoulder met his neck.

He turned in her arms and framed her face with his hands. "We have wandered far off course here. I promised I would treat you honorably and I am not sure that what has gone on tonight qualifies as honorable."

Slowly licking her lips, Naomi drew his attention to her mouth. "I came to you."

"And now I must do what is right."

She rose up on her toes and kissed him. "Tomorrow we can debate what is right. Tonight belongs to me." She kissed him again. "I want you." With her mouth moving against his she finished the sentence, "Inside me."

* * *

He needed to feed.

Making love with Naomi had left him drained and weak. She lay curled against his back, her arm looped over his waist and he didn't want to leave the comfort of her embrace.

Dark hunger clawed at his gut, refusing to subside, so he carefully moved her arm and slipped out of bed. She looked like a child, so peaceful and serene, but Gideon could still feel her writhing beneath him and clawing his back as she found release.

Shaking away the lingering memories, he quietly dressed and walked out into the night. But it was no longer night. Dawn had brushed the sky with the first few shades of morning.

"You better hurry. You waited almost too long to feed."

Gideon cursed beneath his breath, but didn't bother to turn around. He could smell Domieno's stench and feel his evil.

"Let me show you something," Domieno said, a demonic compulsion accompanying the words.

A groan tore from Gideon's throat as his body obeyed. They moved quickly through the shadows, faster than human eyes could see. Beyond the castle walls and into the forest, Gideon struggled against the demon's urging to no avail. The crumbling ruins of some ancient structure came into view and Domieno released his hold.

"Here we are," the demon said. "Human kindness at its finest."

Gideon didn't understand until he looked more closely at the shadows surrounding him. Children lay sleeping in every corner of the ruin, seeking what little shelter the broken walls could provide.

Anger and pity wrestled within him until Gideon forgot his hunger. "Why are they here?" he whispered.

Domieno shrugged, leaning one shoulder against a section of wall still standing. "No one wants them. They are castoffs, orphans. Most of the creatures in the village do well to keep their own children fed."

Awed by their perfect little faces, Gideon moved among the children. He carefully kept his back to Domieno, not wanting the demon to know that his heart was pounding. They were filthy and horribly thin. Some had no shoes and most had no cloaks, despite the crisp, early morning air. They clung to each other for warmth, sleeping in small clusters.

"Pathetic, are they not? Most will not last through the winter. There is no help for it."

Gideon spun to face him, protective instincts surging to the surface. "Why have you brought me here?"

"Do you not see?" His flat soulless eyes suddenly flashed with malevolent intent. "Take your fill. Feed 'til you burst. No one will miss them. No one cares."

Furry spun out of control before Gideon could restrain his reaction. He flew at Domieno and pinned him to the wall with his forearm. "Do not touch these children!"

The demon laughed, his fetid breath fanning Gideon's face. The little girl nearest them tossed restlessly.

"I have no reason to touch them, Gideon." Domieno shoved him away. "But you do. They are going to die anyway. Why cast suspicion on yourself by feeding in the village?"

Gideon glanced at the little girl, worried that she might awaken. "I will not feed on children," he whispered, clenching his teeth.

Domieno grinned. "Then, you will feed on Naomi?"

"Never!"

"Her scent is all over you, friend. You claimed her tonight. Do not bother to deny it. Have you told her? Does she know what you really are?"

Gideon turned, meaning to leave the ruin, but Domieno slammed him against the wall, holding him there just as he had done moments before.

"Stop denying what you are. You made a deal with Michael. You promised to demonstrate your honor and before one day passed in Naomi's presence, you were rutting between her thighs. You are one of us already!"

He shoved against the demon, but Domieno didn't budge. "I promised Michael I would actively seek redemption and that is what I intend to do."

"What you were doing for the past four hours does not lead to redemption, my friend. It leads to—"

"I will not speak of Naomi with you!"

Domieno stepped back, folding his arms across his chest. "You're running out of time. That was true before, but your new agreement makes it doubly so. What were you thinking?"

Gideon resented the amusement in Domieno's tone, but this was neither the time nor the place for a confrontation. "I was thinking of a permanent solution to my unrest."

"We can offer you that and more, but you have to stop pretending. That is all you have been doing—pretending."

The demon dissolved into a cloud of rancid mist.

Covering his nose and mouth with his hand, Gideon fought down the bile rising into his throat.

Why did Domieno persist in tormenting him? And why did his arguments ring true? He didn't regret making love to Naomi, but he should have resolved his future before he—

A distressed cry drew his attention to the little girl. He took an unconscious step back and started to release his corporeal body, but the child didn't scream. She stared back at him with huge, frightened eyes, but she made no sound or movement.

"Fear not," he said softly. "I mean you no harm."

"Something smells bad," she whispered, holding her nose with her finger and thumb.

"Aye, but the air will clear. Go back to sleep."

Scrambling up from her leafy bed, the girl walked toward him. Her head tilted a little more with each step. "You are very tall."

Lazy rays of sunlight sank through the tree limbs and touched the ground near Gideon's foot. He needed to leave. He needed to feed! But the child fascinated him. Her long hair had been braided, but twigs and leaves now adorned the braid. Even through the dirt, Gideon could see the purity of her oval face, the innocence in her wide blue eyes.

His soul ached for all that he had lost.

"What's your name?" she asked.

"Gideon. I'm the night watchman and I stopped by to see that all is well."

Her mouth gaped for a second and then she snapped it shut. "Jack won't like this at all."

"Who is Jack and why will this displease him?"

"Jack be my brother and now you know our secret."

She seemed genuinely distressed, so Gideon bent to one knee and took one of her hands. "What's your name, little one?"

"My name's not little one." She smiled prettily, assuring him that she had intentionally twisted his words. "Midge be my name."

"Very well, Midge. Will Jack be cross with you or will he be cross with me?"

"Jack grumbles and grumps at everyone, but this here is our hideout. No one's supposed to know, but us."

"I see." Gideon stood and brushed the dirt from his hose. "I do not intend to tell anyone, so your secret is safe."

"Can I tell Jack you were here? I'm not supposed to talk to strangers."

"Aye, tell him. I would like to talk with Jack, but I'm the night watchman and `tis nearly day."

"Will you come back tomorrow night?"

"I don't know. I must leave, little one, but I will see you again."

Her eyes followed him as he slipped farther into the trees. He must speak with Roderick about these children. Why would orphans feel it necessary to hide in the forest? Someone should be seeing to their care.

He was exhausted and famished, but he must seek shelter from the sun. Concentrating on the image of a falcon, he spread his arms and launched himself upward. Flapping his wings in strong, even strokes, he held his hunger at bay a moment longer for one precious glimpse of the morning sky.

Chapter Twenty-Two

Naomi spent the morning with Roderick and Kruthers. The bailiff offered information with an economy of words that made Naomi smile. He was knowledgeable and Roderick obviously trusted him, but the man appeared to have been fashioned without a personality.

She retreated to her tower room late in the afternoon, hoping to finish her sketch of Brother Gabriel before the light faded. The desk was surprisingly comfortable. A pad had been attached to the bench, and being able to adjust the angle of the workspace was a luxury she had never before experienced.

With careful strokes of the pen and gentle sweeps of the brush, Naomi added the finishing touches to her guardian's beloved features. Tapping the end of the brush against the edge of the workspace, she studied the drawing.

Sadness crept over her for a moment, but tenderness chased it away. She missed him terribly. Her childhood had been filled with warmth and security because of Brother Gabriel. He had been a truer father to her than many children knew.

But more importantly, he had helped shape her character. He had helped her develop attitudes and perspectives that would serve her well as she took her place in the world.

"He knows you love him. You never need to worry about that."

Naomi glanced at the door. Gideon stood there, but she had not heard him enter.

"Sometimes I get impatient," he told her with a sardonic smile.

He had bound his hair, accenting the harsh angles of his face and his sword was strapped to his side. Naomi pushed back the bench and stood. He always looked fierce, but right now he looked dangerous. "You were gone when I awakened. I was disappointed."

"I will try harder tonight."

She smiled at his brash response. With slow calculated steps he approached her. Immediately, her breathing sped up and her pulse raced. "You look ready for battle," she said softly as he reached her.

He cupped her cheek in his palm and stroked her lips with his thumb. "Were your guards at their posts today?"

"Aye. They have followed me around like puppies all day. You do realize if you had arranged the rotation last night—"

"I shall guard you each night, so nothing would have changed."

Rubbing her cheek against his hand, she nipped the pad of his thumb and smiled. "Why are you wearing your sword?"

"What sort of guard would I be if I came unarmed?"

"Well, I know you have other weapons at your disposal, but I see your point."

He kissed her gently, yet thoroughly and Naomi sighed. "If only there was a pallet in this room…"

He chuckled and slapped her rounded behind. "Do not tempt me. I will strip you naked and keep you locked in this tower. You can work on your drawings all day and pleasure me all night."

"Grandfather might have something to say about that arrangement." She moved out of his arms. "Do you have plans for this evening?"

"Actually, I was hoping to show you something."

She grinned at him. "Something more than you showed me last night?"

He growled and reached for her. She laughed and scurried away. "You tempt me sorely to show you a pallet is not necessary."

Smiling prettily, she asked, "What did you wish to show me?"

All playfulness fled from his tone and expression. "How extensive was your tour of the villages?"

"Leon took me through them." Concern eroded her smile. "I didn't notice anything out of the ordinary. Is something amiss?"

"I believe so, but I would like your opinion."

He took her hand and led her from the room. They paused in the great hall while Elspeth fetched her cloak.

"We can walk or ride, which would you prefer?" Gideon asked as he fastened the cloak around her shoulders.

"Where are we going?"

"To the ruins of the old manor house, just west of Monthamn Major."

Had he planned some romantic surprise? Were they to spend the night in the forest beneath the stars? Her stomach gave a little flutter and she tried not to let her expression reveal her excitement. "I would prefer to walk, if it's not too far."

Cool evening air brushed her cheeks as they left the castle compound. The fresh scents of pine and smoke from cook fires drifted on the breeze. Most of the villagers were in their cottages and the workshops were empty.

Passing through Monthamn Major, they moved into the forest beyond. Naomi reached over and took Gideon's hand. He had been tense and silent since they left the castle. She didn't understand his mood.

"What is this about? I take it this is not a ploy to be alone with me."

He squeezed her hand, but his expression remained hard and distant. "Roderick told me that a fever swept through the area about five years past. Lady Naomi, Roderick's wife, responded to the crisis in a rather unusual way. She closed the castle to the people in the villages."

"That is not unusual. It is a wise precaution."

"I agree, but that is not all she did. The fever seemed to affect adults more so than children. So if any member of a family fell ill, Naomi brought the children to the castle."

"Why are you telling me this?"

He stopped walking and turned to face her. "Naomi left the castle to help tend the sick and was never able to return. She sacrificed herself trying to save her people. By the time the illness had run its course, Roderick was left alone with a castle full of orphans."

Naomi's heart sank into the pit of her stomach. Roderick must have been devastated by the loss. "What became of the orphans? They are not at the castle now."

"Nay, they are not," Gideon said. "Roderick was tortured by their presence. They were a continual reminder of Naomi's death, so he made arrangements with Father John for their care."

He offered no more information. Threading his fingers through hers, he led her farther into the trees.

Silhouetted against the coming night, the ruins cast ragged shadows across the forest floor. Naomi heard a voice speak urgently and then silence. A bird shifted restlessly in the branches to her left and she spotted the distant flicker of a tiny fire.

As they neared the doorless entrance, a boy stepped into the open arch. Ragged clothing draped his too thin frame and defiance blazed in his dark eyes. Naomi could only guess at the color of his tangled hair. His suspicious gaze shifted to Gideon and Naomi rubbed her arms, suddenly feeling the cold evening air.

"Are you the man Midge told me about?" he demanded, eyeing Gideon overtly.

"If you are Jack," Gideon replied. "I am the night watchman."

"Night watchman, my arse," the boy grumbled. "No castle guard would bother with the likes of us. Who sent you? What do you want?"

Naomi couldn't decide if she wanted to enlist him as her champion or paddle his behind. Never had she seen such a confounding mixture of pride and vulnerability. Not even the faintest hint of a beard marred his jaw and yet he faced Gideon as if they were equals.

She stepped toward him. His pointed chin lifted and he crossed his arms over his chest.

"Who are you?"

"My name is Naomi, and this is Gideon."

His gleaming, dark eyes narrowed. "That supposed to mean something to me?"

"It means you will show the lady the respect she is due or answer to me." Gideon stepped up beside her, but Naomi held him off with an upraised hand.

"I give everyone the respect *they have earned,"* Jack said.

Naomi laid her hand on Gideon's arm and the muscles flexed beneath her fingers. "Why do you know this place?" she asked Gideon, hoping to distract him from the lad's belligerence.

"I stumbled upon it."

He said nothing more, so she turned her attention back to Jack. "May we enter your keep, kind sir?"

With a rather disrespectful snort, he moved aside. "Only half the walls still stand. If I say you, nay, you'll only go around."

"Are you always so agreeable?" Naomi asked as she moved passed the boy and into the gaping space that had once been a great hall. Only one section of the roof remained intact. In the far corner, a group of perhaps fifteen children huddled around the fire she had seen earlier. Their curious expressions and anxious eyes tore at her heart.

"How many children are in your charge, Master Jack?" Naomi moved around the room, looking into the adjoining spaces, but not venturing too near any of the children.

"What's it to you?"

Gideon reached him before Naomi could intervene. He grabbed the boy by the scruff of the neck and scowled down into his dirty face. "Listen well, pup. We are here to help you and those within your care, but I will not tolerate your insolence. You will address her as Lady Naomi and you will speak respectfully."

Naomi held her breath, waiting for Jack to react. If the lad rebelled, Gideon would be forced to punish him. Jack glared into the distance for a moment, but then his stance relaxed. He shook off Gideon's hand and faced her.

"There be nine and twenty now, Lady Naomi. We've lost six since the fever fled."

She wanted to reassure the boy, to comfort him, but Gideon was right. He needed to accept their authority. "Who is the youngest?"

"Tot. She were only two when the fever came."

He motioned toward a dark-haired girl to Naomi's right. If five years had passed since the fever, then the girl was seven. She was tiny and frail. Naomi would never have thought her as old as seven. "Do you know her Christian name?"

"Tot is all I know her by."

"How old are you, Master Jack?" She tried to see beneath the grime.

"I was nearly eight when the fever came."

He referenced everything back to the horrible event. Naomi's insides twisted. Why were they hiding in a tumbledown ruin? "Did the fever take all of your families?"

"Nay. Some of us still have families. I have Midge and Tot has two sisters. Thom and—"

"Your parents, Jack," she interrupted him gently. "Did the fever take all of your parents?"

"Most. A few was orphans before."

He kicked at the dirt with his bare toes and scratched subtle furrows in the dirt on one cheek.

"How long have you been living here?"

"This will be the second winter."

Naomi was so distracted by the conversation that she gasped when a tiny hand slid into hers. She looked down to find a cherub smiling up at her. Wide blue eyes studied her with curiosity and fascination.

"Midge, leave Lady Naomi be," Jack said.

Naomi knelt and smiled at the girl. "Hello, Midge. You sure have pretty eyes."

The girl beamed. "Are you the watchman's wife?"

Gideon's gaze smoldered, daring her to answer.

"I am Lady Naomi. It is nice to meet you." Ignoring the mockery in Gideon's stare, she turned back to Jack. "Where did you live before you came…here?"

"Ask Father John." In a flash the tiger cub returned. He spun on Gideon, his features scrunched into a snarl. "What do you want with us? Why are you here? Have you not…we will not go back there. I will not go back!"

Jack dashed into the darkness and Naomi knew he was racing tears.

"We must speak with Father John," Gideon muttered, heading toward the doorway.

"We cannot leave them here," Naomi said vehemently.

He took her hand and guided her from the ruin. When curious ears could no longer hear them, he drew her near. "We must first earn Jack's trust. The children will not trust us until Jack trusts us and I would not force my will upon these children."

"But the night is chilly and—"

"We will send food and blankets back with a guard, but whatever we decide to do with the orphans must be accepted by Jack."

She smiled, rubbing her thumb across his fingers. "How do you know so much about children?"

Gideon recoiled from the question. He released her hand and tromped off through the woods. "I know nothing about children, but I know about pride. This battle will be won or lost with Jack."

"Battle? Why must this be a battle? Why is everything a battle?"

He could hear her scurrying to keep up with his angry strides, but he didn't slow his pace. Ever since they'd made love, Gideon had been inundated with feelings he thought long dead within him.

Protectiveness was a strong, masculine emotion. He could accept that he wanted to keep her safe. Nay, he *needed* to keep her safe. But this...tenderness. Why did his gut turn to mush each time he looked at her?

And the children? Why should he care that they slept in the cold with no real shelter and little food? They were nothing to him. Why did he feel this overwhelming urge to throttle Father John?

"Gideon!"

She grabbed his arm, bringing him up short and forcing his attention back to her.

"What do you intend to do?" she asked. "Stomp into the rectory and beat a hapless priest?"

"Aye. If this *hapless* priest has intentionally neglected these children, I will beat him senseless."

She laughed, releasing his arm. "If what you suspect is true, I will assist you, but we need information. We need to know the specifics of his arrangement with Roderick. If you accuse him now, he will simply deny…"

"How can he deny neglecting the orphans? They live alone in a crumbling ruin with nothing to eat."

"And we must find out why. It cannot be as simple as his ignoring their plight." She stroked his face with her hand, tracing the sharp angle of his cheekbone with her thumb. "Something is at work here, something more sinister than neglect."

He turned into her touch. Closing his eyes, he let the heat of her hand soothe him. "Then, what do you suggest?"

"We must speak with Roderick. Find out the exact nature of his arrangement with Father John. We need to know where the children were taken when they left the castle. Jack said this was the second winter they've passed in the ruins, so they were under Father John's care for the previous three. We need to know what happened. What changed?"

Kissing her palm, Gideon said, "Give me till sunrise with the priest and I will have your answers."

She smiled, moving closer still. "I suspect he deserves that and more, but I prefer a less violent approach. The children will watch how we conduct ourselves. What message do you want to send them?"

He framed her face with his hands and kissed her gently, slowly. "I would tell them I trust their Lady and bow to her expertise in this matter."

Naomi circled his neck with her arms and smiled into his eyes. "For how long?"

Chuckling softly, he pulled her against him. "For as long as I feel we are making progress. But if the time comes that I feel your gentler methods are not working, I will visit Father John."

Chapter Twenty-Three

After escorting Naomi back to the castle, Gideon went to find Daniel. Naomi's determination to investigate the situation with the orphans frustrated Gideon to no end. Information was for monks and scholars. He was a man of action. The children had immediate needs and he intended to address them.

Daniel stood before the barracks with two of the knights they had recruited for Naomi's private guard. Gideon motioned Daniel to him, out of earshot of the other men.

"What ails you now?" Daniel asked, his dark eyes flashing.

Three days into their grand adventure, Gideon convinced Alyssa that England was as good a place as any for their relocation. Daniel hadn't been pleased.

"I need your assistance."

Daniel's eyes narrowed and he tossed back his mantle, freeing his sword arm. "Why do I have the feeling this is more along the lines of scrubbing floors than slaying giants?"

Gideon grinned. His restlessness had quieted upon his arrival at Monthamn, but his friend's discontent grew in keeping with Gideon's calm.

"We have uncovered a great injustice that must be put to rights." It was really unfair to utilize the one call to arms Daniel couldn't resist, but the orphans needed help.

"You're a manipulative fiend," Daniel said, but amusement stirred within his black gaze. "May I presume that `we' is you and Lady Naomi?"

"You may."

"What is the nature of the injustice?"

"I will show you, but provisions must be gathered and loaded into some sort of cart," Gideon explained.

"What sort of provisions?"

Gideon steered him toward the stables. "Food, blankets, the basic essentials of life. Would you please find the marshal and see to the cart? I will begin gathering what we will need."

"You have Alyssa playing nursemaid to your—"

"Watch which words you choose to describe Lady Naomi," he said tersely.

Daniel's dark gaze turned intent. "What is so special about this human?"

"She is unique, Daniel," Alyssa answered from behind them. "She is warm and caring, shrewd, yet innocent."

"She is not all *that* innocent. I know where she spent last night."

Gideon sprang. Twisting his fists in the front of Daniel's tunic, he slammed him back against the stable wall. "You will not mock her. Do you understand? You will-"

"I do not believe this!" Daniel shoved him back. "You are in love with her. *You.* In love with a human! This is unreal."

Gideon didn't deny it. He hadn't applied a name to the emotions Naomi unleashed within him, but he refused to lie to himself any longer.

Ignoring Daniel's indignation, he turned to Alyssa. She looked adorable in her servant's garb, the flame-red hair now soft strawberry blonde. "Where is she—*Elspeth?*"

Alyssa smiled and dropped into a quick curtsy. "My lady is in the great hall with her Lord Uncle." She slipped effortlessly into her role.

"You are both acting like fools," Daniel muttered.

Gideon pulled Alyssa against his side, but met Daniel's angry gaze. "Will you find the marshal?"

"Aye," Daniel said, obviously annoyed.

* * *

Roderick coughed repeatedly into a cloth, his thin shoulders shaking. Kruthers handed him a cup of heated cider as the spasm ended and Naomi's heart lurched. In the few short days since she had come to Monthamn Castle, her grandfather had become incredibly dear. She didn't want to watch him die, and if she were brutally honest, she didn't want to face the responsibilities of Monthamn without him.

"So, what's this about the orphans?" Roderick asked.

They sat at the small table in Roderick's counting room. Kruthers handed Naomi a cup with the spiced apple cider and then silently slipped from the room, leaving the door ajar.

"What did Father John agree to do for the children and how is he compensated for the service?" Naomi gently took his hand in hers.

"Father John found homes for the orphans." Roderick's voice was thin and hoarse. "He had them housed in the old cloister down by the mill for a time, but their numbers dwindled until a separate building was no longer necessary. He kept the last few with him at the parish church until they were placed with families. As for compensation, I gave him whatever he needed and he asked for support from the Bishop of Chichester. This parish is in his diocese."

She stroked the back of his fingers, reassured by the warmth of his skin and his responding squeeze. "Is Father John the only priest in this parish?"

"Aye." Roderick stifled a cough by taking a long drink from his cup. "He had an underling a few years back, but I do not know why he left. Probably too ambitious for his own good. Priests usually are."

Naomi fidgeted on the narrow wooden bench. Perhaps Gideon had it right. She imagined engaging Father John in a decidedly physical confrontation. Already, it was evident that he had been lying to Roderick.

"You said he housed them in a cloister. Were the nuns available to care for the children?"

"The cloister was abandoned. The nuns are long gone. What is this about?"

She started to explain but could not bring herself to speak the words. Roderick had borne enough already. He had more than earned what peace he could find.

"Nothing, Grandfather. I just overheard someone talking about the orphans and wondered what had become of them." She set her cup on the table and offered him a beaming smile. "I never got the opportunity to thank you for the tower room. It was a wonderful surprise."

Roderick returned her smile with a bit less enthusiasm. "That was Gideon's doing. He has been a godsend."

Naomi bristled at the phrase. It had been many years since God sent him anywhere.

"I'll not keep you." Naomi scooted off the end of the bench. "You need your rest."

"I have everything I need, young lady. But you do not."

The sudden strength in Roderick's tone drew her attention. She paused beside the table.

"What do I need that I lack?"

"A husband." He paused for a moment before he said, "I will be frank, Naomi. I know where you spent last night."

Her heartbeat sped up and she worried her lower lip. Had she really believed that no one would notice?

"Sir Roderick." Gideon spoke from the doorway. "I have every intention of wedding with Lady Naomi. I had hoped to secure her agreement before I brought my petition to you."

"You seem to have the cart before the horse here, lad." He pushed to his feet, but his legs wobbled beneath him. Mustering a scowl that must have been fierce in his prime, Roderick stared down the younger man. "Generally a man asks permission of the guardian before he woos the woman."

"I am asking your permission now."

"Don't see that there's much of a choice. The wedding is supposed to come before the bedding, too." He shook his head. "If your intentions are honorable, I'll leave the details to you."

Tension emanated from every nuance of Naomi's posture. Her jaw was set, her eyes narrowed, her hands tightly fisted at her sides. This was not good. She met his gaze, but Gideon could not read her expression. She offered her farewell to Roderick and followed Gideon out into the great hall.

He watched the tempest gather within her eyes. She wasn't ready to accept him as her mate. He braced for the coming storm.

"Do you age?" she asked as they started across the room. "You told me that you have been banished from the light for nearly a century, and yet you look to be a man in his prime."

"There has been no change in my physical appearance since I was banished," he said.

"You cannot...you told me that you are unable to father children. God took the ability away, and you have hated humans ever since."

"I do not hate you, Naomi."

She ducked his outreached hand. "But you are unable to father children."

"Aye." He took a deep breath. "Why is this of such importance now? You were contemplating your final vows when I first met you. Nuns do not have children."

"My circumstances have changed, Gideon. I have changed." She was silent for a long time. Her lips trembled and she clutched the embroidered edge of her sleeves. "What happens when your punishment ends? Will you return to Heaven?"

"I do not know."

Releasing her sleeves she made a broad gesture with both hands. "Then how can you expect me to wed with you?"

"I expect nothing," he said softly. "I want you with me. That is all."

Silence descended again.

He hadn't expected her to relent easily, but it didn't make the disappointment any less painful. Raking his fingers through his hair, he squared his shoulders and asked, "Where are you bound?"

"I'm going back to the ruins to speak with Jack," she said, stubbornly fighting back tears. "Will you please accompany me?"

Quickly averting his gaze, he made certain she didn't see how well the question pleased him. "Daniel and Al—err, Elspeth are gathering provisions. Wait for me here."

Naomi watched him walk out into the night. Her heart hung heavy in her breast and tension banded her middle. If only he were human. If only...

Just like Gideon's passionate interest in the orphans. *We always want most what we cannot have.*

But how could she accept a husband who could not give her children? She must produce an heir to solidify her claim to Monthamn Castle.

And she wanted no other husband but Gideon.

She forced away the useless thoughts and retrieved her cloak from the chair where she had laid it earlier. He had asked that she wait, but he knew where she was bound and she was anxious to question Jack. Gideon would catch up with her.

Walking briskly through the moonlit night, Naomi soon reached Monthamn Major. Why had the orphans left the cloister? If Father John was attempting to find them homes, why had they abandoned his care for the uncertainty of the forest? Something was not right and she intended to find out what it was.

She paused before the huge stone church in the center of the village, tempted to pound on the door and demand answers from the priest. Gideon would have approved of the plan, but the time was not yet right. She moved on along the rutted lane.

Swirling mist curled around her ankles as she moved deeper into the trees. Naomi shivered. Moonlight silvered the area, creating eerie silhouettes and pockets of darkness. A leafy branch brushed against her arm, a twig snagged her cloak. She walked faster, suddenly wishing she had waited for Gideon.

Something rustled in the bushes to her right. She veered sharply to the left and collided with a tree.

"This is ridiculous," she muttered, rubbing her bruised shoulder. "You are frightening yourself."

She stood there for a moment, dragging the crisp night air into her lungs. The fresh scent of damp earth soothed her and the evening breeze cooled her skin. Lifting her face to the moonlight, Naomi released the tension in her body with a long exhale.

"You should not be wandering in the forest alone."

Naomi spun to face the speaker. She didn't recognize his voice. A tall figure lurked in the shadows, the details of his appearance concealed by the night.

"Who are you?"

"Who I am is not important. I have come to help you."

"Help me with what?" Naomi asked casually, but her eyes searched the ground for a weapon. If she ran toward the ruins, she would lead this person to the children. He blocked her way back to the village and the underbrush on either side of the trail was dense.

So, if he tried to harm her, she must fight!

"You cannot fight me, Naomi. You would be foolish to try."

The faintest taint of sulfur colored the air, as if she could smell his breath. "Who are you?" she asked again, fear tightening her stomach. He knew her name; this was no random act. "What do you want with me?"

"I want only to warn you." He took a step forward and moonlight touched his face.

Naomi recoiled from the creature, ready to scream. In an instant he stood in front of her, his hand clasped around her throat. The scream became a strangled sob and waves of revulsion washed over her. His flesh was icy and his nails bit into her skin. She grabbed his wrist with both hands, but his hold remained steady.

His features were ordinary, his hair light and long, falling to his shoulders in lank strands. But his blank, soulless eyes radiated evil.

A demon held her—a demon that knew her by name.

Trembling within his hold, Naomi could do nothing but await his next move. She was helpless and they both knew it.

His fingers loosened but didn't leave her throat.

"Warn me about what?" she whispered.

"Gideon belongs to us. He always has. He always will! The longer you continue to confuse him, the harder it will be for him to accept the inevitable end."

She tensed, repelled by his touch, yet more appalled by his words. "I do not accept that his end is inevitable, and neither does Gideon."

"I know. That is why I have sought you out. Gideon will Fall. The only real question is, will he drag you down with him?"

Feeling the pressure of his fingers relax, she shoved his hand away and took a quick step backward. "Gideon will not Fall. He has made great strides toward the light. You fear you are losing him; that is why you have sought me out."

He laughed, his putrid breath gagging her.

"The first thing he did when he saw you again was to take your virginity. Was that his stride toward the light or your descent into darkness?"

"You know nothing about it. He has shown kindness and selflessness in the past few days. He is trying to improve himself. He wants—"

"Not even Gideon knows what he wants." The demon sneered at her. "A few pots of ink and a kind word to orphans do not change the basic nature of a *predator*. That is what Gideon is, Naomi. He is a predator."

She stared at the creature and doubt flickered to life within her. What did he mean?

"He has not told you, has he?"

Laughter lightened his tone and Naomi stiffened. Anything that amused this creature could not bode well for her. "Told me what?"

"What Michael did to him."

"Michael?" Naomi relaxed just a bit. "Michael banished Gideon from the light. He already told me about his punishment."

"Did he now? And what did he tell you?"

Tension gripped her again. Why did he still sound smug? "Sunlight burns his skin and drains his strength."

"That is true, but it is incidental. Did he tell you what he must do to survive? Did he tell you how he *feeds?*"

"I will not listen to any more of your lies." She turned toward the ruins, but he was in front of her again.

"I do not lie. Ask your lover on what he feeds."

She watched in fascinated horror as the demon disintegrated into a cloud of foul- smelling vapor.

Ask your lover on what he feeds.

Fear and dread held her motionless on the moonlit trail as the words echoed over and over through her mind.

Chapter Twenty-Four

"Why did you not wait for me?" Gideon asked, carefully restraining his anger.

After confirming that a cart had been readied with food, clothing and blankets, Gideon returned to the great hall and discovered that Naomi had left without him. She sat now against a section of the ruined wall, little Midge curled on her lap.

"You knew where I was going," she said. "I was too anxious to just sit still."

Gideon searched her steady gaze, not understanding the quiver in her tone or the tightness in her expression. She raised her hand to stroke the child's hair. Her hand trembled. If Gideon didn't know better, he would think she was afraid—of him.

She averted her gaze and continued to cuddle the child. Gideon braced his feet apart and inhaled deeply. The scent was subtle, but he could definitely smell fear.

"What is amiss?" he asked gently.

Her throat worked nervously and Gideon shifted his gaze to her mouth. She had been angry when he left her, but not afraid. He had overcome her fear long ago. What had rekindled it now? Clasping his hands behind his back, he fought down his own anxiety.

"Where is Jack?" he asked, when she didn't respond to his first question.

"No one has seen him since he rushed into the forest earlier."

His heart leapt within his chest. Was her fear for the boy? Had he misunderstood her expression? Energized by hope, Gideon relaxed his stance. "I will find him. Wait here." He paused and smiled at her. "May I have your word that you will?"

She only nodded.

If her mood didn't lighten once he had found the boy, Gideon would question her more closely. Much had happened this day. Perhaps she was just overwrought.

Transforming into a falcon, Gideon circled the area and spotted Jack on a fallen log near a narrow creek. Diving back into the trees, Gideon regained his human shape and waited a moment before he walked out of the woods.

"Lady Naomi is worried about you."

In one hand Jack held a fistful of pebbles, with the other he threw them into the sluggish creek. "Lady Naomi…weren't the other one named Lady Naomi, too?"

Gideon straddled the log, facing the boy. "Aye. Roderick's wife was Lady Naomi as well."

"She means to save us, but she will only make it worse." Jack threw a rock hard enough to span the creek and bounce off a tree trunk.

"How can it be worse?" Gideon asked, his tone just a bit challenging. "You are living like animals in the forest. You are strong, Jack, but what about Midge and Tot? Do they not deserve something better?"

The boy's defiant gaze slashed through the darkness. "They deserve many things I cannot give them."

"You cannot, but Lady Naomi can. Do you realize who she is, Jack? She is Lord Roderick's granddaughter and Lady of Monthamn Castle."

Jack jumped up from the log and dumped the rocks back into the dirt. Planting his fists on his hips, he faced Gideon. "The Lady of Monthamn Castle wants to save us?"

The question snapped with sarcasm, but he chose not to reprimand the boy. "Speak with her. Tell her all that has happened. We already know that Father John is at the heart of this, but we need to understand what transpired."

"Why should I trust you? Father John seemed to be kind and understanding in the beginning. I still think it's best if I just care for the little ones here."

"I'm not asking you to trust blindly. I ask only for the opportunity to understand."

Jack didn't argue, so Gideon led him back to the ruins. Naomi sat just where he'd left her, but Midge had moved off to play with several of the other girls. Naomi'd drawn her knees up, tenting her skirts and was poking at the tiny fire with a long stick.

Firelight accented the beauty of her features and reflected in her wide blue eyes. But her expression was so forlorn Gideon wanted to shake her and demand an explanation. Or take her back to the castle and kiss away her pain.

"You were looking for me," Jack said, drawing her attention from the fire.

She raised her troubled gaze to the boy and motioned to the large rock across the fire pit. "Please, sit. I have some questions for you."

Gideon stayed back a pace, leaning his shoulder against the wall. She hadn't so much as glanced his way.

The boy sat, silently waiting for her to speak.

She curled her legs to one side. "Jack, I need you to tell me everything that has happened since you were taken from the castle five years past."

"Now, that would take five years, would it not?" He offered her a cheeky grin.

She smiled and Gideon's heart pulsed out of time. She was so beautiful. His senses smoldered just looking at her.

"Lord Roderick explained that Father John took all the orphans to the abandoned cloister, where the nuns used to live. But he is under the impression that Father John found homes for all of you."

Jack pulled a piece of leaf off his filthy ankle and tossed it into the fire. "Oh, he found homes for us all right. He started with the older boys and worked his way down through the ranks. Two men came and carted off the strong ones all at once."

"Do you know who the men were or where the boys were taken?" Her brows crinkled slightly above her expressive eyes.

"Father John refused to say, but no family wants five sons, unless they have lots of work for them to do."

Naomi shifted restlessly. "They may not have been taken to one place, Jack. They may—"

"Same men came back twice more. I thought for sure I'd be taken the third time, but I've always been scrawny."

"They took only the older, bigger boys?" she asked.

"Until there weren't none left."

Crossing her arms over her chest, Naomi finally glanced at Gideon. He sucked in a startled breath. Her gaze churned with a potent mixture of pity and desolation. This was a tragic tale, but why was she reacting so strongly to events she could not change?

Gideon sat down beside her and tried to put his arm around her shoulders. She rose abruptly, pacing beside the fire. Why wouldn't she let him comfort her?

"What became of the girls?" she asked.

Jack looked around before he began his tale, and Gideon seethed. The lad didn't want to share the story if the other orphans could hear.

"A fancy man took Esther and Mary. They were sisters and I don't think it was a bad thing. But that red-haired devil kept coming back."

"Red-haired devil?" she asked. "Did Father John ever call him by name?"

"Not that I heard."

"What did he look like?"

Jack shrugged. "Like a man. Had hair sort of like yours only brighter."

She touched the end of her braid where it extended beyond her wimple. "Why did he keep coming back?"

He looked around again and then lowered his voice. Gideon had to strain to hear, while Naomi sat down next to the boy and rested her hand lightly on his shoulder. "I found Megan crying after he left one time. She wouldn't tell me what was wrong, but I knew. He came back twice and then Megan disappeared."

"It was the same man each time?" Naomi asked. "A man with red hair?"

Jack was responding well to Naomi, so Gideon held his tongue.

"Aye. There were three more after Megan. I know he…hurt them and then Father John sent them away. That's when I took the little ones and left. Father John tried dragging us back, but the last time, I broke his nose before he knocked me on the head. I guess he figured I was more trouble than I was worth. Besides, none of the girls are…they have not…the red-haired man said they need to ripen."

Naomi gave Jack a quick hug. "You have been very brave, Master Jack. I appreciate your honesty."

"The red-haired man said no one could touch him, 'cause it would always be my word against his," Jack said.

"We shall see about that," she insisted stubbornly.

Gideon was relieved by the determination in her words. "I brought provisions for you, Master Jack."

"Provisions?"

"Aye. Blankets and tunics and…" he paused for effect, "food. And a very good friend of mine will be patrolling the perimeter. His name is Daniel and you can trust him."

Naomi stood and grabbed the sleeve of Jack's ragged tunic before he could dash toward the cart. "Everyone must bathe in the creek before they don new tunics."

"But we will freeze to death," he objected.

"It can wait till morning," she said. "Then the sun will warm your hides."

"Oh, aye."

Gideon led Naomi to the cart and motioned toward his lifelong comrade. "Lady Naomi, this is Daniel."

Naomi looked at the tall, somber man standing beside the cart. Dressed all in black, his features were nearly as arresting as Gideon's. Pitch-black eyes watched her closely, and he made no attempt to smile.

"He is a friend of yours, as Gabriel is a friend of yours?" she asked, dragging her gaze back to Gideon.

"More so," he said meaningfully.

Daniel was one of the rebels. Naomi crossed her arms in front of her, shivering. These creatures surrounded her.

The orphans. She must focus on the orphans. Daniel handed her a bundle of blankets with a mocking smirk. Her anxiety obviously amused him.

"If you harm one hair—"

"I have sworn to protect them. I may be many things, Lady Naomi, but an abuser of children is not one of them."

Naomi tossed the bundle to Jack.

"If Sir Gideon trusts him..." Jack's words trailed off uncertainly.

"All is well...?" she assured him, but her gaze moved to Gideon, making the words a question.

"All is well." His firm words reinforced Naomi's promise.

Jack handed the blankets to another child and reached around her to grab the bag of food. With one last uncertain glance at Daniel, he headed back to the fire.

Naomi arranged the children in three neat rows. She passed out the food and stood back to watch them wolf it down.

"How do creatures so tiny consume so much food?" Gideon asked, awe obvious in his glistening eyes.

Naomi studied his chiseled profile and felt her heart lodge in her throat. *What do you consume? On what do you feed?* The questions rang through her brain like the sharp toll of an iron bell.

She had a bag ready to collect the scraps, but nothing was left after the children had finished eating. Jack ate his portion, while keeping careful watch over the "little ones." How had his narrow shoulders borne such a burden for so long?

Jack promised to see each child scrubbed clean in the morning, but Naomi intended to return and supervise the task. They distributed the blankets and Naomi received countless hugs before she was ready to depart.

Daniel remained in the shadows, an unobtrusive sentinel. She offered him a silent nod as she left the encampment, comforted to know the children would be watched.

Gideon fell into step beside her, leading his horse.

"Are you going to tell me what's wrong?" he asked, after a long period of strained silence.

The need to understand overrode her fear. "I spoke with a friend of yours on my way to the ruins."

"Male or female?"

"Male."

"Daniel is my only male friend in England."

"This friend came from much farther away."

He dropped the horse's lead and grasped her shoulders. "Domieno appeared to you? Did he touch you? Where you harmed?"

She swallowed past the lump in her throat, refusing to be moved by his concern. "He failed to introduce himself, but I assure you he was not human and he was far more menacing than Daniel. This was a demon, Gideon. From the pit of hell."

He attempted to pull her into his arms, but Naomi twisted away.

"What did he tell you?"

"That you are going to Fall and I will be dragged down with you unless I stop confusing you with my...love."

Time stood still. Naomi could hear her blood rushing in her ears. They had never spoken of love. But surely he knew that she loved him. Tears blurred her eyes. He was not human and yet she loved him.

"I will not Fall, Naomi. I *want* to—"

"How do you feed?" she cried, before she lost her nerve. "What did he mean? He told me to ask you on what you *feed.*"

He staggered back a step, his expression a contortion of self-loathing. "I will change. I am working to change."

"You...must...tell me." She felt as broken as her words.

He reached for her again, but Naomi couldn't let him touch her. The world fell away whenever he touched her and this could not go on. Once and for all, she must understand who and what he was.

Shaking, his eyes filled with pain, Gideon responded to her demand. "After Lucifer Fell, I was filled with useless rage. I longed for violence and hungered for bloodshed. We told Michael he was a slave to God's will, that we were all slaves. So,

Michael set us free. He loosed the boundaries within our beings, allowing our spirits to corrupt themselves according to our individual contentions."

"And what was your contention? What did your spirit choose?"

He glanced away and took a long, shuddering breath. "My thirst for blood became literal."

Her hand flew to cover her mouth and Naomi tasted bile in the back of her throat. "You feed on human blood?" she whispered behind her hand.

"Aye. I feed on human blood."

He sounded almost relieved, but Naomi's head went reeling. "Have you ever…how is it done?"

Slowly moving toward her, Gideon opened his mouth and showed her his fangs. Naomi gasped, her knees gave out beneath her, and she found herself in Gideon's arms.

"Please do not hurt me," she whimpered.

Tension rippled through his entire body. She felt his arms tighten and then relax. "I will never hurt you, Naomi."

She clutched his tunic, but arched away, needing his comfort, but terrified of him at the same time. "I cannot do this. I cannot love you. I cannot…"

She squirmed and twisted until he let her go. Gideon watched her run into the night. Desperation crept over him with insidious intensity. He couldn't do this alone.

If she turned from him—he would Fall.

Emotion choked him. Tears blurred his vision.

He could feel the darkness closing in.

Chapter Twenty-Five

Naomi threw herself onto the bed and buried her face against the mattress. Hard, wracking sobs shook her entire body, but nothing eased the oppressive emptiness within her chest. She rolled to her side, covering her face with her hands.

Gideon was a demon, a monster, a beast who fed on the blood of humans. She shuddered and sobbed. How could she love such a creature? How could she long to be with him, to share her life and her future with him?

Even as the questions tore her world apart, images filled her mind. She saw his gentle smile. She remembered the pleasure he found in arranging her tower room. The orphans revealed glimpses of his nature that she had never imagined. He could be kind. He could be caring. He could be tender.

"He can be vicious. He can be deadly. He can rip out your throat and gorge on your blood."

Naomi scrambled off the bed and tossed her hair over her shoulders, facing the demon. "Get out! Get out of my house. Get out of my life."

Domieno laughed and putrid currents stirred the air. "But then who would amuse me? Nay, you and I must come to an understanding. Gideon is clinging to hope and I am running out of patience."

His demonic nature surged and rolled beneath his skin. Naomi fell back against the bedpost, clutching it for support. "He told me everything. You cannot frighten me."

Domieno stalked toward her, but she had nowhere to retreat. "You are frightened, Naomi. You reek of it. Yet, I am not certain I inspire the fear." He leaned in. She shrank back, turning her face away. "Gideon confessed the depravity of his nature and you love him still. What sort of creature does that make you?"

Naomi ducked and turned, quickly putting the bed between them. Her heart hammered and the world tipped out of balance. Why was he here? What did he hope to—

"Just as Jack is the key to the orphans, you are the key to Gideon." Domieno answered her silent question. "I hoped you would reject him utterly and he would come running to me. But he senses your indecision. He is as much of a monster as I. How can you still care for him?"

"There is good in Gideon. There is *nothing* but evil in you." She glanced around for something to hurtle at him, but she had witnessed the speed with which he could move.

His empty eyes narrowed and he stroked his chin with skeletal fingers. "There is another way. Less pleasant, I admit, but we are determined to add Gideon to our ranks. If your nature were evil, he would follow you into darkness."

Dragging air into her lungs, Naomi intended to scream the house down.

Domieno closed her throat with a look. "We have been through this before. I know your thoughts before you think them. Stop provoking me!"

Naomi gasped and rubbed her neck as her airway opened. She must do something. The demon's influence enveloped her like a cloud, dampening her senses and muddling her mind. She sank to her knees, folded her hands and desperately prayed for help.

The demon went wild. He grabbed her by the hair and dragged her to her feet. Naomi cried out. Pain stretched across her scalp, but she continued to pray. She steadied herself and covered his hand with hers.

"Stop it!" He sneered into her face.

He drew back his hand, but someone caught his wrist, preventing the blow.

"Release her," Gideon said, his tone calm and deadly.

Domieno obeyed so suddenly, that Naomi stumbled backward and fell. Pain ricocheted up her spine as she slammed against the wooden floor.

"It is me you want," Gideon snarled. "Leave Naomi out of this!"

"I am not the one who dragged her into this. You should have stayed away. You should have accepted what you are before others became involved."

"I will not Fall!" Heaven's light ignited within Gideon. He felt his eyes dilate and knew they glowed. "Leave this place!"

The demon glowered at Naomi, his lips curled back from his yellow teeth. "We will meet again." Then, with a threatening hiss, he disappeared.

Gideon turned to Naomi. She huddled against the wall, eyes huge, face devoid of color, lips ashen and trembling. His breath lodged in his throat as the impact of her terror kicked him in the chest. Protective fury screamed through his being.

Slowly, he took a step toward her. "Naomi."

Her eyes shifted to his face, but her gaze seemed unfocused. Gideon knelt before her and reached for her hand. She snatched it away and pressed herself against the wall.

"This cannot be real," she whispered. "How can this be real?"

Tracing the contour of her face with his fingertip, Gideon tucked her hair beneath her wimple. He didn't know what to say. He didn't know how to ease her fear.

"I love you, Naomi." The words escaped in a sudden rush. "I will do anything you want. Tell me what you need."

Tears rolled down her cheeks, launched by the sweep of her long lashes. "I need...I want..."

She wrapped her arms around her legs and hid her face against her knees.

"I'm sorry," he whispered. "I'm so sorry."

Naomi heard him leave the room. Part of her desperately wanted to call him back, but—he drank human blood. She trembled, waiting for her emotions to run their course.

He loved her.

He drank human blood.

He had protected her.

He drank human blood.

He could be so wonderful.

He drank human blood!

"He *survives* on human blood," a female voice interrupted her thoughts. "You make it sound like he hunts for pleasure."

Naomi raised her head, no longer surprised that someone had responded to her thoughts. Elspeth stood before her—yet, it was not Elspeth. This woman's hair was a vivid shade of red, her eyes a brighter blue.

Tugging off her wimple, Naomi dried her face with the soft linen. "You are a *friend* of Gideon's, as well?"

"As well as Daniel, aye. But do not dare to connect me in any way with Domieno."

"Do all of you...?"

"Survive on human blood?" she finished.

"Aye? Do all of Gideon's friends survive on human blood?"

"Nay. Gideon is the only one. Our abilities and our torments are uniquely our own."

Naomi struggled to her feet. "What do you want? Is Elspeth your name?"

"I'm known by many names, but most often I'm called Alyssa."

"Why pretend to be a servant?" Her breath shuddered, but gradually Naomi regained her composure. "What do you want from me?"

Alyssa moved about the room, lightly running her fingertips along the tabletop, the back of a chair, until she stood next to Naomi. "Why must I want something? Why can I not have something *for* you? Or for Gideon?"

Naomi said nothing. She recognized the mischievous gleam in Alyssa's eyes. These rebel angels loved to twist words and manipulate meanings.

"Gideon loves you."

"He told me," Naomi said stiffly.

"I don't think you understand what that means. Gideon has set aside his bitterness, he has subdued the darkness within him and allowed himself to feel—love."

"What would you have me do?" Naomi flared.

"Accept it. Embrace it." She paused. "Return it. He needs you, Naomi. More than you can possibly understand, Gideon needs your love."

"Or he will Fall."

Alyssa didn't respond.

"Will Domieno return?" Naomi asked, unable to contain a shudder.

"Gideon will do his best to keep him away, but it is a possibility. Domieno is desperate, and that alone should tell you how far Gideon has come. He has sacrificed so much for you. It's time to prove yourself worthy."

Chapter Twenty-Six

Accompanied by Karl and Will, the day's rotation of her personal guard, Naomi strolled toward Monthamn Major. She'd not seen Gideon since her disconcerting conversation with Alyssa three days past.

Was he avoiding her? Giving her time to sort out her feelings or...

I love you, Naomi.

The echo of his tormented words cut through her other thoughts, causing her steps to falter.

It's time to prove yourself worthy.

"Where are we bound, Lady Naomi?" one of her guards asked. He was a lanky lad, with shaggy brown hair and sharp gray eyes.

Thankful for the distraction, she said, "To the parish church." She silently struggled to remember if he were Karl or Will.

"Father John will come to the castle to hear your confession, my lady. You need not have troubled yourself," the other guard said. Older and more muscular than the lad, his dark hair was neatly trimmed. The shade of his eyes was more blue than gray, but Naomi wondered if they were kin.

"The sun is shining, the breeze is mild and I can smell baking bread. This is no trouble, I assure you." She averted her gaze and then asked, "So, Karl, are you two kinsmen?"

"Aye, my lady, Will is the youngest of my four brothers," the older man answered.

Naomi smiled; problem solved.

"Don't let my youthful face mislead you, Lady Naomi. I'm fast with a sword and can ride like the wind," Will said.

"Those with impressive abilities don't need to bring them to the attention of others." Karl glared at his brother.

Naomi chuckled softly, enjoying their banter.

The parish church sat in the center of the village, an ostentatious peacock surrounded by humble wrens. Heavy round arches, inset with zigzagging chevrons drew attention to the massive, iron-banded door. Why did this church look forbidding, as if it were built to hold the world at bay?

"Shall we?" She climbed the steep stone steps and Karl heaved the door open for her.

The faint spice of incense teased her nose. Naomi drew her cloak more tightly around her. Should a church feel this cold? Her eyes quickly adjusted to the dim interior and the chill seeped clear to the marrow of her bones. Everywhere she looked, her gaze met the unmistakable gleam of gold. Tall, branched candle stands, a jeweled challis, communion platter...while the orphans starved in the forest!

She must calm down. If she saw Father John, she would claw his eyes out. Dragging slow, deep breaths into her burning lungs, she moved toward the nearest wall.

A large scene depicting the Garden of Eden had been painted directly on the stones. Shrubbery concealed Adam and Eve from the waist down and Eve's long hair protected her modesty. She held an apple toward Adam and a serpent twined around the branch of a tree beside her. The figures were correctly proportioned and positioned realistically, but there was no life, no inspiration—no illumination.

Everything in this church was flat and lifeless.

Shaking her head sadly, she moved on to the next scene.

"May I help you?"

Crushing handfuls of her skirt beneath her cloak, Naomi turned to face Father John. "I was admiring *your* church."

Even in the dimness, his dark eyes gleamed. "The church belongs to God and I to the church."

"The church belongs to the people, as should you." Naomi heard the restless shuffle of Karl and Will behind her. If she attacked this pompous ass, would they restrain her or assist her? "Is it not a priest's sworn duty to meet the needs of the people in his parish?"

His hand closed around the golden cross suspended from his neck. He took a slow step toward her, making the difference in their height more apparent. "The people in my parish want for nothing. They are well fed and happy. If you have something to say to me, lady, then say it."

"Are the ruins of the old manor house in your parish?"

Father John buried his hands in the loose sleeves of his robe. Naomi watched his throat work as he swallowed and his nostrils twitched. She took a step closer and demanded an answer with her hostile gaze.

The orphans were well guarded, safe beyond this...person's reach. Would he betray his guilt by word or deed? If he thought to harm Jack—let him come. Daniel waited for just such a move.

"Do not believe everything that...creature tells you."

"Which creature might that be?" she asked. "The lad, not yet in whiskers, who has taken on *your* responsibilities?"

"Jack lies, my lady," he said calmly.

His nonchalance made her furious. She wanted to jump on him and tear his face to ribbons, but that would not help the orphans. "Fine. I will judge the situation by your information. Was the care of the orphans entrusted to you?"

"Aye, but I—"

"*Just* answer my questions," she cut in and he glared at her. "Are you aware that thirty of the orphans, under your care, are currently living in the forest with no adult supervision and only the—"

"That is not my doing!"

Karl and Will stepped forward, one on either side of Naomi, each with his hand on the hilt of his sword.

Father John cleared his throat and continued in a more respectful tone. "Jack convinced the orphans to flee into the forest with lies and half-truths. I dragged them back twice before I gave up and left them to their own devices."

"And why would Jack feel compelled to *flee* into the forest?"

The priest shrugged and spread his hands, but his dark gaze shifted away from her. "The child has a rich imagination. He concocted all manner of intrigues. According to Jack, I sold the children to the devil himself in exchange for riches and power."

"Odd, the stories he told me were not nearly so dramatic." She crossed her arms under her cloak and studied his ruddy face. "I will not waste my time listening to you refute each of Jack's tales. I need only know one thing."

"How refreshing."

Karl stepped forward threateningly, but Naomi laid her hand on his arm. "Is the Bishop of Chichester still compensating you for the care of the orphans?"

The twitching in his nostrils intensified and a vein in his neck began to pulse. "That is *Church* business. None of *your* affair."

Chapter Twenty-Seven

Gideon paced Naomi's chamber, feeling trapped and torn. Alyssa told him Naomi would return soon from her trip to the village, but he'd never excelled at patience.

He'd stayed away from her, hoping time would allow her to see beyond her fear. But he sensed no stirring, no softening in her attitude. He was open, utterly vulnerable to her rejection. If she turned from him now...

The door opened and he turned, his heart pounding in his throat. She moved into the room and closed the door. She stared at him with wide luminous eyes, but it was only when her chin began to tremble that he realized she was fighting back tears.

Rushing to her, Gideon wrapped his arms around her, holding his breath until she melted into his embrace.

"The world is so confusing," she whispered, her warm mouth moving against his throat. "I think evil is just as easy to find in humankind as it is in your rebel angels."

He eased her away from his chest, needing to see her face. "Of what do you speak?"

"Father John is supposed to be a man of God, but he has allowed horrible things. I want him punished. Can you make that happen, Gideon? Can you see that he pays dearly for the things that he has done?"

Before he could answer, she continued. "I think Frederick is Jack's red-haired man. Jack saw him the day I arrived at Monthamn Castle. He probably heard news of my coming and ventured to Monthamn to question the priest."

"That would make sense."

"I hate them," she said. "With every fiber of my being, I hate them. I know it is wrong, that we are called to forgive, that vengeance belongs to the Lord. But I hate them."

He wiped her tears with his fingertips and kissed her gently on the brow. "Daniel has a talent for extracting information from unusual places. I have asked him to investigate—"

"Then, who guards the children?"

Smiling at her vehemence, he assured her. "I altered the rotation of your personal guard. I didn't think you would mind."

Her gaze turned thoughtful, speculative. "There was a different guard there when I left. I just thought Daniel was sleeping."

"Daniel seldom sleeps," he said. "He is ruthless once he has committed himself to a cause."

"And has he committed himself to this cause?"

"Aye. As have I." He kissed her softly, slowly, pouring all of his newfound tenderness into the caress. Reluctantly, he pulled away. "I want this settled, Naomi. I need to know that I am welcomed here."

She smiled at him and traced his mouth her fingertips. "Welcomed? I welcome you, Gideon. I long for you. I want you, regardless of how irrational that desire may be."

Gideon framed her face with his hands, jealous of the thin material that separated his skin from hers. "Can you accept my love, knowing what I am?"

"I accept it, eagerly, and return it wholeheartedly. Gideon, I love you. Even knowing what you are, I love you."

Her mouth was parted and welcoming when he kissed her again. He traced her teeth and the velvety recesses with hungry abandon. She arched into him, stroking his tongue with hers.

All too soon passion burned through his gentleness, making him restless—making him wild. He drew back, closing his eyes and panting harshly.

"Please, Gideon. Don't hide yourself from me. For the first time there is nothing between us, no secrets, no shadows. I love your wild heart. Your passion thrills me. Love me."

Dark hunger raged in response to her words. He pressed his forehead against hers and drank in her scent. She touched his hair, brushing his temple with her thumb.

"I did not think it was possible to need someone so badly." He spoke quietly, keeping his eyes closed. "I didn't realize how black the darkness had become until I saw your face. I will never let you go, Naomi. I cannot live without you."

"Then, do not try." Raising his face until their eyes met, she said, "I love you, Gideon. Come what may, I love you."

Her arms circled his neck and he molded her body against him. They sank to their knees together, clinging to each other, desperate for each other. Keeping her anchored with one arm about her waist, he flipped the circlet from her head and unfastened her wimple.

"Take down your hair. I want to feel it all around me as I move inside you."

She reached for the end of her braid as he stood to quickly shuck his clothing. By the time he stood before her naked, her thick chestnut hair spread all around her in rippling waves.

Naomi sucked in a ragged breath. Every sculpted contour of his body beckoned her attention. The breadth of his shoulders demanded appreciation. His wide chest made her palms itch. Long and strongly muscled, his legs promised power and aggressiveness. Naomi felt her skin burn as if she had tarried too long in the sun.

"Let me touch you. I need to touch you."

He didn't reply, but moved closer, keeping his hands at his sides. Naomi still knelt, but it felt right. She wrapped her arms around his waist and kissed his abdomen. He shook, his hands raised, but then lowered again to his sides.

She understood the gesture. He offered her control and she didn't hesitate. Stroking his back and exploring the hard curves of his buttocks with her hands, she kissed her way across his abdomen. The heat of his flesh and the taste of his skin excited her as nothing had before. He had used his mouth to pleasure her, but this was just as thrilling. He gasped and groaned beneath her lips, her willing captive.

His shaft jerked between her breasts and Naomi eased away from him, her hands lingering on his hips.

"Do it," he murmured, his tone harsh and needful.

She looked up into his eyes; already they glowed. Curiosity won the battle with her hesitation. Dragging one hand across his hip, she curled her fingers around him and squeezed. His hand covered hers, but she frowned up at him. Immediately, his fingers fell away.

Testing the length and thickness of his shaft with a slow downward stroke, Naomi marveled at the potent power so obvious in his body. She stroked him again, passing her thumb over the plush head, smiling as he trembled.

Looking up at him again she leaned closer, blowing her heated breath across the very tip.

Gideon shifted his feet farther apart and curled his hands into fists. "Do it," he said again.

"Do what?" she taunted, heating his flesh with her breath.

"Kiss me."

Sparks of sensation darted through her body. She felt her nipples gather against the fabric of her chemise and the core of her sex began to throb.

She kissed the very tip then flicked him with her tongue.

"God's blood, woman, do it now!"

Pleased by the urgency she had created, she slowly slipped him into her mouth. His flesh was hot and incredibly hard. She tightened her lips around him and laved with her tongue. His hands moved to her head, steadying her, guiding her. Cupping his heavy sac with one hand, Naomi reveled in the silken friction, the slick movement and his raspy cries.

She slid her mouth forward and back, forward and back, swirling her tongue over the sensitive tip each time she reached the end. His thighs flexed and released as his hips rocked. Hot and hard, his shaft throbbed against her tongue. She tightened her lips and slowly pulled back, stopping when the swollen head still remained within her mouth. Circling the crest over and over with her tongue, she sucked deeply on the very tip, waiting for his strangled groan to start moving again.

"No more." The unsteadiness in his hoarse voice praised her efforts. He pulled her to her feet and attacked her garments.

Naomi laughed, exhilarated by his desperation. Her heart beat frantically and she raised her arms. He tugged each layer off until only her shoes and stockings remained. Kicking aside her shoes, Naomi dragged the stockings off, garters and all.

"Better. Much better."

She laughed again, but the smoldering heat in his golden gaze took her breath away. His desire for her shone brightly in his eyes. Humbled to be the cause of his blatant need, Naomi rose and kissed him deeply.

His hands swept up and down her back, cupping her bottom and pulling her higher, nearly off her feet. Insinuating one hand between their bodies, he covered her breast. He growled into her open mouth and turned her body away from him. Both hands cupped her breasts, dragging her back against him.

"Stand on my feet," he ordered in an urgent whisper.

Hesitating only a second, she did as he asked. His hands moved to her waist, lifting and angling her. She felt him slip into her swollen folds and shuddered. Slowly, inch by glorious inch, he filled her.

Naomi trembled, reaching forward to steady herself against the wall. She could feel her body stretching, adjusting to his penetration. "Oh, Gideon."

"Aye," he muttered.

When he could go no deeper, he nudged her feet to the floor. His entire body molded to her back, warming her skin, cradling her. Naomi shifted restlessly, desperately needing him to move. But he was in no hurry now. He stroked her breasts, working her nipples into aching peaks. He caressed her belly and her thighs, making her gasp and arch.

"Gideon." She tossed her head back, sending her hair spilling over him.

"Be still," he said. "Feel me. Feel me inside you."

His arm circled her waist, holding her still against him. He toyed with her nipples for a few minutes longer and then sank his fingers into the damp curls guarding her mound.

Naomi dug her fingers into his forearms as he petted and parted her most secret flesh. He touched her so gently, so carefully that she felt the shredded remains of her inhibitions disintegrate entirely. She was his. He would never hurt her. She could surrender herself entirely into his care.

Resting her head back against his shoulder, she closed her eyes and let the pleasure unfurl.

Gideon bit his bottom lip to keep from howling like a madman. Her sheath clasped him rhythmically as her pleasure built. The sweet honey of her uninhibited response drenched his fingers and released her scent into the air. Her fingernails bit into his forearms.

"Do it," he whispered into her ear. "Do it for me."

Her whole body shook and her core tightened around him to the point of pain. She moaned as the climax ebbed, leaving her panting and trembling.

Bending slightly, he swept her up into his arms and carried her to the bed. He needed to taste her before he took her; it would strengthen his control. He laid her carefully in the center of the bed and raised a knee to the mattress. She parted her thighs without hesitation and Gideon's heart slammed into his chest. It was the first time she'd offered herself so brazenly.

He slipped his hands beneath her bottom and started to lift her to his mouth, but she squirmed away. "No more teasing. I need you now."

"I need this more," he said gruffly.

She relaxed her legs, a subtle invitation. Lifting her hips upward, he covered her with his mouth. He sank his tongue into her, filling his mouth with her essence. A violent shudder wracked his body. He did it again and again.

She rocked her hips while he used his lips and his teeth and his tongue, always his tongue. He felt her tension, knew she was nearing another climax. His own need responded in time. He surged up along her body, entering her in one forceful thrust. She cried out and he captured the sound with his open mouth. She hesitated, then tentatively touched his tongue with hers.

Gideon was lost. He held tightly to her hips, moving on her with demanding depth. She arched and pulled her legs up high along his sides, offering him more, taking him deeper.

They climbed together, frantic for the culmination of their mutual need. She gasped. He groaned. She clutched his back. He devoured her mouth, matching the thrusts of his tongue to the steady penetration of his body.

Gideon felt the sensations build and gather, spiraling ever tighter. He wrapped his arms under her back and grabbed her shoulders, holding her in place for each forceful thrust. With a hoarse cry, he threw his head back, bared his fangs and spilled his seed deep inside her.

Long moments later, he felt a ticklish pressure against his upper lip. He opened his eyes. Naomi stared up at him, her eyes luminous and content. She carefully traced his fangs with her finger. A jolt of tenderness so powerful it knocked the breath from his lungs responded to her casual gesture.

"I love you, Gideon."

The tight burning in his throat was the only thing that kept him from repeating the endearment.

He kissed her fingertip and rolled until she straddled his hips. The silken swirl of her unbound hair dragged a groan from his throat. Grasping her hips, he rocked into her slowly.

Trepidation hurled him from passion's haze, forcing his instincts into perfect focus. Holding her tightly to him, he sat up and scanned the darkness. He searched the room with all of his senses.

"What is it?" Naomi whispered.

He didn't respond. Evil hovered over and around them, distant and yet distinct.

"Is it Domieno?"

Gideon shook his head, pulling her more firmly against him. "Nay. This is something—more."

He felt her tremble and wrap her arms securely around his back. "Will this never end?"

"It will end, my love," he promised her. "Once and for all, this will come to an end."

Chapter Twenty-Eight

Naomi spent the following day with the orphans. She encouraged them to "play" in the brook, and then scrubbed their matted hair before they realized it was not part of the game.

Jack helped her create a log of names and ages, but at times she still saw suspicion in his dark brown eyes. Midge, on the other hand, followed Naomi about like a talkative shadow. The little girl quizzed her incessantly, most of her questions about Gideon.

Late in the afternoon, Naomi returned to the castle. She wanted to bathe and change her clothing before Gideon awoke. But the moment she stepped into the great hall, she knew something was dreadfully wrong.

All conversation hushed and every eye turned her way. Stumbling to a stop, she searched the sea of faces, trying to understand their odd behavior.

Kruthers pushed his way through the throng. "We have been searching everywhere for you, my lady."

"Searching for me? Why?" Anxious flutters danced through her belly. She had never seen Kruthers so animated.

"It is Roderick."

Those three words filled her with dread. "Take me to him."

The crowd parted and let them pass. Naomi felt sorrow mount with each step she took. She didn't want to lose her grandfather so soon.

Countless candles burned and a massive fire roared, making the room stiflingly hot. Naomi paused in the doorway, shocked and horrified. Roderick rested in the center of the bed, a mountain of pillows stacked behind his back. Fear and grief held her motionless. Was she too late already?

"My lord," Kruthers said loudly, easing past her, "Naomi is here."

She didn't notice Father John until she stepped into the room. He stood silently in one corner of the room, carefully distanced from the sick bed. Their eyes met and clashed, but neither spoke.

Roderick stirred slowly. His breath rattled and wheezed and then his eyes opened. "Naomi, my love."

She stepped up to the bed and took his frail hand. His fingers were icy.

"I am so cold, Naomi," he whispered. "Cannot a fire be lit?"

"I will see to it, my love," she responded automatically. It didn't matter that he thought she was his wife. She would do anything to make him more comfortable.

He blinked so slowly that she feared his eyes would not open again, but when they did his gaze was more focused, clearer.

"Has he returned, yet?" Roderick asked.

"Has who returned?"

"Gideon," he said. "He went to fetch a special license. I want to see you wed before I leave this earth."

Naomi smiled and gently squeezed his hand. "Stubborn to the bitter end. I wondered where that trait came from."

"There is much of me in you. I only wish we'd had more time."

His gaze clouded and his eyes drifted shut. Naomi held her breath. She had never witnessed death, but she could sense it heavy in the room. His spirit was restless and ready.

"Come, my lady." Kruthers cupped her elbow and guided her away from the bed. "If he stirs again, I will fetch you."

"She would be more easily fetched if she would remain where she belongs."

Father John muttered the words under his breath, but Naomi heard him. She started toward him, but Kruthers held her back.

"Not here," he said firmly.

She stepped into the corridor, her legs wobbly. "Is there no other priest to attend him? I despise that man."

"We have sent for another, but time is short. I am not sure Roderick will survive." Kruthers sounded impatient and annoyed.

"I apologize. I'm sure you know what's best for Roderick."

"The time for changes will come, my lady, but Roderick deserves to pass peacefully."

"Of course. I will be in the hall or in my chamber."

He nodded and returned to Roderick's side.

Naomi started down the corridor, her steps lethargic. She needed to stay busy or this sadness would overwhelm her. She must arrange food for the orphans, but she would send word explaining why she didn't return herself.

She rounded a corner and fell back against the wall. The putrid stench of demons hung like fog in the air. Clasping her hand over her mouth, she forced down her nausea and pushed away from the wall. The corridor was empty, but something was there.

"Leave me alone," she whispered.

The icy brush of unseen fingers passed along her arms. She shrieked, jerking sharply to one side. "Stop it!"

She took several quick steps and the cold sensation brushed against her legs. Choking back a second scream, she ran. The tormenting sensations continued until she reached the staircase leading to the great hall. Then suddenly, the air around her cleared, lightened, until Naomi knew that the entity had vanished.

Pressing her hand against her chest, Naomi felt the wild gallop of her heart. "You better be right, Gideon. I cannot take much more of this," she whispered to the empty corridor.

Karl rushed to meet her as she reached the great hall. "Is Lord Roderick…"

"Not yet. But I fear he'll not last the night." Her voice sounded as raw as she felt.

"Come, sit by Will. Let me fetch you some wine."

She didn't argue. Everyone here was waiting for Roderick to die. The realization felt awful. She wanted to weep and wail, but her people expected her to be strong.

"Here, this will soothe you."

Naomi accepted the cup from Karl, but set it aside without taking a sip. She had caught a glimpse of dark red hair out of the corner of her eye. Searching the crowd with a careful gaze, she tried in vain to locate the person again.

"What is it, my lady?" Karl asked.

"I'm not sure. Do you know Frederick of Westerville?"

"I know the knave," Will volunteered, even though she had posed the question to Karl. "He is a regular bas—"

"Will!" Karl cut him off. "Why do you ask, my lady?"

"Is he here in the hall?" Naomi asked.

"I've not seen him," Karl said. "Shall I search the crowd?"

"Nay. It was probably my imagination." She picked up the cup and raised it to her lips. The wine was cool and light. She drank deeply.

"You believe he is Jack's red-haired man."

Karl had not posed it as a question, but Naomi responded, "Aye, I do." She took another drink before she said, "I promised Jack a meal for the little ones. I must go arrange it."

"Please, my lady," Karl said. "Relax. Allow me to see to the arrangements."

"I'll come with you." Will offered, obviously impressed by his brother's gallantry.

"Then, who will protect Lady Naomi?"

Will laughed, realizing his folly. "Carry on. I will not leave her side."

Naomi had just finished her wine when Karl returned.

"Two reluctant knights and a scullery maid are on their way to the ruins with a meal for the orphans," Karl told her.

"You have my thanks." Naomi pushed back the bench. "Let us away to the tower room."

"Will you be able to see well enough to draw?" Will asked as they fell in behind her. "Shall we fetch more candles?"

He was attempting to anticipate her needs as his brother had. But Naomi thought of Roderick's suffocating bedchamber and shook her head. "Nay. I will be fine."

Karl preceded her into the room. He moved to the shelves and quickly lit several candles with the flame from the one he had carried from the hall.

Naomi's gaze touched the back corner of the room and she gasped. Will was beside her in an instant, his sword pointed directly at the intruder.

Frederick of Westerville stood there calmly, his sword still in its scabbard. He slowly raised his hands and smiled. "I mean you no harm. I want only a word with you, away from the chaos in the hall."

"Nothing you have to say interests me."

"You have a rather pronounced opinion of me. Why is that, when we have never really spoken to one another?"

She motioned for Will to sheath his sword, but he ignored her. He moved back a step, but his weapon remained at ready.

"In our one and only conversation you called me a whore." Naomi glared. "Grandfather has made it clear—"

"Roderick is a stubborn old man. He believed lies and half-truths—"

"That is the exact phrase Father John used to defend himself." Naomi responded without pause. "I didn't believe him then and I don't believe you now. I trust Grandfather's judgment."

He stepped away from the wall. Candlelight caught in his hair, accenting the red tones. Naomi's gut twisted. She had no patience for this, no tolerance left for anyone today.

"I don't see why you and I can't determine our own course." He approached her cautiously, his gaze watchful. "We need not base our relationship on the opinion of others."

"We have no relationship, *Frederick.* Let me be perfectly clear. You are not welcome here."

"We are blood kin, *Naomi.*" He took the same liberty. "That has to mean something to an orphan."

Naomi shoved him hard with both hands. He stumbled back and collided with the wall. "You want to talk about orphans, you vile bastard? I know how you choose to use orphans."

Momentarily stunned by her unexpected aggression, Frederick quickly recovered. "Do not lay hands on me again or I will take it as an invitation to do likewise."

"Get out! Get off my land before I have you hanged."

"Father John told me this would be futile. He assured me you are no more rational than your grandfather. Just remember, I tried to settle this peacefully. I tried!"

Naomi stepped aside and let Will have his way. The younger man escorted Frederick from the room at sword point.

Shaking, unable to name the swarm of emotions seething within her, Naomi tore off her wimple and tossed it into the corner Frederick had just vacated. The golden circlet pinged against the stone and rolled across the room.

"My lady."

She didn't turn around. She was too close to tears. Raising her hand to ward Karl off she said, "I am fine."

"My lady."

When he spoke the second time, Naomi realized it wasn't Karl. She turned. Kruthers stood in the doorway, his devastated expression foretelling his announcement.

"Roderick has passed."

*   *   *

Gideon felt her sorrow as he entered the upper bailey. With a whispered explanation to his companions, he melted into the shadows and rapidly turned to mist. She needed him. Her heart cried out for comfort, even as her spirit grieved.

Focusing on her pain, he easily found her. She sat on the floor in the wardrobe, her legs drawn up, her face buried against her knees. Her quiet sobs tore at Gideon's heart. He knew in an instant Roderick was dead, but why was she alone?

"Naomi," he said softly, kneeling beside her.

She raised her head and blinked the tears from her eyes. "Gideon. You've returned."

He pulled her onto his lap and cradled her against his chest. "Aye. Why is no one with you? No one should feel such sorrow alone."

"I asked them to leave. I must be strong for them, but I could be strong no longer."

He kissed the top of her head and arranged her more comfortably against his chest. Rubbing his cheek against the softness of her hair, he just held her.

"Were you able to see him before he gave up the ghost?" he asked quietly.

"Aye. But Frederick was here and—"

"Frederick?" Protective anger made his arms tighten around her. "Frederick of Westerville came to the castle?"

Naomi turned to face him. Kneeling between his legs, she rested her hands on his shoulders. His heart leaped toward her.

"He attempted to convince me that Roderick was wrong about him, that he had been maligned."

"What a fool," he muttered. "Where were Karl and Will? How did this man get near you?"

"I was never in any danger." Her beautiful eyes darted away. "At least not from Frederick."

He turned her face back toward his. "Then from whom?"

She licked her lips, her eyes wide and frightened. "I sensed a presence in the corridor. I don't think it was Domieno. This felt different, as if it were everywhere at once."

"Or there were many, all in the same place."

She nodded. "Do you know who—or what this was?"

"Aye. It is called Legion. It is many and yet it is one."

"Why is it here?"

Gideon hesitated to tell her too much. Understanding demons could make them less frightening, but only to a point. "Domieno is desperate. He is under tremendous pressure to deliver me to Lucifer, and Domieno knows he's failing."

She smiled and kissed his mouth.

"You have a visitor," Gideon whispered against her willing lips. "Dry your tears. He's waiting in the great hall."

Chapter Twenty-Nine

"Brother Gabriel!"

Naomi flew across the hall and into his waiting arms. She clung to him, absorbing the familiar rasp of his coarse robes and the way his hand gently stroked her hair. Her heart flipped and tumbled, and brilliant beams of light penetrated the darkness that had gathered all day.

Easing back far enough to see his face, she smiled into his warm brown eyes. "How? Where did you come from? Why are you here?"

"Do I need a reason?" he teased her, touching the tip of her nose with his fingertip. "Are you not pleased to see me?"

"I'm thrilled. I'm ecstatic." She took a step back, her gaze locked on his beautiful face. She was afraid if she blinked he would disappear. "I'm also confused. This can't be coincidence. How did you know what was going on here?"

Gabriel glanced around the crowded hall. "Is there somewhere we can speak more privately?"

"Of course." She reached for Gideon's hand, but he shook his head.

"I'll join you shortly," Gideon said.

Gabriel took her hand instead and tucked it into the bend of his elbow. They crossed to the counting room in the back corner of the hall. The room was cold and gloomy, but at least they could speak freely.

Gabriel sat, while Naomi faced him, leaning her hips against the counting table.

"Does Michael know you're here?" she asked tentatively. "Can he hear me when I speak? Is he aware of everything that transpires on the earth?"

Gabriel laughed and reached over to squeeze her hand. "That ability is reserved for God alone. Michael can easily find out anything he wants to know, but he is not omniscient."

"Does he know you're here?" she asked again.

"Aye. In fact, he suggested I come."

"Really? Michael has been suspiciously cooperative of late. First the tower room, and now he allows you to visit. What inspired his good humor?"

Gabriel smiled, his eyes sparkling with golden light. "What did Gideon tell you about the tower room?"

Naomi picked up the end of her braid and toyed with the cord tied there. "Only that he had negotiated with Michael so you'd be allowed to assist him."

"Did he explain the conditions to which he agreed?"

"Not in detail." She had sensed Gideon's reluctance to talk about it and let the issue lie.

"My prideful, often irrational brother agreed to strict limitations on the use of his power. He agreed to actively pursue the light and he agreed to make his final decision before the new moon rises."

Naomi gasped. Only four days remained before the new moon rose. "What does this mean? What happens to Gideon once he makes his final decision?"

"The outcome will depend on what he decides."

She fidgeted, shifting her weight against the table. If Gideon resolved his conflict with God, would he return to Heaven? He'd never answered the question, didn't seem to know the answer. She wouldn't even consider the possibility that he would Fall. They'd come too far. Gideon had accomplished too much. But a future together seemed uncertain regardless of his decision.

"His agreement with Michael isn't the only evidence of Gideon's progress. His attachment to the orphans is encouraging. Michael is pleased." Gabriel paused. "I know it upsets you to discuss it, but Gideon is also losing his taste for blood. He feeds only when he must now, and he no longer enjoys it."

She shuddered. Her love for Gideon allowed her to accept the darkest element of his nature, but part of her still recoiled from the thought. "Are you here to influence his decision?" she asked softly.

"Nay. My reason for being here is even more surprising than all the rest." Gabriel punctuated the statement with a grin. "Gideon asked for help."

"Domieno has enlisted others," Gideon said from the doorway. "Why is it surprising that I would do the same?"

"It's a wise and necessary precaution," Gabriel said. "It's just refreshing that you're being so reasonable."

Gideon waved away the issue with one long-fingered hand.

"So, who shall we vanquish first?" Gabriel asked.

"Father John," Gideon immediately suggested.

He came to stand beside Naomi and she slipped her hand into his. "He is here, in the castle. I think he is still receiving compensation from the Bishop of Chichester."

"Aye, he is," Gabriel said. "I spoke with the bishop this morning. Father John can only be tried by the Church, so I asked that he be called up to answer for his crimes. The bishop is a good man. He was enraged to learn of Father John's misdeeds and I am confident that he will see the priest punished."

"We arrived with his replacement and the bishop's own guards to escort Father John." Gideon smiled in satisfaction.

"Does he know any of this?" she asked.

Gabriel shook his head. "Nay. We wanted you to tell him."

Naomi hugged them both. "It would be my pleasure."

* * *

Naomi sat in Roderick's high-backed chair. It had been draped in black, but Leon assured her that no one would find it disrespectful for her to take her rightful place. The trestle tables had been taken down and many of the villagers had returned to their cottages for the night. There was much to be done over the next few days, but one task would wait no longer.

Gideon stood on her right and Gabriel on her left, a united front against injustice.

Father John walked across the great hall, his stride quick, his expression impatient. "What do you want? I have duties awaiting me."

"Actually, you do not," she responded casually. "What you did to the orphans was reprehensible and you—"

"I am only accountable to Canon Law. You have no authority over me."

"Perhaps, but the Bishop of Chichester does." She lifted the sealed message that Gabriel had given her. "This is a summons from the bishop. You are relieved of all duties pending the outcome of his investigation."

He snatched the parchment from her hand. "That is impossible. You could not have contacted him..."

His words trailed away as he looked at the seal on the message. Naomi motioned the guards forward as he broke the seal and unfolded the parchment. She waited until his eyes widened and the color drained from his face before she launched the final blow. "These men will see that you arrive safely to answer for your deeds."

"This is outrageous," he protested as the guards grabbed his arms. He twisted and jerked at their restraining hold. "I will not be treated like a common criminal! Release me!"

Naomi tried not to let her pleasure show. He continued to object and struggle, while the guards dragged him from the hall.

"I would like you to meet Father Thomas, if you are not overwrought."

"I feel invigorated, knowing that beast is safely locked away."

Gabriel motioned to the priest standing silently to one side. His robes were sturdy and simply made, and the cross around his neck was carved and polished, but made of wood. She liked him already.

"Father Thomas, this is Lady Naomi of Monthamn Castle." Gabriel made the introduction.

The priest bowed his head. "May the Lord bless and keep you."

His features were ordinary, but his sky-blue eyes met hers directly with no deceit or arrogance.

"Brother Gabriel told me you were raised believing you were an orphan," Father Thomas explained. She nodded. "I, too, am an orphan. I lost my parents when I was eleven. I was taken in by a convent when no one else would have me and I entered the priesthood when I was nineteen. The bishop believes that I will be quite at home in this parish."

Naomi smiled at him. "I agree."

* * *

"I missed you, Gideon. I know it was only a few days, but it felt like an eternity."

He locked the door to the tower room and leaned back against it. "I know what an eternity feels like, my love, and you've not waited nearly so long."

She smiled at him. "It is rude for us to sneak away like this, so why did you want to come up here? I would much rather have gone to my bedchamber and made better use of our rudeness."

"My intentions are entirely dishonorable, I assure you."

Heat crept along her throat and her belly began to tingle. "Then, why are we here?"

"Because I don't need a bed to ravage your lovely body." He stalked toward her, his lustful intentions clearly written in his gleaming gaze. "We don't have much time, before we're missed below, so let your ravishment commence."

He swept her into his arms and kissed her. Naomi responded without hesitation, trusting him implicitly. His hands stroked her breasts and kneaded her hips, but they were soon restless and needful.

"I'll strip you naked and we'll make slow, leisurely love after every one else has gone to sleep."

She chuckled, nipping his bottom lip. "That sounds suspiciously like an apology."

"I beg your pardon." He turned her away from him and urged her to her knees. Bunching her skirts up over her hips, he knelt behind her and nudged her thighs apart. "Lean forward and give yourself to me."

Lowering her shoulders and arching her back, she assumed a wanton position that would have shocked her a fortnight before. She expected his forceful entry, but instead she felt his hands stroking her bottom, delving deeply into the crack between her cheeks. "Gideon?"

"Let me," he whispered and she smiled. There was nothing she would deny him when he used that silken tone.

He traced her slit with his fingertips, while his mouth explored the silken curves so blatantly displayed for him. He laved her smooth skin, his fingers busy in the damp curls below. Gently parting her folds, he entered her with two fingers. She thrust back, needing more than this teasing substitute.

"Gideon, please."

His mouth pressed against her, his tongue reaching places she hadn't realized he could access from behind. He circled her swollen nub. His fingers slid in and out, teasing her, taunting her with hints of what she really needed.

He pulled his fingers out and used them to flick her ruthlessly, bringing her quickly to a sharp, pulsing climax. His tongue thrust into her core and savored the essence of her release. Licking and swirling, he built her need again. She squirmed and arched, keeping her legs spread wide, while he pleasured her.

In one lightning-fast movement, he surged up and over her. She cried out, her body stretched tight by his. He pulled back and thrust in. She braced against the impact, thrilled by the fullness, the completeness of having him deep inside her.

He wasn't gentle. She couldn't have borne it if he were. This fierce passion was just as much a part of their love as the patient tenderness they shared more often. She embraced him with her body, arching into each violent thrust with equal vigor.

She buried her face in the crook of her arm as his hands clasped her hips. He drove fully into her and stayed there, throbbing and fully erect.

"Why did you stop?" she panted.

"It will be over too quickly." He caressed her hips, her sides, sneaked inside her dress to cup her breasts. "No matter how long I make it last, it will end too quickly."

Tightening her inner muscles in a way that drove him crazy, she said, "We can always start over again."

He continued to tease her with his hands, stroking her back, her hips, and her thighs. The longer he made her wait, the more forcefully she squeezed him. Soon they were both moaning and laughing and moaning again.

He pulled out slowly, until only the flared head remained inside her. She tightened her muscles, but without his shaft filling her she felt hollow and achy. His fingers circled her sensitive nub and he eased back in.

Their lovemaking took on a new rhythm. His fingers flicked, her inner muscles squeezed and he filled her. Her muscles squeezed, he slowly withdrew and his fingers flicked again. Over and over they performed the combination until Naomi's body thrummed with vibrations of pleasure, so intense she trembled with it.

"No more." She ground out the words.

Wicked laughter rumbled deep in his chest and he pushed in completely again. "Then, do it for me, Naomi. Nay, do it for us both."

His fingers, slick with their excitement, caught her nub and gently rolled it. She bit back a scream and the coiled tension released. The powerful ripples of her climax triggered Gideon's pleasure. His body shuddered against her back and his arms wrapped tightly around her.

They collapsed onto their sides. Their harsh breathing echoed in the stillness.

"You're right, it was too soon."

Laughing, he reached down and pinched her bare bottom.

Chapter Thirty

Night had fallen, unfurling its velvet tranquility over Monthamn Castle. Gideon stood beside Naomi on the parapets. They gazed out over the starlit vista, their fingers laced together, their hearts beating as one. But Gideon was not soothed by the darkness.

Beyond the shadows, a storm gathered. The wind carried its crisp tang. The earth rumbled, a distant warning, a promise of danger.

A call to arms.

"We must go," Gideon said.

Naomi nodded. "To the ruins?"

"Aye. We must move the children before it begins. Gabriel will meet us there. He must report our progress to Michael."

"Where are Daniel and Alyssa?"

Gideon chuckled. "Michael will only bend so far. He allowed Gabriel to accompany me with one condition—that Daniel and Alyssa depart."

"You're not supposed to interact with the other rebels?"

"Part of our quest is learning to develop new skills, to build new relationships, and depend—"

"On humans?" she guessed.

"Aye," he admitted. "Depend on humans."

Some of the children were already asleep, but Jack and several others sat around the fire.

"We was just talking about you," Jack said.

"Nothing too damning, I hope," Gideon responded.

Jack tilted his head and pulled a face. "We wasn't talking about you, we was talking about Lady Naomi."

"Then it must have been gracious and respectful, because you know how unpleasant I can be when my lady is insulted."

"Didn't know she was *your* lady."

"That is for Lady Naomi to decide. But the conversation will have to wait in any event. You need to wake the little ones. We're taking everyone to the castle for the night."

Jake stood and planted his fists on his hips. "Maybe I don't want to go to the castle."

Naomi hurried forward. "Jack, there is a dangerous storm moving this way. It is very important that we get the little ones to safety."

His eyes narrowed and Gideon thought he would argue, but then he turned to the others seated by the fire. "Best hurry. There's a storm coming. We need to—"

A shrill scream interrupted Jack's orders. Gideon sprinted in the direction of the cry, focusing with all his senses. A second scream guided him to the stream on the far side of the ruins.

Midge stood there, paralyzed by fear, her hands covering her face. Her tiny body trembled. Each breath she took made a hoarse, keening sound.

Gideon knelt before her and spoke her name. He touched her shoulder gently and she went wild. She screamed and hit at him, lunging toward him, then jerking away.

"Midge," he said more forcefully. "Midge, look at me. It is Gideon, your night watchman."

She collapsed against him weeping pathetically.

"What frightened her?" Naomi asked.

Gideon looked up as he stroked the little girl's hair. Naomi stood beside Jack, her arm wrapped loosely around his shoulders. "I know not."

Wind rustled the trees and the air was suddenly cold. Gideon eased Midge away from his chest and wiped her cheeks with his thumbs. "What's the matter, pumpkin? Tell me what frightened you."

She swallowed and shuddered, and then pointed toward the stream. Gideon picked up Midge and handed her to Naomi.

His boots fought for purchase against the leafy ground as he climbed down the sloping embankment. The acrid scent of fear gave way to something darker, something more vile. Death.

"Jack, take Midge back to the fire and ready the others," he called over his shoulder.

Gideon shook with dread and loathing as he waited for Jack to obey. How much had Midge seen? Had she only stumbled upon the body or had Domieno committed murder in front of her innocent eyes?

The man lay half in and half out of the water, facedown in the mud. Wading into the stream, Gideon grasped the body under the arms and dragged it out onto the grassy bank.

He heard a shuffling above him. "Do not come down here," he called, but Naomi skidded to a stop at the base of the embankment, not far from him.

"Is it one of the orphans?" Her voice shook as she tried to peer beyond him.

"Nay, it is a man. Turn your back. I mean to turn him over." Gideon leaned down and rolled the body.

Hearing Naomi's gasp, Gideon grimaced. He had tried to spare her this.

Fredrick of Westerville's face was contorted in an expression of terror. Gideon quickly shut his lifeless eyes and thanked the darkness for concealing the details of his ravaged throat.

Gideon unfastened his cloak and spread it over the corpse, returning to the creek to wash the blood from his hands.

"Do you think she saw it done?" Naomi asked. Her eyes shone with anxiety and fear.

"Aye. If she had only seen the body as I found it...I do not know. She is very young."

"Oh, that poor baby," she whispered, her fingers covering her mouth.

He gently took her hand and they started up the hill. Halfway up the embankment, Naomi suddenly stopped.

"They will think I did this. Domieno wants suspicion to fall on me."

"No one will suspect you of what was done to that man."

She stepped closer to him, her voice barely a whisper. "I have reason to want him dead. What he did to those girls...and he is the only other person with any claim to Monthamn."

"You're falling into his trap, Naomi. Domieno wants us frightened. He wants us angry. And he wants our doubt! We must stand strong and we must stand together." Gideon took her hand and kissed her fingers before they continued up the hill.

Gabriel sat by the fire, Midge cradled in his arms. He spoke to her softly, his golden head bowed. When he noticed them, he carefully passed the girl to Jack and stood.

"I am ready for war," Gabriel said as he approached them. "Why must evil use innocence?"

"Because it makes angels rage." Naomi sounded tormented.

Gabriel took a deep breath and rolled his shoulders then turned to Gideon. "Can you...take care of this?"

Gideon swallowed. That ability belonged to his dark nature. Did he dare awaken the sleeping beast? "I've not attempted to use any of those abilities since my agreement with Michael."

"Michael could not object to this," Gabriel said. "That child cannot live the rest of her life with the memory of what she saw. I will not allow it."

"I'll try."

Gideon sat beside Jack and stroked Midge's hair. She was nearly asleep in her brother's arms, so he didn't move her. Closing his eyes, he roused the darkness and sank gently into her mind.

His dark nature stirred, stretched and expanded. Her innocence intoxicated him. Greedily, he consumed it. He felt giddy and free. Deeper, he sank deeper, searching for darkness, seeking out evil.

There. He sensed Domieno's imprint, felt his echo, recognized a kindred spirit.

Gideon's angelic nature surfaced, containing his evil. He infused the beast with purpose, focused on the task. He didn't want to experience the memory, but it flashed before him, impossible to ignore. Domieno clutched Frederick, bending him backward, so that Midge could see exactly what he was doing. Frederick flailed and screamed, but Domieno ignored his struggles. He grinned at the child, his demonic nature surged and he bit into Frederick's throat. Ripping and tearing, he savaged the human's flesh until his face was covered in blood and torrents of red streamed into the mud at their feet.

Gideon meticulously gathered every fragment of the memory, every trace and fiber until there was nothing left. Then he withdrew from her mind, taking the images with him.

He shot to his feet, fighting for breath. Naomi stood beside Gabriel and they stared at him expectantly. Turning to face the night, he allowed his mouth to open and ran his tongue over his fangs.

"Were you successful?" Naomi asked carefully. "What is the matter?"

"Give him a moment, Naomi," Gabriel cautioned.

Slowly the darkness submitted to his will. He felt his fangs retract and he was able to relax. He turned to face them. "She will remember nothing."

They quickly gathered the children and Gideon took them to the castle. Jack said not a word and accepted his directives without argument.

Gideon released the orphans into Kruthers' capable hands and returned to the ruins.

"Are you ready?" he asked.

Naomi nodded and stood by his side.

Gabriel joined them, his head bowed in prayer.

Gideon lifted his face to the sky. Spreading his arms wide, he summoned Domieno.

Chapter Thirty-One

Naomi's scream jarred Gideon from his trance. His eyes snapped open and he lunged, but even his supernatural speed was not enough. Domieno held Naomi tightly, his arm wrapped around her waist, trapping her arms to her sides. His skeletal hand grasped her throat, one claw pressed against the throbbing vein in her neck.

Heaven's light radiated from Gabriel, but he too seemed paralyzed by Naomi's peril.

Gideon glanced around the ruins, scanning with his power as well as his senses. Had Domieno actually come alone? Unlikely.

"Let her go," Gideon said.

"Or what?" the demon mocked him. "If I spill her blood, will you tear me limb from limb?"

Gideon's dark nature surged and seethed, drawn by the proximity of the demon and the violence he described. Gabriel's hand came to rest on his shoulder, giving him strength, calming him.

"Nothing you can do will change the outcome, Domieno," Gideon said. "I will not Fall. Recruit someone else."

"Well, you see, therein lies the problem. Either I return with you, or I am no longer welcome. As you know, the only thing that can destroy a demon is to be kept too long from Hell."

"Speak the words and I will disperse your energy, quickly and painlessly," Gabriel volunteered.

Domieno laughed, his breath stirring Naomi's hair. Gideon saw her shudder and felt the need to strike twist within him again.

"Or I can press just a bit harder and we can watch Naomi's blood drain from her body. I've heard that it's painless." His pointed claw scratched her skin, creating a distinct, red line. "If I take her to the very edge, Gideon, will you corrupt her soul to save her life?"

"Never!"

Gideon launched himself into the air, catching Domieno in the face with his foot. For just an instant the demon's hold wavered and Gabriel snatched Naomi out of his grasp.

Landing in a threatening crouch, Gideon growled and glared at his enemy.

Domieno faced him, his manner calm and unafraid. "Did you enjoy my surprise? I know the little girl did."

Naomi came to life within Gabriel's arms. She kicked out at the demon and cried, "You vile, hideous—"

"Listen, human, you're beneath contempt. If it weren't for your connection to Gideon—"

"Go back to the castle, Naomi," Gideon said.

"Oh, we can continue this there, if you like," Domieno taunted him. "I thought you would appreciate the privacy."

Gabriel still held Naomi, so Gideon put himself between them and the demon. "Naomi has nothing to do with this. She need not be here."

"I disagree." He strolled forward, accompanied by a cold rush of air. "Did you not understand my message? If you continue to resist, I will destroy her. I will destroy you both. I will take lives in plain sight of the children until you agree to Fall. I will take on *your* shape as I do it. I will rip out Naomi's throat and paint Jack with her blood. I will—"

"Then, I will Fall," Gideon shouted. "If it means no more will die, I will Fall."

Naomi tore away from Gabriel and threw herself in front of Gideon. "Nay! It is not the same." Panic choked her. Anguish squeezed her chest. She could hardly breathe, could barely speak. "He offers to sacrifice himself. That is not the same as Falling!"

"She's right," Gabriel said. "You cannot deny it."

Domieno just stood there, eyes blazing, chest heaving.

Too terrified to hope they had won so easily, Naomi held her breath.

"Then we fight," Domieno shouted.

The demon leapt, but Gideon was prepared. He pushed Naomi toward Gabriel and accepted the demon's challenge. They collided in midair, the impact shaking the ground. Naomi stumbled back, horrified and fascinated by the spectacle. She had to do something, but she had never felt so helpless, so useless.

"Pray, Naomi," Gabriel directed her. "Pray."

She fell to her knees and folded her hands. The air crackled and hummed. Evil pulsed all around her. The acrid smell was unmistakable. The hairs along her arms and at the nape of her neck prickled and her mouth was suddenly dry.

With every fiber of her being, she began to pray.

Eerie green light flared each time the demon touched Gideon. He flinched and grunted, obviously in pain. Gideon formed Heaven's light in the palm of his hand and hurled it at Domieno. The demon shrieked and flailed as his body absorbed the golden glow.

The creature collapsed onto his hands and knees, his head dangling limply, his lank hair covering his face. Naomi inched forward. Had Gideon drained its strength?

Domieno began muttering phrases, repeating syllables she could not understand. His voice grew louder and more rhythmic. Gideon and Gabriel both covered their ears, moaning and shaking their heads.

The earth beneath her rumbled and vibrated. Streaks of light shot along the ruined walls, sparking and dancing with hypnotic beauty. If it had been golden, Naomi would have enjoyed the phenomenon, but the light was green—demonic.

Gideon staggered, nearly falling to his knees. His dark nature reared and bucked, stimulated by Domieno's chant. His fangs shot out so suddenly that they pierced his lip and the taste of blood provoked him further. Roaring and panting, he released his ears and searched his mind for the angelic counterpart to the demon's words.

Gabriel grasped his hand and began the nearly forgotten song. Gideon let the melody wash over him, soothe him, comfort him. His fangs receded and his raging spirit calmed.

Each note, each phrase renewed his strength and pushed away the night.

A dense shadow formed in the center of the clearing. It rippled and undulated. Gideon knew what would happen next, but tension gripped him, pummeled his hard won composure and demanded that he focus on the light.

The shadow unfolded, growing taller and broader. Domieno's chant ended abruptly and the shadow came to life. It took on shape and definition, twisting and forming a hideous creature—part man, part monster.

It extended a claw-like hand and helped Domieno to his feet. Then, together they faced Gideon and Gabriel. Legion roared, stomping its thick, muscular legs. Each word it uttered was profane. The stench of its breath fouled the air.

"They are evil, Gideon." Gabriel spoke urgently. "Your dark nature will only make them stronger. They can only be destroyed with Heaven's light."

Gideon nodded, acknowledging the wisdom and the warning. "Keep Domieno occupied," he said.

He launched himself at Legion, connecting violently, but the demon shook him aside like a leaf in the wind. Gideon landed with a grunt against the stone wall, then quickly scrambled to his feet. Domieno stalked toward him. Legion uncoiled a thick, spiked tail and Gideon braced himself for the attack.

A flash of light illuminated the darkness. For just a moment everything paused. Gabriel's earthly garments fell away, revealing his heavenly glory. His wings unfurled and Gideon ached at their beauty. In that instant he fully realized all he had lost, all his pride had cost him and what he had nearly become.

Gabriel launched into a series of movements, arches of light following in his wake. He grabbed Domieno and wrestled him away from Gideon. Slamming the demon against the wall, he trapped him there with his wings.

Confident that Gabriel protected his back, Gideon planted his feet far apart and studied Legion. The demon swung his tail. Gideon jumped and spun, barely missing the lethal looking spikes. Fear rippled through him. How could he ever hope to subdue such a creature?

"Unfurl your wings," Gabriel shouted.

Regret choked him.

"I do not remember how," Gideon admitted in an anguished cry. He ducked under Legion's tail and drove himself headfirst into the demon's belly.

The momentum knocked Legion over, but Gideon went tumbling with him. They rolled. Gideon kicked and punched, but Legion hardly noticed the blows.

"Unfurl your wings," Gabriel shouted again.

The battle raging within Gideon suddenly eclipsed the physical fray. His dark nature grappled with his angelic nature and Gideon understood. The war must be won within his soul!

He grasped the darkness by the throat and enveloped it within the memory of Gabriel's unconditional love. He bound it with Naomi's whispered words: *I love you, Gideon. Come what may, I love you.* Then he sealed it with the warmth and tenderness the orphans had released within his heart.

Holding the bundle toward Heaven, he whispered two simple words.

"Forgive me."

Light infused his soul.

With one mighty buck, Gideon flipped Legion off of him. He jumped to his feet and warmth spread along his spine.

"You can do it." He heard Naomi's call. "I know you can."

The tingle intensified, burning and searing until he felt his flesh separate. Brilliant, shimmering wings unfurled, supporting and stabilizing him. Gingerly he moved his wings in a rather unsteady flap. Then again, more confidently.

Legion roared, swinging at Gideon with his tail. Gideon turned to the side and deflected the tail with a powerful sweep of one wing.

Naomi cheered and Gabriel sang a song of praise.

Legion shouted profanity, swinging his tail again and again. Gideon easily blocked his blows with the power of his radiant wings.

Gabriel cried out and Gideon turned to see Domieno break free. He flew through the air and Legion caught him, absorbed him until they were one.

Stunned for a moment, no one moved. Silence filled the ruins. Then Legion screamed, its shape fluctuating grotesquely. The demon split right down the middle, rolling back until it was two separate shapes. Each shape changed into a distinct creature, similar, yet different from the other.

"Dear Heavenly Father, please hear the cry of your humble servant..." Naomi's words trailed off, yet her spirit continued to pray.

A soft swishing sound filled the air and Naomi smelled the spicy scent of incense. Gideon and Gabriel flapped their wings, causing the sound and increasing the golden illumination surrounding them.

Legion stirred restlessly, stomping and snorting. Gabriel took flight, gliding through the night with otherworldly grace. Naomi felt humbled to witness such beauty. He dove suddenly, purposefully, planting his feet in the center of Legion's chest and knocking him backward.

Gideon's flight was less graceful, yet faster, more forceful. He attacked the other demon with several violent kicks and one massive wing slap. The demon hit the wall, stunned and senseless.

"Gideon!"

Gabriel's sharp cry drew Naomi's attention as well. His half of Legion had split again and trapped him between the two. One had its tail wrapped around his ankle, preventing him from flying away.

Naomi quickly snapped a branch off a nearby tree and smacked the demon's tail with all the force she could muster. The tail recoiled and Gideon blocked the demon's frantic lunge for her.

Gabriel drove the demons back, while Gideon repositioned. Naomi glanced back at the demon Gideon had left against the wall. Just as she feared, it had split into two.

Thunder shook the earth, rattling every stone in the ruin. Naomi screamed, but Gabriel shot Gideon a speculative glance. A blinding flash of light split the darkness, forcing the demons to look away.

Michael stood before them, his golden armor illuminated from within. His flowing hair fanned out behind him as he tossed a long, flaming sword to Gabriel, and another to Gideon.

Naomi trembled, shaken by the significance of the gesture. Michael and Gideon fighting side by side.

Each time they swung their swords the metal sizzled and sparks exploded into the night. Clutching the stick to her chest, Naomi watched the battle. They fought in a circle, protecting each other's backs. The demons attacked in pairs, but the flaming swords pierced their flesh effortlessly, dispersing their energy into the darkness. The angels arched their wings in unison as one demon jumped down from a tree above their heads. Michael batted it away, like one would flick a fly, and Gideon skewered it with his sword.

When only one demon remained, Gideon stepped out of formation and angled his sword to strike. "Now and forever, I stand for the light!" He drove the sword into the creature, and it shrieked and flailed as energy spewed forth, scattered forever upon the night wind.

Naomi dropped the branch and ran to Gideon. He tossed his sword to Gabriel and closed his arms around her. She kissed his mouth, filling her head with his scent and his taste. "Is it over, my love? Is it really over?"

He eased her away and kissed her brow. *"Forever,* it is over."

"Forever?" Michael challenged. "We must speak about forever."

Their radiance hurt her eyes, but Naomi couldn't look away. Michael had the power to take Gideon from her. She trembled all the harder when Gideon bowed his head and furled his wings. He appeared human again, devastatingly handsome, but human. Naomi wanted to shake Michael. Why was he making this so difficult?

"What will become of me, sir?" Gideon asked respectfully.

"You cannot return to Heaven. Your angelic nature is irreversibly tainted."

"That is not my wish." He dared a glance at the archangel.

"What is your wish, Gideon? Speak."

Straightening his shoulders, he looked directly at Michael. "I wish to stay with Naomi."

Michael smiled and Naomi felt her heart gallop within her breast. Without his grave expression the archangel was even more beautiful than Gabriel.

"Enough to sacrifice your immortality?" Michael asked, but his tone was almost playful.

"Of course," he said without hesitation. "That is no sacrifice."

"Perhaps not a sacrifice, but an exchange. Tomorrow, with the dawn, you will be transformed. Your angelic nature will be made—*human.*" He chuckled at the irony. "You may reenter the daylight, but you will have no power. And your immortality will be restored in another form."

"Children?" Gideon whispered, his voice husky and unsteady.

"Aye. You will live on through your children." Michael smiled at Naomi. "You did well. We thank you."

Shocked and humbled by his praise, Naomi quickly bowed her head. "It was my pleasure, sir."

He turned to Gabriel. "Say your farewells, Gabriel. Your assignment here is finished, but we have battles yet to fight."

"I will be with you directly."

Michael flashed out of sight and Naomi could contain her emotions no longer. She cried out happily and flung herself into Gideon's arms. Laughing and crying, she clutched him tightly and vowed to never let go. Gideon spun her around and around, laughing and kissing her face.

"Well, this ended rather well." Gabriel chuckled. When Gideon finally set her back on her feet, Gabriel took her hand and kissed her fingers. "As you grew to be a woman, I often tried to imagine your husband. But never once did I picture Gideon."

She laughed.

"I will make her happy, Gabriel. You have nothing to worry about."

"I know," he said, "because I will be visiting from time to time, just to be sure."

* * *

Gideon wrapped his arms around Naomi, molding her back against his chest. They stood on the ramparts, waiting for the rising sun.

"I have the special license," Gideon told her. "We can be married on the morrow."

"But with the danger gone, there is no real hurry."

He pinched her bottom lightly and Naomi laughed.

"I do not want our first child to be conceived until we are lawfully wed," he said.

She rested her head against his shoulder. "Then Father Thomas had better wed us tomorrow. I have no intention of spending another night without you."

"Or another day?"

She turned in his arms, needing to see him. "Oh, to stroll through a sun-drenched meadow with you by my side."

"We will do that and more."

Smiling into his eyes, she asked, "Do you think Father Thomas would mind if I made a few changes to the parish church?"

Gideon tucked a strand of hair behind her ear, his gaze caressing her upturned face. "What changes are needed?"

"Just the paintings on the walls. They are flat and lifeless. I would like to replace them with scenes of angels with glorious wings and flaming swords."

Gideon glanced at the horizon. "You do realize in a moment or two, I will no longer have wings."

"I will have the rest of you," she said. "I think I will survive the disappointment."

He wrapped her in his arms and kissed her deeply, hungrily. As he pulled away, sunlight bathed his features and Naomi could hardly breathe. A swell of happiness constricted her throat. His eyes shone like molten gold, alive with love and laughter.

"What a glorious morning," he said with a beaming smile.

~*~

Cyndi Friberg

Cyndi has been a member of Romance Writers of America since 1999 and also belongs to two local chapters of RWA. She is the winner of multiple national contests including The Molly and The Merritt. In 2003, she was chosen as a finalist in the prestigious Golden Heart, as well as winning the Jasmine with *Born of the Shadows*. After dabbling in freelance journalism and songwriting, she returned to her true passion: paranormal romance.

NOW AVAILABLE In Print

ROMANCE AT THE EDGE: In Other Worlds
MaryJanice Davidson, Angela Knight and Camille Anthony

CHARMING THE SNAKE
MaryJanice Davidson, Camille Anthony and Melissa Schroeder

WHY ME?
Treva Harte

THE PRENDARIAN CHRONICLES
Doreen DeSalvo

HARD CANDY
Angela Knight, Morgan Hawke and Sheri Gilmore

TAKING CHARGE
Stephanie Vaughan and Lena Austin

SHE BLINDED ME WITH SCIENCE FICTION
Kally Jo Surbeck

FOR THE LOVE OF…
Kally Jo Surbeck

AVAILABLE FROM YOUR FAVORITE BOOKSELLER!

Publisher's Note: All titles published in print by Loose Id® have been previously released in e-book format.

Printed in the United States
43676LVS00002B/103-537